The Woman Destroyed

Simone de Beauvoir, Europe's leading woman novelist, was born in Paris in 1909. A life-long friend of writer and philosopher Jean-Paul Sartre, her books are famous throughout the world.

The Second Sex, published in 1952, was hailed as a revolutionary study of the sexual nature of women. *The Mandarins*, her remarkably frank portrait of the post-war intellectual élite in France, won the coveted Prix Goncourt and was described by Iris Murdoch as 'a novel on the grand scale . . . a superb document containing analyses of great brilliance.'

The Woman Destroyed 'consists of three long short stories all on the theme of woman's vulnerability: in the first, to the process of ageing; in the second, to loneliness; and, in the third, to the growing indifference of the loved one.'

Sunday Telegraph

The
Woman
Destroyed

Simone de Beauvoir

Translated by Patrick O'Brian

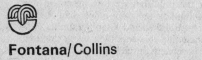

Fontana/Collins

First published in France by Editions Gallimard
under the title 'La Femme Rompue'
First published in Great Britain by
William Collins 1969
First issued in Fontana Books 1971
Fifth Impression May 1979

© in the French edition, Editions Gallimard
1967
© in the English translation, William Collins
Sons & Co Ltd, London and Glasgow, and
G. P. Putnam's Sons, New York, 1969

Made and printed in Great Britain by
William Collins Sons and Co Ltd, Glasgow

THE AGE OF
DISCRETION

Has my watch stopped? No. But its hands do not seem to be going round. Don't look at them. Think of something else—anything else: think of yesterday, a calm, ordinary, easy-flowing day, in spite of the nervous tension of waiting.

Tender awakening. André was in an odd, curled-up position in bed, with the bandage over his eyes and one hand pressed against the wall like a child's, as though in the confusion and distress of sleep he had needed to reach out to test the firmness of the world. I sat on the edge of his bed; I put my hand on his shoulder.

'Eight o'clock.'

I carried the breakfast-tray into the library: I took up a book that had arrived the day before—I had already half leafed through it. What a bore, all this going on about non-communication. If you really want to communicate you manage, somehow or other. Not with everybody, of course, but with two or three people. Sometimes I don't tell André about my moods, sorrows, unimportant anxieties; and no doubt he has his little secrets too; but on the whole there is nothing we do not know about one another. I poured out the China tea, piping hot and very strong. We drank it as we looked through our post: the July sun came flooding into the room. How many times had we sat there opposite one another at that little table with piping hot, very strong cups of tea in front of us? And we should do so again tomorrow, and in a year's time, and in ten years' time . . . That moment possessed the sweet gentleness of a memory and the gaiety of a promise. Were we thirty, or were we sixty?

André's hair had gone white when he was young: in earlier days that snowy hair, emphasizing the clear freshness of his complexion, looked particularly dashing. It looks dashing still. His skin has hardened and wrinkled—

7

old leather—but the smile on his mouth and in his eyes has kept its brilliance. Whatever the photograph-album may say to the contrary, the pictures of the young André conform to his present-day face: my eyes attribute no age to him. A long life filled with laughter, tears, quarrels, embraces, confessions, silences, and sudden impulses of the heart: and yet sometimes it seems that time has not moved by at all. The future still stretches out to infinity.

He stood up. 'I hope your work goes well,' he said.

'Yours too,' I replied.

He made no answer. In this kind of research there are necessarily times when one makes no progress: he cannot accept that as readily as he used to do.

I opened the window. Paris, sweltering beneath the crushing summer heat, smelt of asphalt and impending storms. My eyes followed André. Maybe it is during those moments, as I watch him disappear, that he exists for me with the most overwhelming clarity: his tall shape grows smaller, each pace marking out the path of his return; it vanishes and the street seems to be empty; but in fact it is a field of energy that will lead him back to me as to his natural habitat: I find this certainty even more moving than his presence.

I paused on the balcony for a long while. From my sixth floor I see a great stretch of Paris, with pigeons flying over the slate-covered roofs, and those seeming flowerpots that are really chimneys. Red or yellow, the cranes—five, nine, ten: I can count ten of them—hold their iron arms against the sky: away to the right my gaze bumps against a great soaring wall with little holes in it—a new block: I can also see prism-like towers—recently-built tall buildings. Since when have cars been parked in the tree-lined part of the boulevard Edgar-Quinet? I find the newness of the landscape staringly obvious; yet I cannot remember having seen it look otherwise. I should like two photographs to set side by side, Before and After, so that I could be amazed by the differences. No: not really. The world brings itself into being before my eyes in an everlasting present: I grow used to its different aspects so quickly that it does not seem to me to change.

The card-indexes and blank paper on my desk urged me to work; but there were words dancing in my head that prevented me from concentrating. 'Philippe will be here this evening.' He had been away almost a month. I went into his room. Books and papers were still lying about—an old grey pull-over, a pair of violet pyjamas—in this room that I cannot make up my mind to change because I have not the time to spare, nor the money; and because I do not want to believe that Philippe has stopped belonging to me. I went back into the library, which was filled with the scent of a bunch of roses, as fresh and simple-minded as so many lettuces. I was astonished that I could ever have thought the flat forlorn and empty. There was nothing lacking. My eyes wandered with pleasure over the cushions scattered on the divans, some softly coloured, some vivid: the Polish dolls, the Slovak bandits and the Portuguese cocks were all in their places, as good as gold. 'Philippe will be here . . .' I was still at a loss for anything to do. Sadness can be wept away. But the impatience of delight—it is not so easy to get rid of that.

I made up my mind to go out and get a breath of the summer heat. A tall negro in an electric blue raincoat and a grey felt hat was listlessly sweeping the pavement: before, it used to be an earth-coloured Aigerian. In the boulevard Edgar-Quinet I mingled with the crowd of women. As I almost never go out in the morning any more, the market had an exotic air for me (so many morning markets, beneath so many skies). The little old lady hobbled from one stall to another, her sparse hair carefully combed back, her hand grasping the handle of her empty basket. In earlier days I never used to worry about old people; I looked upon them as the dead whose legs still kept moving. Now I see them—men and women: only a little older than myself. I had noticed this old lady at the butcher's one day when she asked for scraps for her cats. 'For her cats!' he said when she had gone. 'She hasn't got a cat. Such a stew she's going to make for herself!' The butcher found that amusing. Presently she will be picking up the leavings under the stalls before the tall negro sweeps everything into the gutter. Making ends meet on a hundred and eighty francs a month: there are more than a million in the same plight: three million more scarcely less wretched.

I bought some fruit, some flowers, and sauntered along. Retired: it sounds rather like rejected, tossed on to the scrap-heap. The word used to chill my heart. The great stretch of free time frightened me. I was mistaken. I do find the time a little too broad over the shoulders; but I manage. And how delightful to live with no imperatives, no kind of restraint! Yet still from time to time a bewilderment comes over me. I remember my first appointment, my first class, and the dead leaves that rustled under my feet that autumn in the country. In those days retirement seemed to me as unreal as death itself, for between me and that day there lay a stretch of time almost twice as long as that which I had so far lived. And now it is a year since it came. I have crossed other frontiers, but all of them less distinct. This one was as rigid as an iron curtain.

I came home; I sat at my desk. Without some work I should have found even that delightful morning insipid. When it was getting on for one o'clock I stopped so as to lay the table in the kitchen—just like my grandmother's kitchen at Milly (I should like to see Milly again)—with its farmhouse table, its benches, its copper pots, the exposed beams: only there is a gas-stove instead of a range, and a refrigerator. (What year was it that refrigerators first came to France? I bought mine ten years ago, but they were already quite usual by then. When did they begin? Before the war? Just after? There's another of those things I don't remember any more.)

André came in late; he had told me he would. On leaving

the laboratory he had attended a meeting on French nuclear weapons.

'Did it go well?' I asked.

'We settled the wording of a new manifesto. But I have no illusions about it. It will have no more effect than the rest of them. The French don't give a damn. About the deterrent, the atomic bomb in general—about anything. Sometimes I feel like getting the hell out of here—going to Cuba, to Mali. No, seriously, I do think about it. Out there it might be possible to make oneself useful.'

'You couldn't work any more.'

'That would be no very great disaster.'

I put salad, ham, cheese and fruit on the table. 'Are you as disheartened as all that? This is not the first time you people have been unable to make headway.'

'No.'

'Well, then?'

'You don't choose to understand.'

He often tells me that nowadays all the fresh ideas come from his colleagues and that he is too old to make new discoveries: I don't believe him. 'Oh, I can see what you are thinking,' I said. 'I don't believe it.'

'You're mistaken. It is fifteen years since I had my last idea.'

Fifteen years. None of the sterile periods he has been through before have lasted that long. But having reached the point he has reached, no doubt he needs a break of this kind to come by fresh inspiration. I thought of Valéry's lines

> *Chaque atome de silence*
> *Est la chance d'un fruit. mûr.*

Unlooked-for fruit will come from this slow gestation. The adventure in which I have shared so passionately is not over—this adventure with its doubt, failure, the dreariness of no progress, then a glimpse of light, a hope, a hypothesis confirmed; and then after weeks and months of anxious perseverance, the intoxication of success. I do not understand much about André's work, but my obstinate confidence used to reinforce his. My confidence is still unshaken. Why can I no longer convey it to him? I will *not* believe that I am never again to see the feverish joy of discovery blazing in his eyes. I said, 'There is nothing to prove that you will not get your second wind.'

'No. At my age one has habits of mind that hamper inventiveness. And I grow more ignorant year by year.'

'I will remind you of that ten years from now. Maybe you will make your greatest discovery at seventy.'

'You and your optimism; I promise you I shan't.'

'You and your pessimism!'

We laughed. Yet there was nothing to laugh about. André's defeatism has no valid basis: for once he is lacking in logical severity. To be sure, in his letters Freud did say that at a given age one no longer discovers anything new, and that it is terribly sad. But at that time he was much older than André. Nevertheless this extreme gloominess still saddens me just as much, although it is unjustified. And the reason why André gives way to it is that he is in a state of general crisis. It surprises me, but the truth of the matter is that he cannot bring himself to accept the fact that he is over sixty. For my own part I still find countless things amusing: he does not. Formerly he was interested in everything: now it is a tremendous business to drag him as far as a cinema or an exhibition, or to see friends.

'What a pity it is that you no longer like walking,' I said. 'These days are so lovely! I was thinking just now how I should have liked to go back to Milly, and into the forest at Fontainebleau.'

'You are an amazing woman,' he said with a smile. 'You know the whole of Europe, and yet what you want to see again is the outskirts of Paris!'

'Why not? The church at Champeaux is no less beautiful because I have climbed the Acropolis.'

'All right. As soon as the laboratory closes in four or five days' time, I promise you a long run in the car.'

We should have time to go for more than one, since we are staying in Paris until the beginning of August. But would he want to? I said, 'Tomorrow is Sunday. You're not free?'

'No, alas. As you know there's this press-conference on apartheid in the evening. They've brought me a whole pile of papers I have not looked at yet.'

Spanish political prisoners; Portuguese detainees; persecuted Persians; Congolese, Angolan, Cameroonian rebels; Venezuelan, Peruvian and Colombian resistance fighters; he is always ready to help them as much as ever he can. Meetings, manifestoes, public gatherings, tracts, delegations —he jibs at nothing.

'You do too much.'

What is there to do when the world has lost its savour? All that is left is the killing of time. I went through a wretched period myself, ten years ago. I was disgusted with my body; Philippe had grown up; and after the success of my book on Rousseau I felt completely hollow inside. Growing old filled me with distress. But then I began to work on Montesquieu, I got Phillipe through his *agrégation** and managed to make him start on a thesis. I was given a lectureship at the Sorbonne and I found my teaching there even more interesting than my university-scholarship classes. I became resigned to my body. It seemed to me that I came to life again. And now, if André were not so very sharply aware of his age, I should easily forget my own altogether.

He went out again, and again I stayed a long while on the balcony. I watched an orange-red crane turning against the

* A difficult, competitive post-graduate examination for university and lycée posts.

blue background of the sky. I watched a black insect that drew a broad, foaming, icy furrow across the heavens. The eternal youth of the world makes me feel breathless. Some things I loved have vanished. A great many others have been given to me. Yesterday evening I was going up the boulevard Raspail and the sky was crimson; it seemed to me that I was walking upon an unknown planet where the grass might be violet, the earth blue. It was trees hiding the red glare of a neon-light advertisement. When he was sixty André was astonished at being able to cross Sweden in less than twenty-four hours, whereas in his youth the journey had taken a week. I have experienced wonders like that. Moscow in three and a half hours from Paris!

A cab took me to the Parc Montsouris, where I had an appointment with Martine. As I came into the gardens the smell of cut grass wrung my heart—the smell of the high Alpine pastures where I used to walk with André with a sack on my shoulders, a smell so moving because it was that of the meadows of childhood. Reflexions, echoes, reverberating back and back to infinity: I have discovered the pleasure of having a long past behind me. I have not the leisure to tell it over to myself, but often, quite unexpectedly, I catch sight of it, a background to the diaphanous present; a background that gives its colour and its light, just as rocks or sand show through the shifting brilliance of the sea. Once I used to cherish schemes and promises for the future; now my feelings and my joys are smoothed and softened with the shadowy velvet of time past.

'Hallo!'

Martine was drinking lemon juice on the café terrace. Thick black hair, blue eyes, a short dress with orange and yellow stripes and a hint of violet: a lovely young woman. Forty. When I was thirty I smiled to hear André's father describe a forty-year-old as a 'lovely young woman'; and here were the same words on my own lips, as I thought of

Martine. Almost everybody seems to me to be young, now. She smiled at me. 'You have brought me your book?'

'Of course.'

She looked at what I had written in it. 'Thank you,' she said, with some emotion. She added, 'I so long to read it. But one is so busy at the end of the school year. I shall have to wait for July 14.'

'I should very much like to know what you think.'

I have great trust in her judgment: that is to say we are almost always in agreement. I should feel on a completely equal footing with her if she had not retained a little of that old pupil-teacher deference towards me, although she is a teacher herself, married and the mother of a family.

'It is hard to teach literature nowadays. Without your books I really should not know how to set about it.' Shyly she asked, 'Are you pleased with this one?'

I smiled at her. 'Frankly, yes.'

There was still a question in her eyes—one that she did not like to put into words. I made the first move. 'You know what I wanted to do—to start off with a consideration of the critical works published since the war and then to go on to suggest a new method by which it is possible to make one's way into a writer's work, to see it in depth, more accurately than has ever been done before. I hope I have succeeded.'

It was more than a hope: it was a conviction. It filled my heart with sunlight. A lovely day: and I was enchanted with these trees, lawns, walks where I had so often wandered with friends and fellow-students. Some are dead, or life has separated us. Happily—unlike André, who no longer sees anyone—I have made friends with some of my pupils and younger colleagues: I like them better than women of my own age. Their curiosity spurs mine into life: they draw me into their future, on the far side of my own grave.

Martine stroked the book with her open hand. 'Still, I shall dip into it this very evening. Has anyone read it?'

'Only André. But literature does not mean a very great deal to him.'

Nothing means a very great deal to him any more. And he is as much of a defeatist for me as he is for himself. He does not tell me so, but deep down he is quite sure that from now on I shall do nothing that will add to my reputation. This does not worry me, because I know he is wrong. I have just written my best book and the second volume will go even farther.

'Your son?'

'I sent him proofs. He will be telling me about it—he comes back this evening.'

We talked about Philippe, about his thesis, about writing. Just as I do she loves words and people who know how to use them. Only she is allowing herself to be eaten alive by her profession and her home. She drove me back in her little Austin.

'Will you come back to Paris soon?'

'I don't think so. I am going straight on from Nancy into the Yonne, to rest.'

'Will you do a little work during the holidays?'

'I should like to. But I'm always short of time. I don't possess your energy.'

It is not a matter of energy, I said to myself as I left her: I just could not live without writing. Why? And why was I so desperately eager to make an intellectual out of Philippe when André would have let him follow other paths? When I was a child, when I was an adolescent, books saved me from despair: that convinced me that culture was the highest of values, and it is impossible for me to examine this conviction with an objective eye.

In the kitchen Marie-Jeanne was busy getting the dinner ready: we were to have Philippe's favourite dishes. I saw that everything was going well. I read the papers and I did a difficult crossword-puzzle that took me three quarters of an hour: from time to time it is fun to concentrate for a long while upon a set of squares where the words are potentially there although they cannot be seen: I use my brain as a photographic developer to make them appear— I have the impression of drawing them up from their hiding-places in the depth of the paper.

When the last square was filled I chose the prettiest dress in my wardrobe—pink and grey foulard. When I was fifty my clothes always seemed to me either too cheerful or too dreary: now I know what I am allowed and what I am not, and I dress without worrying. Without pleasure either. That very close, almost affectionate relationship I once had with my clothes has vanished. Nevertheless, I did look at my figure with some gratification. It was Philippe who said to me one day, 'Why, look, you're getting plump.' (He scarcely seems to have noticed that I have grown slim again.) I went on a diet. I bought scales. Earlier on it never occurred to me that I should ever worry about my weight. Yet here I am! The less I identify myself with my body the more I feel myself required to take care of it. It relies on me, and I looked after it with bored conscientiousness, as I might look after a somewhat reduced, somewhat wanting old friend who needed my help.

André brought a bottle of Mumm and I put it to cool; we talked for a while and then he telephoned his mother. He often telephones her. She is sound in wind and limb and she is still a furious militant in the ranks of the Communist Party; but she *is* eighty-four and she lives alone in her house at Villeneuve-lès-Avignon. He is rather anxious about her. He laughed on the telephone; I heard him cry out and protest; but he was soon cut short—Manette is very talkative whenever she has the chance.

'What did she say?'

'She is more and more certain that one day or another fifty million Chinese will cross the Russian frontier. Or else that they will drop a bomb anywhere, just anywhere, for the pleasure of setting off a world war. She accuses me of taking their side: there's no persuading her I don't.'

'Is she well? She's not bored?'

'She will be delighted to see us; but as for being bored, she doesn't know the meaning of the word.'

She had been a school-teacher with three children, and, for her, retirement is a delight that she has not yet come to the end of. We talked about her and about the Chinese, of whom we, like everybody else, know so very little. André opened a magazine. And there I was, looking at my watch, whose hands did not seem to be going round.

All at once he was there: every time it surprises me to see his face, with the dissimilar features of my mother and André blending smoothly in it. He hugged me very tight, saying cheerful things, and I leant there with the softness of his flannel jacket against my cheek. I released myself so as to kiss Irène: she smiled at me with so frosty a smile that I was astonished to feel a soft, warm cheek beneath my lips. Irène. I always forget her; and she is always there. Blonde; grey-blue eyes; weak mouth; sharp chin; and something both vague and obstinate about her too-wide forehead. Quickly I wiped her out. I was alone with Philippe as I used to be in the days when I woke him up every morning with a touch on his forehead.

'Not even a drop of whisky?' asked André.

'No, thanks. I'll have some fruit-juice.'

How sensible she is! She dresses with a sensible stylishness; sensibly stylish hair-do—smooth, with a fringe hiding her big forehead. Artless make-up: severe little suit. When I happen to run through a woman's magazine I often say to myself, 'Why, here's Irène!' It often happens too that when I see her I scarcely recognize her. 'She's pretty,' asserts André. There are days when I agree—a delicacy of ear and nostril: a pearly softness of skin emphasized by the dark blue of her lashes. But if she moves her head a little her face slips, and all you see is that mouth, that chin. Irène. Why? Why has Philippe always gone for women of that kind—smooth, stand-offish, pretentious? To prove to himself that he could attract them, no doubt. He was not fond of them. I used to think that if he fell in love . . . I used to think he would not fall in love; and one evening he said to me, 'I have great news for you,' with the somewhat over-excited air of a birthday-child who has been playing too much, laughing too much, shouting too much. There was that crash like a gong in my bosom, the blood mounting to my cheeks, all my strength concentrated on stopping the trembling of my lips. A winter evening, with the curtains drawn and the lamplight on the rainbow of cushions, and this suddenly-opened gulf, this chasm of absence. 'You will like her: she is a woman who has a job.' At long intervals she works as a script-girl. I know these with-it young married women. They have some vague kind of a job, they claim to use their minds, to go in for sport, dress well, run their houses faultlessly, bring up their children perfectly, carry on a social life—in short, succeed on every level. And they don't really care deeply about anything at all. They make my blood run cold.

Philippe and Irène had left for Sardinia the day the university closed, at the beginning of June. While we were having dinner at that table where I had so often obliged Philippe to eat (come, finish up your soup: take a little more beef: get something down before going off for your lecture), we talked about their journey—a handsome wed-ding-present from Irène's parents, who can afford that sort of thing. She was silent most of the time, like an intelligent woman who knows how to wait for the right moment to produce an acute and rather surprising remark: from time to time she did drop a little observation, surprising—or at least surprising to me—by its stupidity or its utter ordinari-ness.

We went back to the library. Philippe glanced at my desk. 'Did the work go well?'

'Pretty well. You didn't have time to read my proofs?'

'No; can you imagine it? I'm very sorry.'

'You'll read the book. I have a copy for you.' His care-lessness saddened me a little, but I showed nothing. I said,

'And what about you? Are you going to get back to serious
work on your thesis again now?' He did not answer. He
exchanged an odd kind of look with Irène. 'What's the
matter? Are you going to set off on your travels again?'

'No.' Silence again and then he said rather crossly, 'Oh,
you'll be vexed; you'll blame me; but during this month I
have come to a decision. It is altogether too much, teaching
and working on a thesis at the same time. But unless I do
a thesis there is no worthwhile future for me in the university. I am going to leave.'

'What on earth are you talking about?'

'I'm going to leave the university. I'm still young enough
to take up something else.'

'But it's just not possible. Now that you have got this
far you cannot drop it all,' I said indignantly.

'Listen. Once upon a time being a don was a splendid
career. These days I am not the only one who finds it
impossible to look after my students and do any work of
my own: there are too many of them.'

'That's quite true,' said André. 'Thirty students is one
student multiplied by thirty. Fifty is a mob. But surely we
can find some way that will give you more time to yourself
and let you finish your thesis.'

'No,' said Irène, decisively. 'Teaching and research—
they really are too badly paid. I have a cousin who is a
chemist. At the National Research Centre he was earning
eight hundred francs a month. He has gone into a dye
factory—he's pulling down three thousand.'

'It's not only a question of money,' said Philippe.

'Of course not. Being in the swim counts too.'

In little guarded, restrained phrases she let us see what
she thought of us. Oh, she did it tactfully—with the tact
you can hear rumbling half a mile away. 'Above all I don't
want to hurt you—don't hold it against me, for that would
be unfair—but still there are some things I have to say to
you and if I were not holding myself in I'd say a great deal
more.' Andrè is a great scientist of course and for a woman

I haven't done badly at all. But we live cut off from the world, in laboratories and libraries. The new generation of intellectuals wants to be in immediate contact with society. With his vitality and drive, Philippe is not made for our kind of life; there are other careers in which he would show his abilities far better. 'And then of course a thesis is totally old hat,' she ended.

Why does she sometimes utter grotesque monstrosities? Irène is not really as stupid as all that. She does exist, she does amount to something: she has wiped out the victory I won with Philippe—a victory over him and for him. A long battle and sometimes so hard for me. 'I can't manage this essay; I have a head-ache. Give me a note saying I'm ill.' 'No.' The soft adolescent face grows tense and old; the green eyes stab me. 'How unkind you are.' Andrè stepping in—'Just this once . . .' 'No.' My misery in Holland during those Easter holidays when we left Philippe in Paris. 'I don't want your degree to be botched.' And with his voice full of hatred he shouted, 'Don't take me, then; I don't care. And I shan't write a single line.' And then his successes and our understanding, our alliance. The understanding that Irène is now destroying. I did not want to break out in front of her: I took hold of myself. 'What do you mean to do, then?'

Irène was about to answer. Philippe interrupted her. 'Irène's father has various things in mind.'

'What kind of things? In business?'

'It's still uncertain.'

'You talked it over with him before your journey. Why did you say nothing to us?'

'I wanted to turn it over in my mind.'

A sudden jet of anger filled me: it was unbelievable that he should not have spoken to me the moment the idea of leaving the university stirred in his mind.

'Of course you two blame me,' said Philippe angrily. The green of his eyes took on that stormy colour I knew so well.

'No,' said André. 'One must follow one's own line.'

'And you, do you blame me?'

'Making money does not seem to me a very elevating ambition,' I said. 'I am surprised.'

'I told you it is not a question of money.'

'What is it a question of, then? Be specific.'

'I can't. I have to see my father-in-law again. But I shan't accept his offer unless I think it worth while.'

I argued a little longer, as mildly as possible, trying to persuade him of the value of his thesis and reminding him of earlier plans for papers and research. He answered politely, but my words had no hold on him. No, he did not belong to me any more; not any more at all. Even his physical appearance had changed: another kind of hair-cut; more up-to-date clothes—the clothes of the fashion-able sixteenth arrondissement. It was I who moulded his life. Now I am watching it from outside, a remote spec-tator. It is the fate common to all mothers; but who has ever found comfort in saying that hers is the common fate?

André saw them to the lift and I collapsed on to the divan. That void again . . . The happy day, the true pre-sence underlying absence—it had merely been the certainty of having Philippe here, for a few hours. I had waited for him as though he were coming back never to go away again: he will always go away again. And the break be-tween us is far more final than I had imagined. I shall no longer share in his work; we shall no longer have the same interests. Does money really mean all that to him? Or is he only giving way to Irène? Does he love her as much as that? One would have to know about their nights together. No doubt she can satisfy his body to the full, as well as his pride: beneath her fashionable exterior I can see that she might be capable of remarkable outbursts. The bond that physical happiness brings into being between a man and woman is something whose importance I tend to under-estimate. As far as I am concerned sexuality no longer

exists. I used to call this indifference serenity: all at once
I have come to see it in another light—it is a mutilation;
it is the loss of the sense. The lack of it makes me blind to
the needs, the pains and the joys of those who do possess it.
It seems to me that I no longer know anything at all about
Philippe. Only one thing is certain—the degree to which
I am going to miss him. It was perhaps thanks to him that
I adapted myself to my age, more or less. He carried me
along with his youth. He used to take me to the twenty-four
hour race at Le Mans, to op-art shows and even, once, to a
happening. His mercurial, inventive presence filled the
house. Shall I grow used to this silence, this prudent, well-
behaved flow of days that is never again to be broken by
anything unforeseen?

I said to André, 'Why didn't you help me try to bring
Philippe to his senses? You gave way at once. Between us
we might perhaps have persuaded him.'

'People have to be left free. He never terribly wanted to
teach.'

'But he was interested in his thesis.'

'Up to a point, a very vaguely defined point. I understand him.'

'You understand everybody.'

Once André was as uncompromising for others as he
was for himself. Nowadays his political attitudes have not
weakened but in private life he keeps his rigour for himself
alone: he excuses people, he explains them, he accepts
them. To such a pitch that sometimes it maddens me. I
went on, 'Do you think that making money is an adequate
goal in life?'

'I really scarcely know what our goals were, nor whether
they were adequate.'

Did he really believe what he was saying, or was he
amusing himself by teasing me? He does that sometimes,
when he thinks me too set in my convictions and my prin-
ciples. Usually I put up with it very well—I join in the

game. But this time I was in no mood for trifling. My voice rose. 'Why have we led the kind of life we have led if you think other ways of life just as good?'

'Because *we* could not have done otherwise.'

'We could not have done otherwise because it was our way of life that seemed to us valid.'

'No. As far as I was concerned knowing, discovering, was a mania, a passion, even a kind of neurosis, without the slightest moral justification. I never thought everybody else should do the same.'

Deep down I *do* think that everybody else should do the same, but I did not choose to argue the point. I said, 'It is not a question of everybody, but of Philippe. He is going to turn into a fellow concerned with dubious money-making deals. That was not what I brought him up for.'

André reflected. 'It is difficult for a young man to have over-successful parents. He would think it presumptuous to suppose that he could follow in their steps and rival them. He prefers to put his money on another horse.'

'Philippe was making a very good start.'

'You helped him: he was working under your shadow. Frankly, without you he would not have got very far and he is clear-sighted enough to realize it.'

There had always been this underlying disagreement between us about Philippe. Maybe André was chagrined because he chose letters and not science: or maybe it was the classic father-son rivalry at work. He always looked upon Philippe as a mediocre being, and that was one way of guiding him towards mediocrity.

'I know,' I said. 'You have never had any confidence in him. And if he has no confidence in himself it is because he sees himself through your eyes.'

'Maybe,' said André, in a conciliatory tone.

'In any case, the person who is really responsible is Irène. It is she who is pushing him on. She wants her husband to earn a lot of money. And she's only too happy to draw him away from me.'

'Oh, don't play the mother-in-law! She's quite as good as the next girl.'

'What next girl? She said monstrous things.'

'She does that sometimes. But sometimes she is quite sharp. The monstrosities are a mark of emotional unbalance rather than a lack of intelligence. And then again, if she had wanted money more than anything else she would never have married Philippe, who is not rich.'

'She saw that he could become rich.'

'At all events she picked him rather than just any pretentious little nobody.'

'If you like her, so much the better for you.'

'When you love someone, you must give the people he loves credit for being of some value.'

'That's true,' I said. 'But I do find Irène disheartening.'

'You have to consider the background she comes from.'

'She scarcely comes from it at all, unfortunately. She is still there.'

Those fat, influential, important bourgeois, stinking with money, seem to me even more loathsome than the fashionable, shallow world I revolted against as a girl.

We remained silent for a while. Outside the window the neon advertisement flicked from red to green: the great wall's eyes blazed. A lovely night. I would have gone out with Philippe for a last drink on the terrace of a café . . . No point in asking André whether he would like to come for a stroll; he was obviously half asleep already. I said, 'I wonder why Philippe married her.'

'Oh, from outside, you know, there is never any understanding these things.' He answered in an offhand tone. His face had collapsed: he was pressing a finger into his cheek at the level of his gum—a nervous habit he caught some time ago.

'Have you got tooth-ache?'

'No.'

'Then why are you messing about with your gum?'

'I'm making sure it doesn't hurt.'

Last year he used to take his pulse every ten minutes. It is true his blood-pressure was a little high, but treatment steadied it at a hundred and seventy, which is perfect for our age. He kept his fingers pressed against his cheek; his eyes were vacant; he was playing at being an old man and he would end by persuading me that he was one. For a horrified moment I thought, 'Philippe has gone and I am to spend the rest of my life with an old man!' I felt like shouting, 'Stop, I can't bear it.' As though he had heard me, he smiled, became himself again, and we went to bed.

He is still asleep. I shall go and wake him up: we will drink piping hot, very strong China tea. But this morning is not like yesterday. I must learn that I have lost Philippe —learn it all over again. I ought to have known it. He left me the moment he told me about his marriage: he left me at the moment of his birth—a nurse could have taken my place. What had I imagined? Because he was very demanding I believed I was indispensable. Because he is easily influenced I imagined I had created him in my own image. This year, when I saw him with Irène or his in-laws, so unlike the person he is with me, I thought he was falling in with a game: I was the one who knew the real Philippe. And he has preferred to go away from me, to break our secret alliance, to throw away the life I had built for him with such pains. He will turn into a stranger. Come! André often accuses me of blind optimism: maybe this time I am harrowing myself over nothing. After all, I do not really think that there is no salvation outside the world of the university, nor that writing a thesis is a categorical imperative. Philippe said he would only take a worthwhile job . . . But I have no confidence in the jobs Irène's father can offer him. I have no confidence in Philippe. He has often hidden things from me, or lied: I know his faults and I am resigned to them—and indeed they move me as a physical ugliness might do. But this time I am indignant because he did not tell me about his plans as they were forming. Indignant and worried. Up until now, whenever he hurt me he always knew how to make it up to me after-wards: I am not so sure that this time he can manage it.

Why was André late? I had worked for four hours without a pause; my head was heavy and I lay down on the divan. Three days, and Philippe had not given any signs of life: that was not his way, and I was all the more surprised by his silence since whenever he is afraid he has hurt me he keeps ringing up and sending little notes. I could not under-stand; my heart was heavy and my sadness spread and spread, darkening the world; and the world gave it back food to feed upon. André. He was growing more and more morose. Vatrin was the only friend he would still see and yet he was cross when I asked him to lunch. 'He bores me.' Everyone bores him. And what about me? A great while ago now he said to me, 'So long as I have you I can never be unhappy.' And he does not look happy. He no longer loves me as he did. What does love mean to him, these days? He clings to me as he might cling to anything he had been used to for a long while but I no longer bring him any kind of happiness. Perhaps it is unfair, but I resent it: he accepts this indifference—he has settled down into it.

The key turned in the lock; he kissed me; he looked preoccupied. 'I'm late.'

'Yes, rather.'

'Philippe came to fetch me at the Ecole Normale. We had a drink together.'

'Why didn't you bring him here?'

'He wanted to speak to me alone. So that I should be the one to tell you what he has to say.' (Was he leaving for abroad, a great way off, for years and years?) 'You won't like it. He could not bring himself to tell us the other evening but it is all settled. His father-in-law has found him a job. He is getting him into the Ministry of Culture. He tells me that for anyone of his age it is a splendid post. But you see what it implies.'

'It's impossible! Philippe?'

It was impossible. He shared our ideas. He had taken great risks during the Algerian war—that war which had torn our hearts and which now seems never to have taken place at all—he had got himself beaten up in anti-Gaullist demonstrations; he had voted as we did during the last elections . . .

'He says he has developed. He has come to understand that the French left wing's negativism has led it nowhere, that it is done for, finished, and he wants to be in the swim, to have a grip on the world, accomplish something, construct, build.'

'Anyone would think it was Irène speaking.'

'Yet it was Philippe,' said André in a hard voice.

Suddenly everything fell into place. Anger took hold of me. 'So that's it? He's an arriviste—a creature that's going to succeed whatever it costs? He's turning his coat out of vulgar ambition. I hope you told him what you thought of him.'

'I told him I was against it.'

'You didn't try to make him change his mind?'

'Of course I did. I argued.'

'Argued! You ought to have frightened him—told him that we should never see him again. You were too soft: I know you.' All at once it crashed over me, an avalanche of suspicions and uneasy feelings that I had thrust back. Why had he never had anything but pretentious, fashionable, too-well-dressed young women? Why Irène and that great frothy marriage in church? Why did he display such an eager desire to please his in-laws—why so winning? He was at home in those surroundings, like a fish in its native water. I had not wanted to ask myself any questions, and if ever André ventured a criticism I stood up for Philippe. All my obstinate trust turned into bitterness of heart. In an instant Philippe showed another face. Unscrupulous ambition: plotting. 'I'm going to have a word with him.'

I went angrily towards the telephone. André stopped me. 'Calm down first. A scene will do nobody any good.'

'It will relieve my mind.'

'Please.'

'Leave me alone.'

I dialled Philippe's number. 'Your father has just told me you're joining the Ministry of Culture right up at the top. Congratulations!'

'Oh, please don't take it like that,' he said to me.

'How am I to take it, then? I ought to be glad you're so ashamed of yourself that you didn't dare tell me to my face.'

'I'm not ashamed at all. One has the right to reconsider one's opinions.'

'Reconsider? Only six months ago and you were utterly condemning the régime's entire cultural policy.'

'There you are, then! I'm going to try and change it.'

'Come, come, you aren't of that calibre and you know it. You'll play their little game as good as gold and you'll carve yourself out a charming little career. Your motive is mere ambition, nothing more . . .' I don't know what else I said to him. He shouted, 'Shut up, shut up.' I went on: he interrupted, his voice filled with hatred, and in the end he shouted furiously, 'I'm not a swine just because I won't share in your senile obstinacy.'

'That's enough. I shall never see you again as long as I live.'

I hung up: I sat down, sweating, trembling, my legs too weak to hold me. We had broken off for ever more than once; but this clash was really serious. I should never see him again. His turning his coat sickened me, and his words had hurt me deeply because he had meant them to hurt deeply.

'He insulted us. He spoke of our senile obstinacy. I shall never see him again and I don't want you to see him again either.'

'You were pretty hard, too. You should never have treated it on an emotional basis.'

'And just why not? He has not taken our feelings into

account at all. He has put his career first, before us, and he is willing to pay the price of a break . . .'

'He had not expected any break. Besides, there won't be one: I won't have it.'

'As far as I'm concerned it's there already: everything's over between Philippe and me.' I closed my mouth: I was still quivering with anger.

'For some time now Philippe has been very odd and shifty,' said André. 'You would not admit it, but I saw clearly enough. Still, I should never have believed he could have reached that point.'

'He's just an ambitious little rat.'

'Yes,' said André in a puzzled voice. 'But why?'

'What do you mean, why?'

'As we were saying the other evening, we certainly have our share of responsibility.' He hesitated. 'It was you who put ambition into his mind; left to himself he was comparatively apathetic. And no doubt I built up an antagonism in him.'

'It's all Irène's fault,' I burst out. 'If he had not married her, if he had not got into that environment he would never have ratted.'

'But he did marry her, and he married her partly because he found people of that environment impressive. For a long time now his values have no longer been ours. I can see a great many reasons . . .'

'You're not going to stand up for him.'

'I'm trying to find an explanation.'

'No explanation will ever convince me. I shall never see him again. And I don't want you to see him, either.'

'Make no mistake about this. I disapprove of him. I disapprove very strongly. But I shall see him again. So will you.'

'No I shan't. And if you let me down, after what he said to me on the telephone, I'll take it more unkindly—I'll resent it more than I have ever resented anything you've done all my life. Don't talk to me about him any more.'

But we could not talk of anything else, either. We had dinner almost in silence, very quickly, and then each of us took up a book. I felt bitter ill-will against Irène, against André, against the world in general. 'We certainly have our share of responsibility.' How trifling it was to look for reasons and excuses. 'Your senile obstinacy': he had shouted those words at me. I had been so certain of his love for us, for me: in actual fact I did not amount to anything much—I was nothing to him; just some old object to be filed away among the minor details. All I had to do was to file him away in the same fashion. The whole night through I choked with resentment. The next morning, as soon as André was gone, I went into Philippe's room, tore up the old letters, flung out the old papers, filled one suitcase with his books, piled his pull-over, pyjamas and everything that was left in the cupboards into another. Looking at the bare shelves I felt my eyes fill with tears. So many moving, overwhelming memories rose up within me. I wrung their necks for them. He had left me, betrayed me, jeered at me, insulted me. I should never forgive him.

Two days went by without our mentioning Philippe. The third morning, as we were looking at our post, I said to André, 'A letter from Philippe.'

'I imagine he is saying he's sorry.'

'He's wasting his time. I shan't read it.'

'Oh, but have a look at it, though. You know how hard he finds it to make the first step. Give him a chance.'

'Certainly not.' I folded the letter, put it into an envelope and wrote Philippe's address. 'Please post that for me.'

I had always given in too easily to his charming smiles and his pretty ways. I should not give in this time.

Two days later, early in the afternoon, Irène rang the bell. 'I'd like to talk to you for five minutes.'

A very simple little dress, bare arms, hair down her back: she looked like a girl, very young, dewy and shy. I had never yet seen her in that particular role. I let her in. She had come to plead for Philippe, of course. The sending back of his letter had grieved him dreadfully. He was sorry for what he had said to me on the telephone; but he did not mean a word of it; but I knew his nature—he lost his temper very quickly and then he would say anything at all, but it was really only so much hot air. He absolutely had to have it out with me.

'Why didn't he come himself?'

'He was afraid you would slam the door on him.'

'And that's just what I should have done. I don't want to see him again. Full stop. The end.'

She persisted. He could not bear my being cross with him: he had never imagined I should take things so much to heart.

'In that case he must have turned into a half-wit: he can go to hell.'

'But you don't realize. Papa has worked a miracle for him: a post like this, at his age, is something absolutely extraordinary. You can't ask him to sacrifice his future for you.'

'He had a future, a clean one, true to his own ideas.'

'I beg your pardon—true to your ideas. He has developed.'

'He will go on developing: it's a tune we all know. He will make his opinions chime with his interests. For the moment he is up to his middle in bad faith—his only idea is to succeed. He is betraying himself and he knows it; that is what is so tenth-rate,' I said passionately.

Irène gave me a dirty look. 'I imagine your own life has always been perfect, and so that allows you to judge everybody else from a great height.'

I stiffened. 'I have always tried to be honest. I wanted Philippe to be the same. I am sorry that you should have turned him from that course.'

She burst out laughing. 'Anyone would think he had become a burglar, or a coiner.'

'For a man of his convictions, I do not consider his an honourable choice.'

Irène stood up. 'But after all it is strange, this high moral stand of yours,' she said slowly. 'His father is more committed, politically, than you; and he has not broken with Philippe. Whereas you . . .'

I interrupted her. 'He has not broken . . . You mean they've seen one another?'

'I don't know,' she replied quickly. 'I know he never spoke of breaking when Philippe told him about his decision.'

'That was before the phone call. What about since?'

'I don't know.'

'You don't know who Philippe sees and who he doesn't?'

Looking stubborn she said, 'No.'

'All right. It doesn't matter,' I said.

I saw her as far as the door. I turned our last exchanges over in my mind. Had she cut herself short on purpose—a cunning stroke—or was it a blunder? At all events my mind was made up. Almost made up. Not quite enough for it to find an outlet in rage. Just enough for me to be choked with distress and anxiety.

As soon as André came in I went for him. 'Why didn't you tell me you had seen Philippe again?'

'Who told you that?'

'Irène. She came to ask me why I didn't see him, since you did.'

'I warned you I should see him again.'

'I warned you that I should resent it most bitterly. It was you who persuaded him to write to me.'

'No: not really.'

'It certainly was. Oh, you had fun with me, all right: "You know how hard it is for him to make the first step." And it was you who had made it! Secretly.'

'With regard to you, he did make the first step.'

'Urged on by you. You plotted together behind my back. You treated me like a child—an invalid. You had no right to do so.'

Suddenly there was red smoke in my brain, a red mist in

front of my eyes, something red shouting out in my throat. I am used to my rages against Philippe; I know myself when I am in one of them. But when it happens (and it is rare, very rare) that I grow furious with André, it is a hurricane that carries me away thousands of miles from him and from myself, into a desert that is both scorching and freezing cold.

'You have never lied to me before! This is the first time.'

'Let us agree that I was in the wrong.'

'Wrong to see Philippe again, wrong to plot against me with him and Irène, wrong to make a fool of me, to lie to me. That's very far in the wrong.'

'Listen . . . will you listen to me quietly?'

'No. I don't want to talk to you any more; I don't want to see you any more. I must be by myself: I am going out for a walk.'

'Go for a walk then, and try to calm yourself down,' he said curtly.

I set off through the streets and I walked as I often used to do when I wanted to calm my fears or rages or to get rid of mental images. Only I am not twenty any more, nor even fifty, and weariness came over me very soon. I went into a café and drank a glass of wine, my eyes hurting in the cruel glare of the neon. Philippe: it was all over. Married, a deserter to the other side. André was all I had left and there it was—I did not have him either. I had supposed that each of us could see right into the other, that we were united, linked to one another like Siamese twins. He had cast himself off from me, lied to me; and here I was on this café bench, alone. I continually called his face, his voice to mind, and I blew on the fire of the furious resentment that was burning me up. It was like one of those illnesses in which you manufacture your own suffering—every breath tears your lungs to pieces, and yet you are forced to breathe.

I left, and I set off again, walking. So what now? I asked

myself in a daze. We were not going to part. Each of us alone, we should go on living side by side. I should bury my grievances, then, these grievances that I did not want to forget. The notion that one day my anger would have left me made it far worse.

When I got home I found a note on the table: 'I have gone to the cinema.' I opened our bedroom door. There were André's pyjamas on the bed, a packet of tobacco and his blood-pressure medicines on the bedside table. For a moment he existed—a heart-piercing existence—as though he had been taken far from me by illness or exile and I were seeing him again in these forgotten, scattered objects. Tears came into my eyes. I took a sleeping-pill; I went to bed.

When I woke up in the morning he was asleep, curled in that odd position with one hand against the wall. I looked away. No impulse towards him at all. My heart was as dreary and frigid as a deconsecrated church in which there is no longer the least warm flicker of a lamp. The slippers and the pipe no longer moved me; they no longer called to mind a beloved person far away; they were merely an extension of that stranger who lived under the same roof as myself. Dreadful anomaly of the anger that is born of love and that murders love.

I did not speak to him. While he was drinking his tea in the library I stayed in my room. Before leaving he called, 'You don't want to have it out?'

'No.'

There was nothing to 'have out'. Words would shatter against this anger and pain, this hardness in my heart.

All day long I thought of André, and from time to time there was something that flickered in my brain. Like having been hit on the head, when one's sight is disordered and one sees two different images of the world at different weights, without being able to make out which is above and which below. The two pictures I had, of the past André and the present André, did not coincide. There was an error somewhere. This present moment was a lie: it was not we

who were concerned—not André, nor I: the whole thing
was happening in another place. Or else the past was an
illusion, and I had been completely wrong about André.
Neither the one nor the other, I said to myself when I
could see clearly again. The truth was that he had changed.
Aged. He no longer attributed the same importance to
things. Formerly he would have found Philippe's behaviour utterly revolting: now he did no more than disapprove. He would not have plotted behind my back; he
would not have lied to me. His sensitivity and his moral
values had lost their fine edge. Will he follow this tendency? More and more indifferent . . . I can't bear it. This
sluggishness of the heart is called indulgence and wisdom:
in fact it is death settling down within you. Not yet: not
now.

That day the first criticism of my book appeared. Lantier
accused me of going over the same ground again and again.
He's an old fool and he loathes me; I ought never to have
let myself feel it. But in my exacerbated mood I did grow
vexed. I should have liked to talk to André about it, but
that would have meant making peace with him: I did not
want to.

'I've shut up the laboratory,' he said that evening, with
a pleasant smile. 'We can leave for Villeneuve and Italy
whatever day you like.'

'We had decided to spend this month in Paris,' I answered shortly.

'You might have changed your mind.'

'I have not done so.'

André's face darkened. 'Are you going to go on sulking
for long?'

'I'm afraid I am.'

'Well, you're in the wrong. It is out of proportion to
what has happened.'

'Everyone has his own standards.'

'Yours are astray. It's always the same with you. Out of
optimism or systematic obstinacy you hide the truth from

yourself and when it is forced upon you you either collapse or else you explode. What you can't bear—and of course I bear the brunt of it—is that you had too high an opinion of Philippe.'

'You always had too low a one.'

'No. It was merely that I never had much in the way of illusions about his abilities or his character. Yet even so I thought too highly of him.'

'A child is not something you can evaluate like an experiment in the laboratory. He turns into what his parents make him. You backed him to lose, and that was no help to him at all.'

'And you always back to win. You're free to do so. But only if you can take it when you lose. And you can't take it. You always try to get out of paying; you fly into a rage, you accuse other people right and left—anything at all not to own yourself in the wrong.'

'Believing in someone is not being in the wrong.'

'Pigs will fly the day you admit you were mistaken.'

I know. When I was young I was perpetually in the wrong and it was so difficult for me ever to be in the right that now I am very reluctant ever to blame myself. But I was in no mood to acknowledge it. I grasped the whisky bottle. 'Unbelievable! *You* as prosecuting counsel against me!'

I filled a glass and emptied it in one gulp. André's face, André's voice: the same man, another; beloved, hated; this anomaly went down inside my body. My sinews, my muscles contracted in a tetanic convulsion.

'From the very beginning you refused to discuss it calmly. Instead of that you have been swooning about all over the place . . . And now you're going to get drunk? It's grotesque,' he said, as I began my second glass.

'I shall get drunk if I want. It's nothing to do with you: leave me alone.'

I carried the bottle into my room. I settled in bed with a spy-story but I could not read. Philippe. I had been so wholly taken up with my fury against André that his image had faded a little. Suddenly he was there smiling at me with unbearable sweetnesss through the swimming of the whisky. Too high an opinion of him: no. I had loved him for his weaknesses: if he had been less temperamental and less casual he would have needed me less. He would never have been so adorably tender if he had nothing to beg forgiveness for. Our reconciliations, tears, kisses. But in those days it was only a question of peccadilloes. Now it was something quite different. I swallowed a brimming glass of whisky, the walls began to turn, and I sank right down.

The light made its way through my eyelids. I kept them closed. My head was heavy: I was deathly sad. I could not remember my dreams. I had sunk down into black depths—liquid and stifling, like diesel-oil—and now, this morning, I was only just coming to the surface. I opened my eyes. André was sitting in an armchair at the foot of the bed, watching me with a smile. 'My dear, we can't go on like this.'

It was he, the past, the present André, the same man; I acknowledged it. But there was still that iron bar in my chest. My lips trembled. Stiffen even more, sink to the bottom, drown myself in the depths of loneliness and the night. Or try to catch this outstretched hand. He was talking in that even, calming voice I love. He admitted that he had been wrong. But it was for my sake that he had spoken to Philippe. He knew we were both so miserable that he had determined to step in right away, before our break could become definitive.

'You are always so gay and alive, and you have no idea how wretched it made me to see you eating your heart out! I quite understand that at the time you were furious with me. But don't forget what we are for one another: you mustn't hold it against me for ever.'

I gave a weak smile; he came close and put an arm round my shoulders. I clung to him and wept quietly. The warm physical pleasure of tears running down my cheek. What a relief! It is so tiring to hate someone you love.

'I know why I lied to you,' he said to me a little later. 'Because I'm growing old. I knew that telling you the truth would mean a scene: that would never have held me back once, but now the idea of a quarrel makes me feel weary. I took a short cut.'

'Does that mean you are going to lie to me more and more?'

'No, I promise you. And in any case I shan't see Philippe often: we haven't much to say to one another.'

'Quarrels make you feel tired: but you bawled me out very thoroughly yesterday evening, for all that.'

'I can't bear it when you sulk. It's much better to shout and scream.'

I smiled at him. 'Maybe you're right. We had to get out of it.'

He took me by the shoulders. 'We are out of it, really out of it? You aren't cross with me any more?'

'Not any more at all. It's over and done with.'

It was over: we were friends again. But had we said everything we had to say to one another? I had not, at all events. There was still something that rankled—the way André just gave in to old age. I did not want to talk about it to him now: the sky had to be quite clear again first. And what about him? Had he any mental reservations? Was he serious in blaming me for what he called my systematically stubborn optimism? The storm had been too short to change anything between us: but was it not a sign that for some time past—since when?—something had in fact been imperceptibly changing?

Something has changed, I said to myself as we drove down the motorway at ninety miles an hour. I was sitting next to André; our eyes saw the same road and the same sky; but between us, invisible and intangible, there was an insulating layer. Was he aware of it? Yes, certainly he was. The

reason why he had suggested this drive was that he hoped
it might bring to life the memory of other drives in the past
and so bring us wholly together again: it was not like
them at all, however, because he did not look forward to
deriving the least pleasure from it. I ought to have been
grateful for his kindness: but I was not. I was hurt by his
indifference. I had felt it so distinctly that I had almost
refused, but he would have taken the refusal as a mark of
ill-will. What was happening to us? There had been quarrels in our life, but always over serious matters—over the
bringing up of Philippe, for example. They were genuine
conflicts that we resolved violently, but quickly and for
good. This time it had been a great whirling of fog, or
smoke without fire; and because of its very vagueness two
days had not quite cleared it away. And then again, in
former times bed was the place for our stormy reconciliations. Trifling grievances were utterly burnt away in
amorous delight, and we found ourselves together again,
happy and renewed. Now we were deprived of that re-
source.

I saw the signpost; I stared and stared again. 'What?
Already? We only set off twenty minutes ago.'

'I drove fast,' said André.

Milly. When Mama used to take us to see Grandmama,
what an expedition it was! It was the country, vast golden
wheat-fields, and we picked poppies at their edges. That
remote village was now nearer to Paris than Neuilly or
Auteuil had been in Balzac's day.

André found it hard to park the car, for it was market-
day—swarms of cars and pedestrians. I recognized the old
covered market, the Lion d'Or, the houses and their faded
tiles. But the square was completely changed by the stalls
that were set up in it. The plastic pots and toys, the
millinery, tinned food, scent and the jewellery were in no
way reminiscent of the old village fairs. It was Monoprix
or Inno shops spread out in the open air. Glass doors and
walls: a big glittering stationery shop, filled with books

and magazines with shiny covers. Grandmama's house, once a little outside the village, had been replaced by a five-storey building, and it was now right inside the town.

'Would you like a drink?'

'Oh, no!' I said. 'It's not my Milly any more.' Nothing is the same any more, and that's certain: neither Milly, nor Philippe, nor André. Am I?

'Twenty minutes to reach Milly is miraculous,' I said as we got back into the car. 'Only it's not Milly any longer.'

'There you are. The sight of the changing world is miraculous and heart-breaking, both at the same time.'

I reflected. 'You'll laugh at my optimism again, but for me it's above all miraculous.'

'But so it is for me too. The heart-breaking side of growing old is not in the things around one but in oneself.'

'I don't think so. You do lose in yourself as well, but you also gain.'

'You lose much more than you gain. To tell you the truth, I don't see what gain there is, anyhow. Can you tell me?'

'It's pleasant to have a long past behind one.'

'You think you *have* it? I don't, as far as mine is concerned. Just you try telling it over to yourself.'

'I know it's there. It gives depth to the present.'

'All right. What else?'

'You have a much greater intellectual command of things. You forget a great deal, certainly; but in a way even the things one has forgotten are available to one.'

'In your line, maybe. For my part, I am more and more ignorant of everything that is not my own special subject. I should have to go back to the university like an ordinary undergraduate to be up to date with quantum physics.'

'There's nothing to stop you.'

'Perhaps I will.'

'It's strange,' I said. 'We agree about everything; yet not in this. I can't see what you lose in growing old.'

He smiled. 'Youth.'

'It's not in itself a valuable thing.'

'Youth and what the Italians so prettily call *stamina*. The vigour, the fire, that enables you to love and create. When you've lost that, you've lost everything.'

He had spoken in such a tone that I dared not accuse him of self-indulgence. There was something gnawing at him, something I knew nothing about—that I did not want to know about—that frightened me. It was perhaps that which was keeping us apart.

'I shall never believe that you can no longer create,' I said.

'Bachelard says, "Great scientists are valuable to science in the first half of their lives and harmful in the second." They consider me a scientist. All I can do now is try not to be too harmful.'

I made no reply. True or false, he believed what he was saying: it would have been useless to protest. It was understandable that my optimism should often irritate him: in a way it was an evasion of his problem. But what could I do? I could not tackle it for him. The best thing was to be quiet. We drove in silence as far as Champeaux.

'This nave is really beautiful,' said André as we went into the church. 'It reminds me very much of the one at Sens, only its proportions are even finer.'

'Yes, it is lovely. I have forgotten Sens.'

'It's the same thick single pillars alternating with slender twinned columns.'

'What a memory you have!'

Conscientiously we looked at the nave, the choir, the transept. The church was no less beautiful because I had climbed the Acropolis, but my state of mind was no longer the same as it had been in the days when we systematically combed the Ile de France in an aged second-hand car. Neither of us was really taking it in. I was not really interested in the carved capitals, nor in the misericords that had once amused us so.

As we left the church, André said to me, 'Do you think the Truite d'Or is still there?'

'Let's go and see.'

The little inn at the water's edge, with its simple, delightful food, had once been one of our favourite places. We celebrated our silver wedding there, but we had not been back since. This village, with its silence and its little cobbles, had not changed. We went right along the high street in both directions: the Truite d'Or had vanished. We did not like the restaurant in the forest where we stopped: perhaps because we compared it with our memories.

'And what shall we do now?' I asked.

'We had thought of the Château de Vaux and the towers at Blandy.'

'But do you want to go?'

'Why not?'

He did not give a damn about them, and nor indeed did I; but neither of us liked to say so. What exactly was he thinking of, as we drove along the little leaf-scented country roads? About the desert of his future? I could not follow him on to that ground. I felt that there beside me he was alone. I was, too. Philippe had tried to telephone me several times. I had hung up as soon as I recognized his voice. I questioned myself. Had I been too demanding with regard to him? Had André been too scornfully indulgent? Was it this lack of harmony that had damaged him? I should have liked to talk about it with André, but I was afraid of starting a quarrel again.

The Château de Vaux, the towers at Blandy: we carried out our programme. We said, 'I remember it perfectly, I did not remember it at all, these towers are quite splendid . . .' But in one way the mere sight of things is neither here nor there. You have to be linked to them by some plan or some question. All I saw was stones piled one on top of the other.

The day did not bring us any closer together; I felt that

we were both disappointed and very remote from one another as we drove back to Paris. It seemed to me that we were no longer capable of talking to one another. Might all one heard about non-communication perhaps be true, then? Were we, as I had glimpsed in my anger, condemned to silence and loneliness? Had this always been the case with me, and had it only been that stubborn optimism that had made me say it was not? 'I must make an effort,' I said to myself as I went to bed. 'Tomorrow morning we will discuss it. We will try to get to the bottom of it.' The fact that our quarrel had not been dissipated was because it was merely a symptom. Everything would have to be gone into again, radically. Above all not to be afraid of talking about Philippe. A single forbidden subject and our dialogue would be wholly frustrated.

I poured out the tea and I was trying to find the words to begin this discussion when André said, 'Do you know what I should like? To go to Villeneuve straight away. I should rest there better than in Paris.'

So that was the conclusion he had drawn from the failure of yesterday: instead of trying to come closer he was escaping! It sometimes happens that he spends a few days at his mother's house without me, out of affection for her. But this was a way of escaping from our tête-à-tête. I was cut to the quick.

'A splendid idea,' I said curtly. 'Your mother will be delighted. Do go.'

'Wouldn't you like to come?' he asked, in an unnatural tone.

'You know very well that I haven't the least wish to leave Paris so early. I shall come at the date we fixed.'

'As you like.'

I should have stayed in any case: I wanted to work and also to see how my book would be received—to talk to my friends about it. But I was much taken aback at the way he did not press me. Coldly I asked, 'When do you think of going?'

'I don't know: soon. I have absolutely nothing to do here.'

'What does soon mean? Tomorrow? The day after?'

'Why not tomorrow morning?'

So we should be away from one another for a fortnight: he never used to leave me for more than three or four days, except for congresses. Had I been so very unpleasant? He ought to have talked things over with me instead of running away. And yet it was not like him, avoiding an issue. I could only see one explanation for it—always the same explanation—he was getting old. I thought crossly, 'Let him go and get over his ageing somewhere else.' I was certainly not going to raise a finger to keep him here.

We agreed that he should take the car. He spent the day at the garage, shopping, telephoning: he said good-bye to his colleagues. I scarcely saw him. When he got into the car the next day we exchanged kisses and smiles. Then I was back in the library, quite at a loss. I had the feeling that André, ditching me in this way, was punishing me. No: it was merely that he wanted to get rid of me.

Once my first amazement was over I felt lightened. Life as a couple implies decisions. 'When shall we eat? What would you like to have?' Plans come into being. When one is alone things happen without premeditation: it is restful. I got up late; I stayed there lapped in the gentle warmth of the sheets, trying to catch the fleeting shreds of my dreams. I read my letters as I drank my tea, and I hummed 'I get along without you very well . . . of course I do.' Between working hours I strolled about the streets.

This state of grace lasted for three days. On the afternoon of the fourth someone rang with little quick touches on the bell. Only one person rings like that. My heart began to thump furiously. Through the door I said, 'Who is that?'

'Open the door,' cried Philippe. 'I shall keep my finger on the bell until you do.'

I opened, and immediately there were his arms around me and his head leaning on my shoulder. 'Darling, sweetheart, please, please don't hate me. I can't bear life if we are cross with one another. Please. I do so love you!'

How often this imploring voice had melted away my resentment! I let him come into the library. He loved me; I could have no doubt of that. Did anything else matter? The familiar words 'My little boy' were just coming to my lips, but I thrust them back. He was not a little boy.

'Don't try to soften my heart: it's too late. You've spoilt everything.'

'Listen. Perhaps I was wrong, perhaps I have behaved badly—I don't know. It keeps me awake all night. But I don't want to lose you. Have pity on me. You're making me so unhappy!' Childish tears shone in his eyes. But this was not a child any more. A man, Irène's husband, an entirely adult person.

'That's too easy altogether,' I said. 'You quietly go about your business, knowing perfectly well that you are setting us poles apart. And you want me to take it all with a smile —you want everything to be just the same as it was before! No, no, no.'

'Really, you are too hard—you have too much Party spirit altogether. There are parents and children who love one another without having the same political opinions.'

'It is not a question of differing political opinions. You are changing sides out of mere ambition and a desire to succeed at any price. That is what is so tenth-rate.'

'No, no, not at all. My views *have* changed! Maybe I'm easily influenced but truly I have come to see things in another light. I promise you I have!'

'Then you should have told me about it earlier. Not have carried out your wire-pulling behind my back and then face me with a fait accompli. I shall never forgive you that.'

'I didn't dare. You have a way of looking at me that frightens me.'

'You always used to say that: it has never been a valid excuse.'

'Yet you used to forgive me. Forgive me again this time.

Please, please do. I can't bear it when we are against one another, you and I.'

'There's nothing I can do about it. You have acted in such a way that I cannot respect you any more.'

His eyes began to grow stormy: I preferred that. His anger would keep mine up.

'Sometimes you say the cruellest things. For my part I have never wondered whether I respected you or not. You could do bloody-fool things as much as ever you liked and I shouldn't love you any the less. You think love has to be deserved. Oh yes you do: and I've tried hard enough not to be undeserving. Everything I ever wanted to be—a pilot, a racing driver, a reporter: action, adventure—they were all mere whims according to you: I sacrificed them all to please you. The first time I don't give way, you break with me.'

I cut in. 'You're trying to wear me down. Your behaviour disgusts me: that is why I don't want to see you any more.'

'It disgusts you because it goes against your plans. But after all I'm not going to obey you all my life long. You're too tyrannical. Fundamentally you have no heart, only a love of power.' His voice was full of rage and tears. 'All right! Good-bye. Despise me as much as you bloody well like——I shall get along without you very well.'

He stalked towards the door: slammed it behind him. I stood there in the hall, thinking, 'He will come back.' He always came back. I should no longer have had the strength to stand out against him; I should have burst into tears with him. After five minutes I went back to the library; I sat down, and I wept, alone. 'My little boy . . .' What is an adult? A child puffed with age. I plucked the years away from him and saw him at twelve again: impossible to hold anything against him. Yet now he was a man. There was not the slightest reason to judge him less severely than any-one else. Had I a hard heart? Are there people who can love without respect? Where does respect begin and end? And love? If he had failed in his university career, if he had led a common-place, unsuccessful life, my affection would never have failed him: because he would have needed it. If I had come to be of no use to him any longer, but had remained proud of him, I would cheerfully have gone on loving him. But now he escapes me, and at the same time I condemn him. What have I to do with him?

Sadness came down on me again, and it never left me. From that time on when I stayed late in bed it was because, unsupported, I was reluctant to come to a waking knowledge of the world and of my life. Once I was up I was sometimes tempted to go back to bed again until the evening. I flung myself into my work. I stayed at my desk for hours and hours on end, keeping myself going with fruit-juice. When I stopped at the end of the afternoon my head was on fire and my bones hurt. Sometimes I would go so deeply to sleep on my divan that on waking I felt dazed and intensely distressed—it was as though my consciousness, rising up secretly from the darkness, was hesitating before taking flesh again. Or else I stared round at these familiar surroundings with unbelieving eyes—they were the illusory, shimmering other side of the void into which I had sunk. My gaze lingered with astonishment upon the things I had brought back from every part of Europe. Space had retained no mark of my journeys and my recollection would not trouble to call them to mind; and yet there they were, the dolls, the pots, the little ornaments. The merest trifles fascinated me and preoccupied my mind. The juxtaposition of a red scarf and a violet cushion: when did I last see fuchsias, with their bishop's and their cardinal's robes and their long frail penises? When the light-filled convolvulus, the simple dog-rose, the dishevelled honeysuckle, the narcissus with astonished, wide-open eyes in the midst of its whiteness—when? There might be none left on earth, and I should know nothing about it. Nor water-lilies on the lakes nor buckwheat in the fields. All around me the world lay like an immense hypothesis that I no longer verified.

I wrenched myself out of these dark clouds: I went down

into the streets. I looked at the sky, the shabby houses. Nothing moved me at all. The moonlight and the sunset, the smell of showery spring and hot tar, the brilliance and the changing of the year: I have known moments that had the pure blaze of a diamond. But they have always come without being called for. They used to spring up unexpectedly, an unlooked-for truce, an unhoped-for promise, cutting across the activities that insisted upon my presence; I would enjoy them almost illicitly, coming out of the lycée, or the exit of a métro, or on my balcony between two sessions of work, or hurrying along the boulevard to meet André. Now I walked about Paris, free, receptive, and frigidly indifferent. My overflowing leisure handed me the world and at the same time prevented me from seeing it. Just as the sun, filtering through the closed venetian blinds on a hot afternoon, makes the whole magnificence of summer blaze in my mind; whereas if I face its direct harsh glare it blinds me.

I went home: I telephoned André, or he would telephone me. His mother was more pugnacious than ever; he was seeing old school-fellows, walking, gardening. His cheerful friendliness depressed me. I told myself that we should meet again exactly where we had been before, with this wall of silence between us. The telephone—it is not a thing that brings people nearer: it underlines their remoteness. You are not together as you are in a conversation, for you do not see one another. You are not alone as you are in front of a piece of paper that allows you to talk inwardly while you are addressing the other—to seek out and find the truth. I felt like writing to him: but what? Anxiety began to mingle with my distress. The friends to whom I had sent my book ought to have written to tell me about it: not one had done so, not even Martine. The week after André left there were suddenly a great many articles dealing with it. I was disappointed by Monday's, vexed by Wednesday's, quite crushed by Thursday's. The harshest spoke of wearisome repetition, the kindest of 'an interesting restatement'.

Not one had grasped the originality of my work. Had I not managed to make it clear? I telephoned Martine. The reviews were stupid, she said; I should take no notice of them. As for her own opinion, she wanted to wait until she had finished the book before letting me know it: she was going to finish it and think it over that very evening, and the next day she would be coming to Paris. I hung up with a bitter taste in my mouth. Martine had not wanted to talk to me over the telephone: so her opinion was unfavourable. I could not understand. I do not usually delude myself about my own work.

Three weeks had passed since our meeting in the Parc Montsouris—three weeks that counted among the most unpleasant I had ever known. Ordinarily I should have been delighted at the idea of seeing Martine again. But I felt more anxious than I had when I was waiting for the results of the *agrégation*. After the first quick civilities I plunged straight in. 'Well? What do you think of it?'

She answered me in well-balanced phrases—I could sense that they had been carefully prepared. The book was an excellent synthesis, it clarified various obscurities; it was valuable in emphasizing what was new in my work.

'But in itself, does it say anything new?'

'That was not its intention.'

'It was mine.'

She grew confused: I went on and on, I badgered her. As she saw it I had already, in my earlier books, applied the methods I was now putting forward; indeed, in many places I had spoken of them quite explicitly. No, I was producing nothing new. As Pélissier had said, the book was rather a well-based restatement and summing up.

'I had meant to do something quite different.'

I was both stunned and unbelieving, as it often happens when a piece of bad news hits one. The unanimity of the verdict was overwhelming. And yet still I said to myself, 'I cannot have been so wholly wrong as all that.'

We were having dinner in a garden just outside Paris, and I made a great effort to hide my mortification. In the end I said, 'I wonder whether one's not condemned to repetition once one has passed sixty.'

'What a notion!'

'There are plenty of painters, composers, and even philosophers who have done their very best work in their old age; but can you tell me of a single writer?'

'Victor Hugo.'

'All right. But who else? Montesquieu virtually came to an end at fifty-nine with *L'Esprit des Lois*, which he had had in his mind for years and years.'

'There must be others.'

'But not one of them springs to mind.'

'Come! You mustn't lose heart,' said Martine reproachfully. 'Any body of work has its ups and its downs. This time you have not fully succeeded in what you set out to do: you will have another go.'

'Usually my failures spur me on. This time it's different.'

'I don't see how.'

'Because of my age. André says that scientists are finished well before they are fifty. In writing too no doubt there comes a stage at which one only marks time.'

'In writing I'm sure that's not so,' said Martine.

'And in science?'

'There I'm not qualified to form an opinion.'

I could see André's face again. Had he felt the same kind of disappointment that I was feeling? Once and for all? Or time after time? 'You have scientists among your friends. What do they think of André?'

'That he's a great scientist.'

'But what is their opinion of what he's doing at present?'

'That he has a fine team and that their work is very important.'

'He says all the fresh ideas come from the men who work with him.'

'That may well be. It seems that scientists only make discoveries in the prime of life. Nearly all the Nobel prizes for science go to young men.'

I sighed. 'So André was right, then. He'll not discover anything any more.'

'One has no right to make up one's mind about the future in advance,' said Martine, with an abrupt change of tone. 'After all, nothing exists except for particular instances. Generalities do not prove anything.'

'I should like to believe it,' I said, and began to talk of other things.

As she left me, Martine said hesitantly, 'I'm going back to your book. I read it too quickly.'

'You read it, all right, and it doesn't come off. But as you say, it's not very important.'

'Not at all important. I'm quite certain you will still write a great many very good books.' I was almost certain that this was not the case, but I did not contradict her. 'You are so young!' she added.

People often tell me that and I feel flattered. All at once the remark irritated me. It is an equivocal compliment and one that foretells a disagreeable future. Remaining young means retaining lively energy, cheerfulness and vitality of mind. So the fate of old age is the dull daily round, gloom and dotage. I am not young: I am well preserved, which is quite different. Well preserved; and maybe finished and done with. I took some sleeping-pills and went to bed.

When I woke up I was in a very curious state—more feverish than anxious. I stopped telephone calls coming through and set about re-reading my *Rousseau* and *Montesquieu*. I read for ten hours on end, scarcely breaking off to eat a couple of hard-boiled eggs and a slice of ham. It was an odd experience, this bringing to life of pages born of my pen and forgotten. From time to time they interested me—they surprised me as much as if someone else had written them; yet I recognized the vocabulary, the shape of the sentences, the drive, the elliptical forms, the mannerisms. These pages were soaked through and through with myself—there was a sickening intimacy about it, like the smell of a bedroom in which one has been shut up too long. I forced myself to go for a stroll and to dine at the little restaurant nearby: home again I gulped down very strong coffee and I opened this present book. It was all there in my mind, and I knew beforehand what the result of the comparison would be. Everything I had to say had been said in my two monographs. I was doing no more than repeating, in another form, those ideas that had given the monographs their interest. I had deceived myself when I thought I was going on to something new. And what was worse, when my methods were separated from the particular contexts to which I had applied them, they lost their acuity and suppleness. I had produced nothing new: absolutely nothing. And I knew that the second volume would only prolong this stagnation. There it was, then: I had spent three years writing a useless book. Not just a failure, like some others, in which in spite of awkwardness and blunders I did open up certain fresh views. Useless. Only fit for burning.

Do not make up your mind about the future in advance. Easy enough to say. I could see the future. It stretched away in front of me, flat, bare, running on out of sight. Never a plan, never a wish. I should write no more. Then what should I do? What an emptiness within me—all around me. Useless. The Greeks called their old people hornets. 'Useless hornet,' Hecuba called herself in *The Trojan Women*. That was my case. I was shattered. I wondered how people managed to go on living when there was nothing to be hoped for from within.

Out of pride I did not choose to leave any earlier than the fixed date and I did not say anything to André on the telephone. But how long those three days that followed seemed to me! Discs enclosed in their bright-coloured sleeves, books tight-packed on their shelves: neither music nor words could do anything for me. Formerly I had looked to them for stimulus or relaxation. Now they were no more than a diversion whose irrelevance sickened me. See an exhibition, go back to the Louvre? I had so longed to have the leisure to do so in the days when I did not possess it. But if ten days ago all I could see in the churches and châteaux was heaped-up stones, it would be even worse now. Nothing would come over from the canvas to me. For me the pictures would merely be cloth with colours squeezed on from a tube and spread with a brush. Walking bored me: I had already discovered that. My friends were away on holiday and in any case I wanted neither their sincerity nor their falsehoods. Philippe—how I regretted him, and how painfully! I thrust his image aside: it made my eyes fill with tears.

So I stayed at home, brooding. It was very hot, and even if I lowered the sun-blinds I stifled. Time stopped flowing. It is dreadful—I feel like saying it is unfair—that it should be able to go by both so quickly and so slow. I was walking through the gates of the lycée at Bourg, almost as young as my own pupils, gazing with pity at the old grey-haired teachers. Flash, and I was an old teacher myself; and then the lycée gates closed behind me. For years and years my pupils gave me the illusion that my age did not alter: at the beginning of each school year I found them there again, as young as ever; and I adapted myself to this unchanging state. In the great sea of time I was a rock beaten by waves that were continually renewed—a rock that neither moved nor crumbled. And all at once the tide was carrying me away, and would go on carrying me until I ran aground in death. My life was hurrying, racing tragically towards its end. And yet at the same time it was dripping so slowly, so very slowly now, hour by hour, minute by minute. One always has to wait until the sugar melts, the memory dies, the wound scars over, the sun sets, the unhappiness lifts and fades away. Strange anomaly of these two rhythms. My days fly galloping from me; yet the long dragging out of each one makes me weary, weary.

There was only one hope left to me—André. But could he fill this emptiness within me? Where did our relationship stand? And in the first place what had we been for one another, all through this life that is called life together? I wanted to make up my mind about that without cheating. In order to do so, I should have to recapitulate the story of our life. I had always promised myself that I should do so. I tried. Deep in an armchair, staring at the ceiling, I told over our first meetings, our marriage, the birth of Philippe. I learnt nothing that I had not known already. What poverty! 'The desert of time past,' said Chateaubriand. He was right, alas! I had had a general sort of idea that the life I had behind me was a landscape in which I could wander as I pleased, gradually exploring its windings and its hidden valleys. No. I could repeat names and dates, just as a schoolboy can bring out a carefully-learnt lesson on a subject he knows nothing about. And at long intervals there arose worn, faded images, as abstract as those in my old French History: they stood out arbitrarily, against a white background. Throughout all this calling up of the past André's face never changed. I stopped. What I had to do was to reflect. Had he loved me as I loved him? At the beginning I think he did; or rather the question never arose for either of us, for we were so happy together. But when his work no longer satisfied him, did he come to the conclusion that our love was not enough for him? Did it disappoint him? I think he looks upon me as a mathematical constant whose disappearance would take him very much aback without any way altering his destiny, since the heart of the matter lies elsewhere. In that case even my understanding is not much help to him. Would another woman have succeeded in giving him more? Who had set up the barrier between us? Had he? Had I? Both of us? Was there any possibility of doing away with it? I was tired of asking myself questions. The words came to pieces in my mind: love, understanding, disagreement—they were noises, devoid of meaning. Had they ever had any? When

I stepped into the express, the Mistral, early in the afternoon, I had absolutely no idea of what I should find.

He was waiting for me on the platform. After all those mental images and words and that disincarnate voice, the sudden manifestation of a physical presence! Sunburnt, thinner, his hair cut, wearing cotton trousers and a short-sleeved shirt, he was rather unlike the André I had said good-bye to, but it was he. My delight could not be false: it could not dwindle to nothing in a few moments. Or could it? He settled me into the car in the kindest way, and as we drove towards Villeneuve his smiles were full of affection. But we were so much in the habit of talking pleasantly to one another that neither the actions nor the smiles meant much. Was he really pleased to see me again?

Manette placed her dry hand on my shoulder and kissed me quickly on the forehead. 'There you are, my dear child.' When she is dead no one will call me 'dear child' any more. I find it hard to realize that I am now fifteen years older than she was when I first saw her. At forty-five she seemed to me almost as old as she does now.

I sat in the garden with André: the sun-battered roses gave out a scent as heart-touching as a lament. I said to him, 'You've grown younger.'

'That's life in the country. And you, how are you?'

'All right physically. But have you seen my reviews?'

'Some of them.'

'Why didn't you warn me that my book was worth nothing?'

'You exaggerate. It is not so different from the others as you imagined. But it is packed with interesting things.'

'It didn't interest you all that much.'

'Oh, as for me . . . Nothing really holds me any more. I am the world's worst reader.'

'Even Martine thinks poorly of it: and now that I've turned it over in my mind, so do I.'

'You were trying something very difficult and you stumbled a little. But I suppose you see your way clear now: you will put things right in your second volume.'

'No, alas! It is the very conception of the book that is at fault. The second volume would be as bad as the first. I'm giving it up.'

'That's a very hasty decision. Let me read your manuscript.'

'I haven't brought it. I *know* it's bad, believe me.'

He gave me a perplexed look. He knows I am not easily disheartened. 'What are you going to do instead?'

'Nothing. I thought I had my work cut out for two years. All at once there's emptiness.'

He put his hand on mine. 'I can quite see that you are upset. But don't take it too hard. For the moment there is necessarily this emptiness. And then one day an idea will come to you.'

'You see how easy it is to be optimistic where someone else is concerned.'

He went on: that was what was required of him. He spoke of writers that it would be interesting to discuss. But what was the point of starting my *Rousseau* and my *Montesquieu* all over again? I had wanted to hit upon a fresh angle: and that was something I should not find. I remembered the things André had told me. I was discovering those resistances he had spoken of in myself. The way I approached a question, my habit of mind, the way I looked at things, what I took for granted—all this was myself and it did not seem to me that I could alter it. My literary work was over, finished. This did not wound my vanity. If I had died that same night I should still have thought I had made a success of my life. But I was frightened by the waste-land through which I was going to have to drag myself until death came for me. During dinner I found it hard to put a good face upon things. Fortunately Manette and André had a passionate argument about Sino-Soviet relations.

I went up to bed early. My room was filled with the good smell of lavender, thyme and pine-needles: it seemed to me that I had left it only yesterday. A year already! Each year goes by more quickly than the last. I shall not have so very long to wait before I go to sleep for ever. Yet I knew how slowly the hours could drag by. And I still love life too much for the idea of death to be a consolation. In spite of everything I slept, a calming sleep in the silence of the countryside.

'Would you like to go out?' asked André the next morning.

'Indeed I should.'

'I'll show you a charming little place I have discovered. On the banks of the Gard. Bring bathing things.'

'I haven't brought any.'

'Manette will lend you some. You'll be tempted, I assure you.'

We drove along narrow dusty lanes through wild country. André talked away at a great pace. He had not made such a long stay here for years and years. He had had time to explore the country all over again, and to see childhood friends: he seemed markedly younger and more cheerful here than in Paris. It was quite clear that he had not missed me at all. How long would he have gone on cheerfully doing without me?

He stopped the car. 'You see that green patch down there? It's the Gard. It makes a kind of basin: it's perfect for bathing, and the place itself is entrancing.'

'But come, isn't it rather far? We shall have to climb up again.'

'There's nothing to it: I have often done it.'

He darted down the slope, sure-footed and very fast. I followed far behind, holding back and stumbling a little: a fall or a broken bone would not be at all amusing, at my age. I could climb quickly enough, but I had never been much good at going down.

'Isn't it pretty?'

'Very pretty.'

I sat down in the shade of a rock. As for bathing, no. I swim badly. And I am very unwilling to display myself in a bathing-suit, even in front of André. An old man's body, I said to myself, watching him splash about in the water, is after all less ghastly than an old woman's. Green water, blue sky, the smell of the southern hills: I would have been better off here than in Paris. If only he had pressed me I should have come sooner: but that was the very thing he had not wanted.

He sat beside me on the gravel. 'You ought to have come in. It's wonderful!'

'I'm very happy here.'

'What do you think of Mama? She's astonishing, don't you find?'

'Astonishing. What does she do all day?'

'She reads a great deal; she listens to the radio. I suggested buying her a television, but she refused. She said, "I don't let just anyone into my house." She gardens. She goes to the meetings of her cell. She is never at a loss, as she puts it.'

'All in all, it is the best time of her life.'

'Certainly. It's one of those cases in which old age is a happy period—old age after a hard life, one that has been more or less eaten up by others.'

When we began to climb up again it was very hot: the way was longer and harder than André had said. He went up with long strides; and I, who used to climb so cheerfully in former days, dragged along far behind; it was intensely irritating. The sun bored into my head; the shrill death-agony of the love-sick cicadas shattered my ears; I was gasping and panting. 'You're going too fast,' I said.

'You take your time. I'll wait for you at the top.'

I stopped, sweating heavily. I set off again. I was no longer in control of my heart or my breathing; my legs would scarcely obey me, the light hurt my eyes; the pertinacious monotony of the love song, the death song of the cicadas grated on my nerves. I reached the car with my head and my face all afire—I felt as though I were on the very edge of apoplexy.

'I'm done for!'

'You should have come up slower.'

'I remember those easy little paths of yours.'

We drove home without speaking. It was wrong of me to grow cross about a trifle. I had always been quick-tempered; was I going to turn into a shrew? I should have to take care. But I could not get over my vexation. And I felt so unwell that I was afraid I might have sunstroke. I ate a couple of tomatoes and went to lie down in the bedroom, where the darkness, the tiles on the floor and the whiteness of the sheets gave a false impression of coolness. I closed my eyes; in the silence I listened to the tick-tock of a pendulum. I had said to André, 'I don't see what one loses in growing old.' Well, I could see now, all right. I had always refused to consider life as Fitzgerald's 'process of dilapidation'. I had thought my relations with André would never deteriorate, that my body of work would grow continually richer, that Philippe would become every day more and more like the man I had wanted to make of him. As for my body, I never worried about it. And I believed that even silence bore its fruit. What an illusion! Sainte-Beuve's words were truer than Valéry's. 'In some parts one hardens; in others one goes bad: never does one grow ripe.' My body was letting me down. I was no longer capable of writing: Philippe had betrayed all my hopes, and what grieved me even more bitterly was that the relationship between André and me was going sour. What nonsense, this intoxicating notion of progress, of upward movement, that I had cherished, for now the moment of collapse was at hand! It had already begun. And now it would be very fast and very slow: we were going to turn into really old people.

When I went down again the heat had lessened: Manette was reading at a window that gave on to the garden. Age had not taken her powers away; but deep inside her, what went on? Did she think of death? With resignation? With dread? I dared not ask.

'André has gone to play *boules*,' she said. 'He'll be back directly.'

I sat down opposite her. Whatever happened, if I were to reach eighty I should not be like her. I could not see myself calling my solitude freedom and peacefully drawing all the good from each succeeding moment. As far as I was concerned life was gradually going to take back everything it had given me: it had already begun doing so.

'So Philippe has given up teaching,' she said. 'It wasn't good enough for him: he wants to become a bigwig.'

'Yes, alas.'

'The youth of today believes in nothing. And I must say you two don't believe in much, either!'

'André and I? Oh, but we do.'

'André is against everything. That's what's wrong with him. That's why Philippe has turned out badly. One has to be *for* something.'

She has never been able to resign herself to the fact that André will not join the Party. I did not want to argue about it. I told her about our morning's walk and I said, 'Where have you put the photos?'

It is a rite: every year I look through the old album. But it is never in the same place.

She put it down on the table, together with a cardboard box. There are not many very old photographs. Manette on her wedding-day, in a long, severe dress. A group; she and her husband, their brothers, their sisters: a whole generation of which she is the only survivor. André as a child, looking stubborn and determined. Renée at twenty, between her two brothers. We thought we should never get over her death—twenty-four, and she looked forward to so much from life. What would she have got out of it in fact? How would she have put up with growing older? My first meeting with death: how I wept. After that I wept less and less—my parents, my brother-in-law, my father-in-law, our friends. That's something else that ageing means. So many deaths behind one, wept for, forgotten. Often, reading the paper, I see that someone else has died—a writer I liked, a colleague, one of André's former associates, a political fellow-worker, a friend we had lost touch with. It must feel wonderfully strange when, like Manette, one stands there, the only witness to a vanished world.

'You're looking at the photos?' André leant over my shoulder. He leafed through the album and pointed out a picture that showed him at the age of eleven with other boys in his form. 'More than half of them are dead,' he said. 'Pierre, the one here—I saw him again. And this one too. And Paul, who is not in the photo. It's a good twenty years since we met. I scarcely recognized them. You would never imagine they were exactly my age. They have turned into really old men. Much more worn out than Manette. It gave me a jar.'

'Because of the life they've led?'

'Yes. Being a peasant in these parts destroys a man.'

'You must have felt young in comparison with them.'

'Not young. But odiously privileged.' He closed the album. 'I'll take you to Villeneuve for a drink before dinner.'

'All right.'

In the car he told me about the games of *boules* he had just won; he was making great progress since he had come down. His mood seemed to be at set fair; my reverses had not affected it, I observed, rather bitterly. He stopped the car at the edge of a terrace covered with blue and orange sunshades with people drinking pastis under them; the smell of aniseed wafted on the air. He ordered some for us. There was a long silence.

'This is a cheerful little square.'

'Very cheerful.'

'You say that in a funereal voice. Are you sorry not to be in Paris?'

'Oh, no. I don't give a damn about places, just at present.'

'Nor about people either, I take it.'

'What makes you say that?'

'You're not very talkative.'

'I'm sorry. I feel rotten. I had too much sun this morning.'

'Usually you're so tough.'

'I'm getting old.'

There was no friendliness in my voice. What had I expected from André? A miracle? That he should wave a wand and my book would become a good one and the reviews all favourable? Or that my failure should mean nothing any more once I was with him? He had worked plenty of little miracles for me: in the days when he lived tensely reaching out towards his future his eagerness had given life to mine. He gave me confidence, restored my belief in myself. He had lost that power. Even if he had gone on believing in his own future, that would not have been enough to comfort me about mine. He took a letter out of his pocket.

'Philippe has written to me.'

'How did he know where you were?'

'I telephoned him the day I left to say good-bye. He tells me you threw him out.'

'Yes. I don't regret it. I cannot love anyone I do not respect.'

André looked at me hard. 'I don't know that you are being altogether honest.'

'How do you mean?'

'You are setting it all on a moral plane, whereas it is primarily on the emotional plane that you feel you have been betrayed.'

'Both are there.'

Betrayed, abandoned: yes. Too painful a wound for me to be able to talk about. We relapsed into silence. Was it going to settle there between us for good? A couple who go on living together merely because that was how they began, without any other reason: was that what we were turning into? Were we going to spend another fifteen, twenty years, without any particular grievance or enmity, but each enclosed in his own world, wholly bent on his own problem, brooding over his own private failure, words grown wholly useless? We had taken to living out of step. In Paris I was cheerful and he was gloomy. I resented his gaiety now that I had become low-spirited. I made an effort. 'In three days we shall be in Italy. Do you like the idea?'

'I like it if you do.'

'I like it if you like it.'

'Because you really don't give a damn about places?'

'It's the same with you, often enough.'

He made no reply. Something had gone wrong with our communication: each was taking what the other said amiss. Should we ever get out of it? Why tomorrow rather than today: why in Rome rather than here?

'Well, let's go back,' I said, after a pause.

We killed the evening playing cards with Manette.

The next day I refused to face the sun and the strident shrieking of the cicadas. What was the point? I knew that confronted with the palace of the popes, or the Pont du Gard, I should remain as unmoved as I had been at Champeaux. I invented a head-ache so as to stay at home. André had brought a dozen new books and he plunged deep into one of them. I keep up to date and I knew them all. I looked through Manette's library. The Garnier classics; some of the Pléiade collection we had given her as presents. There were many books there that I had not had an opportunity of going back to for ages and ages: I had forgotten them. And yet a feeling of weariness came over me at the idea of reading them again. As you read so you remember; or at least you have the illusion of remembering. The first freshness is lost. What had they to offer me, these writers who had made me what I was and should remain? I opened some volumes and turned a few pages : they all of them had a taste almost as sickening as that of my own books—a taste of decay.

Manette looked up from her paper. 'I'm beginning to think that I'll see men on the moon with my own eyes.'

'Your own eyes? You'll make the journey?' asked André, with laughter in his voice.

'You know very well what I mean. I shall know they are there. And it'll be the Russians, my boy. The Yankees missed by a mile, with their pure oxygen.'

'Yes, Mama, you'll see the Russians on the moon,' said André affectionately.

'And to think we began in caves,' went on Manette meditatively, 'with no more than our ten fingers to help us. And we've reached this point : you must admit it's heartening.'

'The history of mankind is very fine, true enough,' said André. 'It's a pity that that of men should be so sad.'

'It won't always be sad. If the Chinese don't blow the world to pieces, our grandchildren will know socialism. I'd happily live another fifty years to see that.'

'What a woman! Do you hear that?' he said to me. 'She would sign on again for another fifty years.'

'You wouldn't, André?'

'No, Mama : frankly I wouldn't. History follows such very curious paths that I scarcely feel it has anything to do with me at all. I have the impression of being on the touch-line. So in fifty years' time . . .'

'I know : you no longer believe in anything,' said Manette disapprovingly.

'That's not quite true.'

'What do you believe in?'

'People's suffering, and the fact that it is abominable. One should do everything to abolish it. To tell you the truth, nothing else seems to me of any importance.'

'In that case,' I asked, 'why not the bomb? Why not annihilation? Let everything go up and there's an end of it.'

'There are times when one is tempted to wish for it. But I prefer to hope that there can be life, life without suffering.'

'Life to do something with,' said Manette pugnaciously.

André's tone of voice struck me: he was not so uncaring as he seemed. 'It's a pity that that of men should be so sad.' How feelingly he had said that! I looked at him and I felt such a wave of feeling towards him that all at once I was filled with certainty. Never should we be two strangers. One of these days, maybe tomorrow, we should find one another again, for my heart was already with him once more. After dinner it was I who suggested that we should go out. We climbed slowly towards the Fort Saint-André. I said, 'Do you really think that nothing counts, apart from doing away with suffering?'

'What else can count?'

'It's not very cheerful.'

'No. Even less cheerful since one does not know how to set about it.' He was silent for a moment. 'Mama was wrong in saying that we don't believe in anything. But there's virtually no cause that is entirely our own: we are not for the USSR and its compromises; nor for China, either. In France we are neither for the régime nor for any of the parties in the opposition.'

'It's a comfortless situation,' I said.

'It goes some way towards explaining Philippe's attitude: being against everything, when you are thirty, has nothing very exalting about it.'

'Nor when you are sixty either. But there is no reason for betraying one's opinions.'

'Were they really *his* opinions?'

'How do you mean?'

'Oh, of course he is disgusted by flagrant injustice and gross corruption. But he has never been really politically-minded. He took on our opinions because he could not do otherwise—he saw the world through our eyes. But just how deeply was he convinced?'

'What about the risks he ran during the Algerian war?'

'That did genuinely revolt him. And then the speeches and the protests and manifestoes—it was all action and adventure. It does not prove that he was deeply committed to the Left.'

'It's a quaint way of defending Philippe, pulling him to pieces.'

'No. I'm not pulling him to pieces. The more I think it over, the more excuses I find for him. I see just how much we weighed him down: in the end he had to assert himself against us, at any price. And then talking of Algeria—he was sickeningly disillusioned over that. Not one of those fellows he endangered himself for has ever taken any notice of him since. And the great man there is de Gaulle.'

We sat on the grass just under the fort. I listened to André's voice, calm and convincing; we could talk to one another again and something melted inside me. For the first time I thought of Philippe with no anger. With no pleasure, either, but tranquilly: perhaps because André was suddenly so near to me that the picture of Philippe was blurred and indistinct. 'We did weigh him down,' I said, candidly. 'Do you think I ought to see him again?' I asked.

'It would hurt him immensely if you were to go on not being on speaking terms with him: and what would be the point of it?'

'I have no wish to hurt him. I feel indifferent, that's all.'

'Oh, of course, it will never be the same between him and us.'

I looked at André. It seemed to me that between him and me everything was the same again already. The moon was shining, and so was the little star that faithfully accompanies it: a great peace came down upon me. *Little Star that I see, Drawn by the moon.* The old words, just as they were first written, were there on my lips. They were a link joining me to the past centuries, when the stars shone exactly as they do today. And this rebirth and this permanence gave me a feeling of eternity. The world seemed

to me as fresh and new as it had been in the first ages, and
this moment sufficed to itself. I was there, and I was
looking at the tiled roofs at our feet, bathed in the moonlight, looking at them for no reason, looking at them for
the pleasure of seeing them. There was a piercing charm in
this lack of involvement. 'That's the great thing about
writing,' I said. 'Pictures lose their shape; their colours
fade. But words you carry away with you.'

'What makes you think of that?' asked André.

I quoted the two lines of *Aucassin et Nicolette* and I
added regretfully, 'How lovely the nights are here!'

'Yes. It's a pity you didn't come sooner.'

I started. 'A pity? But you didn't want me to come!'

'Me? I like that. It was you who refused. When I said
to you, "Why not leave for Villeneuve right away?" you
answered, "What a good idea. Do go." '

'That was not how it was at all. You said—and I can
remember your words exactly—"What I should like is to
go to Villeneuve." You were sick of me; all you wanted to
do was to get the hell out of it.'

'You're insane! My obvious meaning was I should like
us to go to Villeneuve. And you replied "Go on, then" in a
voice that quite chilled me. But even so, I pressed you.'

'Oh, just as a matter of form. You certainly reckoned on
my refusing.'

'Not in the very least.'

He was so sincere that doubt seized me. Could I have
been mistaken? The scene was there fixed in my mind: I
could not make it change. But I was certain he was not
lying.

'How stupid it is,' I said. 'It gave me such a jar when I
saw you had made up your mind to go off without me.'

'It is stupid,' said André. 'I wonder why you thought
that?'

I reflected. 'I did not trust you.'

'Because I had lied to you?'

'You seemed to me to have changed for some time past.'

'In what way?'

'You were playing at being an old man.'

'It was not a game—you said to me yourself, "I'm growing old" yesterday.'

'But you let yourself go. In all sorts of ways.'

'For example?'

'Mannerisms. That way of messing about with your gum.'

'Oh, that . . .'

'What?'

'My jaw is slightly infected just there; if it gets bad my bridge will go and I shall have to wear false teeth. You see what I mean!'

I saw what he meant. Sometimes I dream that all my teeth fall to pieces in my mouth and all at once there is senile decay developing. False teeth . . .

'Why didn't you tell me?'

'There are some nasty little things one keeps to oneself.'

'That may be a mistake. That's how misunderstandings arise.'

'Maybe.' He stood up. 'Come on: we shall be catching cold.'

I got up too. We walked gently down the grassy slope.

'Yet to a certain extent you were right in saying that I was putting it on,' said André. 'I overdid it. When I saw all those fellows so very much more decrepit than I am and yet still taking things just as they come, without moaning about it at all, I told myself that it really would not do. I decided to pull myself together.'

'Oh, that's it, then! I thought it was my not being here that had made you so good-tempered again.'

'What a notion! Far from it: it was largely on your account that I determined to take myself in hand. I don't want to be an old bore. Old is quite enough: bore, no.'

I took his arm: I squeezed it. I had recovered the André I had never lost and that I never should lose. We walked into the garden and sat on a bench at the foot of a cypress. The moon and its little star were shining over the house.

'Still,' I said, 'it's true that old age does exist. And it's no fun telling oneself that one is done for.'

He put his hand on mine. 'Don't tell yourself any such thing. I think I know why you did not succeed with this book. You set off with a sterile ambition—the ambition of doing something quite new and of excelling yourself. That is a fatal error. To understand Rousseau and Montesquieu and to make them understood, that was a solid plan and one that carried you a long way. If something really grips you again, you may still do good work.'

'All in all, my literary work will remain what it is: I've seen my limits.'

'From a self-regarding point of view you may not go much farther, that's true. But you can still interest readers, make them think and enrich them.'

'Let's hope so.'

'For my part I've taken a decision. I shall go on for one more year and then stop. I shall go back to learning, bring myself up to date and fill in my gaps.'

'You think that after that you will set off again with fresh strength?'

'No. But there are things I don't know and that I want to know. Just as to know them.'

'That will be enough for you?'

'For some time, at all events. Don't let's look too far ahead.'

'You're right.'

We had always looked far ahead. Should we now have to learn to live a short-term life? We sat there side by side beneath the stars, with the sharp scent of the cypress wafting by us; our hands touched. For a moment time stopped still. It would soon start flowing again. What then? Should I be able to work or not? Would my bitterness against Philippe die away? Would the dread of ageing take hold of me again? Do not look too far ahead. Ahead there were the horrors of death and farewells: it was false teeth, sciatica, infirmity, intellectual barrenness, loneliness in a strange world that we would no longer understand and that would carry on without us. Shall I succeed in not lifting my gaze to those horizons? Or shall I learn to behold them without horror? We are together: that is our good fortune. We shall help one another to live through this last adventure, this adventure from which we shall not come back. Will that make it bearable for us? I do not know. Let us hope so. We have no choice in the matter.

THE
MONOLOGUE

The monologue is her form of revenge.

Flaubert

The silly bastards! I drew the curtains they keep the stupid coloured lanterns and the fairy lights on the Christmas trees out of the flat but the noises come in through the walls. Engines revving brakes and now here they are starting their hooters big shots is what they take themselves for behind the wheel of their dreary middle-class family cars their lousy semi-sports jobs their miserable little Dauphines their white convertibles. A white convertible with black seats that's terrific and the fellows whistled when I went by with slanting sunglasses on my nose and a Hermès scarf on my head and now they think they're going to impress me with their filthy old wrecks and their bawling klaxons! If they all smashed into one another right under my windows how happy I should be happy. The swine they are shattering my ear-drums they are utterly repulsive yet still I'd rather have my ears shattered than hear the telephone not ringing. Stop the uproar silence: sleep. And I shan't get a wink yesterday I couldn't either I was so sick with horror because it was the day before today. I've taken so many sleeping-pills they don't work any more and that doctor is a sadist he gives them to me in the form of suppositories and I can't stuff myself like a gun. I've got to get some rest I must be able to cope with Tristan tomorrow: no tears no shouting. 'This is an absurd position. A ghastly mess, even from the point of view of dough! A child needs its mother.' I'm going to have another sleepless night my nerves will be completely frazzled I'll make a cock of it. Bastards! They thump thump in my head I can see them I can hear them. They are stuffing themselves with cheap foie-gras and burnt turkey they drool over it Albert and Madame Nanard Etiennette their snotty offspring my mother: it's flying in the face of nature that my own brother my own mother should prefer my ex-husband to me. I've nothing whatever to say to them only just let them stop preventing me sleeping; you get so you are fit to be shut up you confess everything, true or false, they needn't count on that though I'm tough they won't get me down.

Celebrations with them, how they stank: it was ghastly enough quite ghastly enough on ordinary days! I always loathed Christmas Easter July 14. Papa lifted Nanard on to his shoulders so that he could see the fireworks and I stayed there on the ground squashed between them just at prick-level and that randy crowd's smell of sex and Mama said 'there she is snivelling again' they stuffed an ice into my hand there was nothing I wanted to do with it I threw it away they sighed I couldn't be slapped on a July 14 evening. As for him he never touched me I was the one he liked best: 'proper little God-damn woman.' But when he kicked the bucket she didn't bother to hold in any more and she used to swipe me across the face with her rings. I never slapped Sylvie once. Nanard was the king. She used to take him into her bed in the morning and I heard them tickling one another he says it's untrue I'm disgusting of course he's not going to confess they never do confess indeed maybe he's forgotten they are very good at forgetting anything inconvenient and I say they are shits on account of I do remember: she used to wander about her brothel of a room half-naked in her white silk dressing-gown with its stains and cigarette-holes and he clung around her legs it makes you really sick mothers with their little male jobs and I was supposed to be like them no thank you very much indeed. I wanted decent children clean children I didn't want Francis to become a fairy like Nanard. Nanard with his five kids he's a bugger for all that you can't deceive me you really must hate women to have married that cow.

It's not stopping. How many of them are there? In the streets of Paris hundreds of thousands. And it's the same in every town all over the world: three thousand million and it'll get worse: famines there are not nearly enough more and more and more people: even the sky's infested with them presently they will be as thick in space as they are on the motorways and the moon you can't look at it any more without thinking that there are cunts up there spouting away. I used to like the moon it was like me, and they've mucked it up like they muck everything up they are revolting those photos—a dreary greyish dusty thing anyone at all can trample about on.

I was clean straight uncompromising. No cheating: I've had that in my bones since I was a child. I can see myself now a quaint little brat in a ragged dress Mama looked after me so badly and the kind lady simpering 'And so we love our little brother, do we?' And I answered calmly, 'I hate him.' The icy chill: Mama's look. It was perfectly natural that I should have been jealous all the books say so: the astonishing thing the thing I like is that I should have admitted it. No compromise no act: that proper little woman was me all right. I'm clear I'm straight I don't join in any act: that makes them mad they hate being seen through they want you to believe the stuff they hand out or at least to pretend to.

Here's some of their bloody nonsense now—rushing up the stairs laughter voices all in a tizzy. What the hell sense does that make, all working themselves up at a set date a set time just because you start using a new calendar? All my life it's made me sick, this sort of hysterical crap. I ought to tell the story of my life. Lots of women do it people print them people talk about them they strut about very pleased with themselves my book would be more interesting than all their balls: it's made me sweat but I've lived and I've lived without lies without sham how furious it would make them to see my name and picture in the shop-windows and everyone would learn the real genuine truth. I'd have a whole raft of men at my feet again they're such grovelling creatures that the most dreadful slob once she's famous they make a wild rush for her.

Maybe I should meet one who would know how to love me.

My father loved me. No one else. Everything comes from that. All Albert thought of was slipping off I loved him quite madly poor fool that I was. How I suffered in those days, young and as straight as they come! So of course you do silly things : maybe it was a put-up job what is there to show he didn't know Olivier? A filthy plot it knocked me completely to pieces.

Now of course that just had to happen they are dancing right over my head. My night is wrecked finished tomorrow I shall be a rag I shall have to dope myself to manage Tristan and the whole thing will end in the shit. You mustn't do it! Swine! It's all that matters to me in life sleep. Swine. They are allowed to shatter my ears and trample on me and they're making the most of it. 'The dreary bitch downstairs can't make a fuss it's New Year's Eve.' Laugh away I'll find some way of getting even she'll bitch you the dreary bitch I've never let anyone walk over me ever. Albert was livid. 'No need to make a scene!' oh yes indeed there was! He was dancing with Nina belly to belly she was sticking out her big tits she stank of scent but underneath it you got a whiff of bidet and he was jigging about with a prick on him like a bull. Scenes I've made scenes all right in my life. I've always been that proper little woman who answered 'I hate him' fearless open as a book dead straight.

They're going to break through the ceiling and come down on my head. I can see them from here it's too revolting they're rubbing together sex to sex the women the respectable women it makes them wet they're charmed with themselves because the fellow's tail is standing up. And each one of them is getting ready to give his best friend a pair of horns his dearly beloved girl-friend they'll do it that very night in the bathroom not even lying down dress hitched up on their sweating arse when you go and pee you'll tread in the mess like at Rose's the night of my scene. Maybe it's on the edge of a blue party that couple upstairs they're in their fifties at that age they need whore-house tricks to be able to thread the needle. I'm sure Albert and his good lady have whore-parties you can see from Christine's face she's ready for anything at all he wouldn't have to hold himself back with her. Poor bleeder that I was at twenty-two simple-minded too shame-faced. Touching, that awkwardness: I did really deserve to be loved. Oh I've been done dirt life's given me no sort of a break.

Hell I'm dying of thirst I'm hungry but it would slay me to get up out of my armchair and go to the kitchen. You freeze to death in this hole only if I turn up the central-heating the air will dry out completely there's no spit left in my mouth my nose is burning. What a bleeding mess their civilization. They can muck up the moon but can't heat a flat. If they had any sense they'd invent robots that would go and fetch me fruit-juice when I want some and see to the house without my having to be sweet to them and listen to all their crap.

Mariette's not coming tomorrow fine I'm sick of her old father's cancer. At least I've disciplined *her* she keeps more or less in her place. There are some that put on rubber gloves to do the washing-up and play the lady that I cannot bear. I don't want them to be sluts either so you find hairs in the salad and finger-marks on the doors. Tristan is a cunt. I treat my dailies very well. But I want them to do their jobs properly without making a fuss or telling me the story of their lives. For that you have to train them just as you have to train children to make worth-while grown-ups out of them.

Tristan has not trained Francis: that bitch of a Mariette is leaving me in the lurch. The drawing-room will be a pig-sty after they've been. They'll come with a plushy present everyone will kiss everyone else I will hand round little cakes Francis will make the answers his father has gone over with him he lies like a grown-up man. I should have made a decent child of him. I shall tell Tristan a kid de-prived of his mother always ends up by going to the bad he'll turn into a hooligan or a fairy you don't want that. My serious thoughtful voice makes me feel sick: what I should really like to do is scream it's unnatural to take a child away from its mother! But I'm dependent on him. 'Threaten him with divorce,' said Dédé. That made him laugh. Men hold together so the law is so unfair and he has so much pull that it's him that would get the decree. He would keep Francis and not another penny and you can whistle for the rent. Nothing to be done against this filthy blackmail—an allowance and the flat in exchange for Francis. I am at his mercy. No lolly you can't stand up for yourself you're less than nothing a zero twice over. What a numskull I didn't give a damn about money unselfish halfwit. I didn't twist their arms a quarter enough. If I had stayed with Florent I should have made myself a pretty little nest-egg. Tristan fell for me fell right on his face I had pity on him. And there you are! This puffed-up little pseudo-Napoleon leaves me flat because I don't swoon go down on my knees in admiration before him. I'll fix him. I'll tell him I'm going to tell Francis the truth: I'm not ill I live alone because that swine ditched me he buttered me up then he tortured me about. Go into hysterics in front of the boy bleed to death on their door-mat that or something else. I have weapons I'll use them he'll come back to me I shan't go on rotting all alone in this dump with those people on the next floor who trample me underfoot and the ones next door who wake me every morning with their radio and no one to bring me so much as a crust when I'm hungry. All those fat cows have a man to protect them and kids to wait on them and me nothing: this can't go on. For a fortnight now the plumber hasn't come a woman on her own they think they can do anything how despicable people are when you're down they stamp on you. I kick back I keep my end up but a woman alone is spat on. The concierge gives a dirty laugh. At ten in the morning it is *in concordance with the law* to have the radio on: if he thinks I'm impressed by his long words. I had them on the telephone four nights running they knew it was me but impossible to pin it I laughed and laughed. They've coped by having calls stopped I'll find something else. What? Drips like that sleep at night work all day go for a walk on Sunday there's nothing you can get a hold on. A man under my roof. The plumber would have come the concierge would say good day politely the neighbours would turn the volume down. Bloody hell, I want to be treated with respect I want my husband my son my home like everybody else.

A little boy of eleven it would be fun to take him to the circus to the zoo. I'd train him right away. He was easier to handle than Sylvie. She was a tough one to cope with soft and cunning like that slug Albert. Oh, I don't hold it against her poor little creep they all put her against me and she was at the age when girls loathe their mothers they call that ambivalence but it's hatred. There's another of those truths that make them mad. Etiennette dripped with fury when I told her to look at Claudie's diary. She didn't want to look, like those women who don't go to the doctor because they're afraid of having cancer so you're still the dear little mama of a dear little daughter. Sylvie was not a dear little anything I had a dose of that when I read her diary: but as for me I look things straight in the face. I didn't let it worry me all that much I knew all I had to do was wait and one day she would understand and she would say I was the one who was in the right and not them and cram it down their throats. I was patient never did I raise a hand against her. I took care of myself of course. I told her 'You won't get me down.' Obstinate as a mule whining for hours on end days on end over a whim there wasn't the slightest reason for her to see Tristan again. A girl needs a father I ought to know if anybody does: but nobody's even said she needs two. Albert was quite enough of a nuisance already he was taking everything the law allowed him and more I had to struggle every inch of the way he'd have corrupted her if I hadn't fought. The frocks he gave her it was immoral. I didn't want my daughter to turn into a whore like my mother. Skirts up to her knees at seventy paint all over her face! When I passed her in the street the other day I crossed over to the other pavement. With her strutting along like that what a fool I should have looked if she had put on a great reconciliation act. I'm sure her place is as squalid as ever with the cash she flings away at the hairdresser's she could afford herself a daily woman.

No more hooters I preferred that row to hearing them roaring and bellowing in the street: car-doors slamming they shout they laugh some of them are singing they are drunk already and upstairs that racket goes on. They're making me ill there's a foul taste in my mouth and these two little pimples on my thigh they horrify me. I take care I only eat health foods but even so there are people who muck about with their hands more or less clean there's no hygiene anywhere in the world the air is polluted not only because of the cars and the factories but also these millions of filthy mouths swallowing it in and belching it out from morning till night: when I think I'm swimming in their breath I feel like rushing off into the very middle of the desert: how can you keep your body clean in such a lousy disgusting world you're contaminated through all the pores of your skin and yet I was healthy clean I can't bear them infecting me. If I had to go to bed there's not one of them that would move a finger to look after me. I could croak any minute with my poor overloaded heart no one would know anything about it that terrifies the guts out of me. They'll find a rotting corpse behind the door I'll stink I'll have shat the rats will have eaten my nose. Die alone live alone no I can't bear it. I need to have a man I want Tristan to come back lousy dunghill of a world they are shouting they are laughing and here I am withering on the shelf: forty-three it's too soon it's unfair I want to live. Big-time life that's me: the convertible the flat the dresses everything. Florent shelled out and no horsing around—except a little in bed right's right—all he wanted to do was

to go to bed with me and show me off in the smart joints I
was lovely my loveliest time all my girl-friends were dying
with envy. It makes me sick to think of those days nobody
takes me out any more I just stay here stewing in my own
shit. I'm sick of it I'm sick of it sick sick sick sick sick
sick sick sick sick sick sick sick sick sick sick sick sick sick
sick sick sick sick sick sick sick sick sick sick sick sick sick
sick sick sick sick sick sick sick sick sick sick sick sick sick
sick sick sick sick sick sick sick sick sick sick sick sick sick
sick sick sick sick sick sick sick sick sick sick sick sick sick
sick sick sick sick sick sick sick sick sick sick sick sick sick
sick sick sick sick sick sick sick sick sick sick sick sick sick
sick sick.

That bastard Tristan I want him to have me out to a
restaurant to a theatre I'll insist upon it I don't insist nearly
enough all he does is come drooling along here either by
himself or with the kid sits there with a mealy-mouthed
smirk on his face and at the end of an hour he drools off
again. Not so much as a sign of life even on New Year's
Eve! Swine! I'm bored black I'm bored through the
ground it's inhuman. If I slept that would kill the time. But
there is this noise outside. And inside my head they are
giving that dirty laugh and saying 'She's all alone.' They'll
laugh on the other side of their faces when Tristan comes
back to me. He'll come back I'll make him I certainly will.
I'll go to the couturiers again I'll give cocktail parties evening parties my picture will be in *Vogue* with a neckline
plunging to there I have better breasts than anyone. 'Have
you seen the picture of Murielle?' They will be utterly
fucked and Francis will tell them about how we go to the
zoo the circus the skating-rink I'll spoil him that'll make
them choke on their lies their slanders. Such hatred! Clear-
sighted too clear-sighted. They don't like being seen
through: as for me I'm straight I don't join their act I tear
masks off. They don't forgive me for that. A mother jealous
of her daughter so now I've seen everything. She flung me
at Albert's head to get rid of me for other reasons too no I

don't want to believe it. What a dirty trick to have urged me into that marriage me so vital alive a burning flame and him stuffy middle-class cold-hearted prick like limp macaroni. I would have known the kind of man to suit Sylvie. I had her under control yes I was firm but I was always affectionate always ready to talk I wanted to be a friend to her and I would have kissed my mother's hands if she had behaved like that to me. But what a thankless heart. She's dead and so all right what of it? The dead are not saints. She wouldn't co-operate she never confided in me at all. There was someone in her life a boy or maybe a girl who can tell this generation is so twisted. But there wasn't a precaution she didn't take. Not a single letter in her drawers and the last two years not a single page of diary: if she went on keeping one she hid it terribly well even after her death I didn't find anything. Blind with fury just because I was doing my duty as a mother. Me the selfish one when she ran away like that it would have been in my interest to have left her with her father. Without her I still had a chance of making a new life for myself. It was for her own good that I was having none of it. Christine with her three great lumps of children it would have suited her down to the ground to have had a big fifteen-year-old girl she could have given all the chores to poor lamb she had no notion the hysterics she put on for the benefit of the police . . . Yes the police. Was I supposed to put on kid gloves? What are the police there for? Stray cats? Albert offering me money to give up Sylvie! Always this money how grovelling men are they think everything can be bought anyhow I didn't give a damn about his money it was peanuts compared with what Tristan allows me. And even if I had been broke I'd never have sold my daughter. 'Why don't you let her go? That chick only brings you head-aches' Dédé said to me. She doesn't understand a mother's feelings she never thinks of anything but her own pleasure. But one must not always be at the receiving end one must also know how to give. I had a great deal to give Sylvie I should have made her into a fine girl: and I asked nothing from her for myself. I was completely devoted. Such ingratitude! It was perfectly natural I should ask that teacher's help. According to her diary Sylvie worshipped her and I thought she'd hold her bloody tongue the lousy half-baked intellectual. No doubt there was much more between them than I imagined I've always been so clean-minded I never see any harm these alleged brain-workers are all bull-dykes. Sylvie's snivelling and fuss after it and my mother who told me on the phone I had no right to intermeddle with my daughter's friendships. That was the very word she used *intermeddle*. 'Oh as far as that was concerned you never intermeddled. And don't you begin now, if you please.' Straight just like that. And I hung up. My own mother it's utterly unnatural. In the end Sylvie would have realized. That was one of the things that really shattered me at the cemetery. I said to myself, 'A little later she would have said I was in the right.' The ghastliness of remembering the blue sky all those flowers Albert crying in front of everyone Christ you exercise some self-control. I controlled myself yet I knew very well I'd never recover from the blow. It was me they were burying. I have been buried. They've all got together to cover me over deep. Even on this night not a sign of life. They know very well that nights when there are celebrations everybody laughing gorging stuffing one another the lonely ones the bereaved kill themselves just like that. It would suit them beautifully if I were to vanish they hide me in a hole but it doesn't work I'm a burr in their pants. I don't intend to oblige them, thank you very much indeed. I want to live I want to come to life again. Tristan will come back to me I'll be done right by I'll get out of this filthy hole. If I talked to him now I should feel better maybe I'd be able to sleep. He must be at home he's an early-bedder, he saves himself up. Be calm friendly don't get his back up otherwise my night is shot to hell.

He doesn't answer. Either he's not there or he doesn't

want to answer. He's jammed the bell he doesn't want to listen to what I have to say. They sit in judgment upon me and not one of them ever listens to me. I never punished Sylvie without listening to what she had to say first it was she who clammed up who wouldn't talk. Only yesterday he wouldn't let me say a quarter of what I had to say and I could hear him dozing at the other end of the line. It's disheartening. I reason I explain I prove: patiently step by step I force them to the truth I think they're following me and then I ask 'What have I just said?' They don't know they stuff themselves with mental ear-plugs and if a remark happens to get through their answer is just so much balls. I start over again I pile up fresh arguments: same result. Albert is a champion at that game but Tristan is not so bad either. 'You ought to take me away with Francis for the holidays.' He doesn't answer he talks of something else. Children have to listen but they manage to forget. 'What have I said, Sylvie?' 'You said when one is messy in small things one is messy in big ones and I must tidy my room before I go out.' And then the next day she did not tidy it. When I force Tristan to listen to me and he can't find anything to reply—a boy needs his mother a mother can't do without her child it's so obvious that even the crookedest mind can't deny it—he goes to the door, flies down the stairs four at a time while I shout down the well and cut myself off short in case the neighbours think I'm cracked: how cowardly it is he knows I loathe scenes particularly as I've an odd sort of a reputation in this house of course I have they behave so weirdly—unnaturally—that sometimes I do the same. Oh what the hell I used to behave so well it gave me a pain in the arse Tristan's casualness his big laugh his loud voice I should have liked to see him drop down dead when he used to horse around in public with Sylvie.

Wind! It's suddenly started to blow like fury how I should like an enormous disaster that would sweep everything away and me with it a typhoon a cyclone it would be restful to die if there were no one left to think about me:

give up my body my poor little life to them no! But for everybody to plunge into nothingness that would be fine: I'm tired of fighting them even when I'm alone they harry me it's exhausting I wish it would all come to an end! Alas! I shan't have my typhoon I never have anything I want. It's only a little very ordinary wind it'll have torn off a few tiles a few chimney pots everything is mean and piddling in this world nature's as bad as men. I'm the only one that has splendid dreams and it would have been better to choke them right away everything disappoints me always.

Perhaps I ought to stuff up these sleepings things and go to bed. But I'm still too wide awake I'd only writhe about. If I had got him on the phone if we'd talked pleasantly I should have calmed down. He doesn't give a fuck. Here I am torn to pieces by heart-breaking memories. I call him and he doesn't answer. Don't bawl him out don't begin by bawling him out that would muck up everything. I dread tomorrow. I shall have to be ready before four o'clock I shan't have had a wink of sleep I'll go out and buy petits fours that Francis will tread into the carpet he'll break one of my little ornaments he's not been properly brought up that child as clumsy as his father who'll drop ash all over the place and if I say anything at all Tristan will blow right up he never lets me keep my house as it ought to be yet after all it's enormously important. Just now it's perfect the drawing-room polished shining like the moon used to be. By seven tomorrow evening it'll be utterly filthy I'll have to spring-clean it even though I'll be all washed out. Explaining everything to him from a to z will wash me right out. He's tough. What a clot I was to drop Florent for him! Florent and I we understood one another he coughed up I lay on my back it was cleaner than those capers where you hand out tender words to one another. I'm too soft-hearted I thought it was a terrific proof of love when he offered to marry me and there was Sylvie the ungrateful little thing I wanted her to have a real home and a mother

no one could say a thing against a married woman a
banker's wife. For my part it gave me a pain in the arse to
come it the lady to be friends with crashing bores. Not so
surprising that I burst out now and then. 'You're setting
about it the wrong way with Tristan, Dédé used to tell me.
Then later on 'I told you so!' It's true I'm headstrong I
take the bit between my teeth I don't calculate. Maybe I
should have learnt to compromise if it hadn't been for all
those disappointments. Tristan made me utterly sick I let
him know it. People can't bear being told what you really
think of them. They want you to believe their fine words or
at least to pretend to. As for me I'm clear-sighted I'm
frank I tear masks off. The dear kind lady simpering 'So
we love our little brother do we?' and my collected little
voice: 'I hate him.' I'm still that proper little woman
who says what she thinks and doesn't cheat. It made my
guts grind to hear him holding forth and all those bloody
fools on their knees before him. I came clumping along in
my big boots I cut their fine words down to size for them
—progress prosperity the future of mankind happiness
peace aid for the under-developed countries peace upon
earth. I'm not a racist but don't give a fuck for Algerians
Jews negroes in just the same way I don't give a fuck for
Chinks Russians Yanks Frenchmen. I don't give a fuck for
humanity what has it ever done for me I ask you? If they
are such bleeding fools as to murder one another bomb one
another plaster one another with napalm wipe one another
out I'm not going to weep my eyes out. A million children
have been massacred so what? Children are never anything but the seed of bastards it unclutters the planet a little
they all admit it's overpopulated don't they? If I were the
earth it would disgust me, all this vermin on my back, I'd
shake it off. I'm quite willing to die if they all die too.
I'm not going to go all soft-centred about kids that mean
nothing to me. My own daughter's dead and they've stolen
my son from me.

I should have won her back. I'd have made her into a

worthwhile person. But it would have taken me time. Tristan did not help me the selfish bastard our quarrels bored him he used to say to me 'Leave her in peace.' You ought not to have children in a way Dédé is right they only give you one bloody head-ache after another. But if you do have them you ought to bring them up properly. Tristan always took Sylvie's side: now even if I had been wrong—let's say I might have been sometimes for the sake of argument—from an educational point of view it's disastrous for one parent to run out on the other. He was on her side even when I was right. Over that little Jeanne for example. It quite touches my heart to think of her again her moist adoring gaze: they can be very sweet little girls she reminded me of my own childhood badly-dressed neglected slapped scolded by that concierge of a mother of hers always on the edge of tears: she thought I was lovely she stroked my furs she did little things for me and I slipped her pennies when no one was looking I gave her sweeties poor pet. She was the same age as Sylvie I should have liked them to be friends Sylvie disappointed me bitterly. She whined 'Being with Jeanne bores me.' I told her she was a heartless thing I scolded her I punished her. Tristan stood up for her on the grounds that you can't force liking that battle lasted for ages I wanted Sylvie to learn generosity in the end it was little Jeanne who backed out.

It's quietened down a bit up there. Footsteps voices in the staircase car-doors slamming there's still their bloody fool dance-music but they aren't dancing any more. I know what they're at. This is the moment they make love on beds on sofas on the ground in cars the time for being sick sick sick when they bring up the turkey and the caviar it's filthy I have a feeling there's a smell of vomit I'm going to burn a joss-stick. If only I could sleep I'm wide awake dawn is far away still this is a ghastly hour of the night and Sylvie died without understanding me I'll never get over it. This smell of incense is the same as at the funeral service: the candles the flowers the catafalque.

My despair. Dead: it was impossible! For hours and hours I sat there by her body thinking no of course not she'll wake up I'll wake up. All that effort all those struggles scenes sacrifices—all in vain. My life's work gone up in smoke. I left nothing to chance; and chance at its cruellest reached out and hit me. Sylvie is dead. Five years already. She is dead. For ever. I can't bear it. Help it hurts it hurts too much get me out of here I can't bear the breakdown to start again no help me I can't bear it any longer don't leave me alone . . .

Who to ring? Albert Bernard would hang up like a flash: he blubbered in front of everybody but tonight he's gorged and had fun and I'm the one that remembers and weeps. My mother: after all a mother is a mother I never did her any harm she was the one who mucked up my childhood she insulted me she presumed to tell me . . . I want her to take back what she said I won't go on living with those words in my ears a daughter can't bear being cursed by her mother even if she's the ultimate word in tarts.

'Was it you who rang me? . . . It surprised me too but after all on a night like this it could happen you might think of my grief and say to yourself that a mother and daughter can't be on bad terms all their lives long; above all since I really can't see what you can possibly blame me for . . . Don't shout like that . . .'

She has hung up. She wants peace. She poisons my life the bitch I'll have to settle her hash. What hatred! She's always hated me: she killed two birds with one stone in marrying me to Albert. She made sure of her fun and my unhappiness. I didn't want to admit it I'm too clean too pure but it's staringly obvious. It was she who hooked him at the physical culture class and she treated herself to him slut that she was it can't have been very inviting to stuff her but what with all the men who'd been there before she must have known a whole bagful of tricks like getting astride over the guy I can just imagine it it's perfectly revolting the way respectable women make love. She was too long in the tooth to keep him she made use of me they cackled behind my back and went to work again: one day when I came back unexpectedly she was all red. How old was she when she stopped? Maybe she treats herself to gigolos she's not so poor as she says she's no doubt kept jewels that she sells off in the sly. I think that after you're fifty you ought to have the decency to give it up: I gave it up well before ever since I went into mourning. It doesn't interest me any more I'm blocked I never think of those things any more even in dreams. That old bag it makes you shudder to think of between her legs she drips with scent but underneath she smells she used to make up she titivated she didn't wash not what I call wash when she pretended to use a douche it was only to show Nanard her backside. Her son her son-in-law: it makes you feel like throwing up. They would say, 'You've got a filthy mind.' They know how to cope. If you point out that they're walking in shit they scream it's you that have dirty feet. My dear little girl-friends would have liked to have a go with my husband women they're all filthy bitches and there he was shouting at me, 'You are contemptible.' Jealousy is not contemptible real love has a beak and claws. I was not one of those women who will put up with sharing or whore-house parties like Christine I wanted us to be a clean, proper couple a decent couple. I can control myself but I'm not a complete drip I've never been afraid of making a scene. I did not allow anyone to make fun of me I can look back over my past—nothing unwholesome nothing dubious. I'm the white blackbird.

Poor white blackbird: he's the only one in the world. That's what maddens them: I'm something too far above them. They'd like to do away with me they've shut me up in a cage. Shut in locked in I'll end by dying of boredom really dying. It seems that that happens to babies even, when no one looks after them. The perfect crime that leaves no trace. Five years of this torture already. That ass Tristan

who says travel you've plenty of money. Plenty to travel
on the cheap like with Albert in the old days: you don't
catch me doing that again. Being poor is revolting at any
time but when you travel . . .! I'm not a snob I showed
Tristan I wasn't impressed by de luxe palace hotels and
women dripping with pearls the fancy doormen. But
second-rate boarding-houses and cheap restaurants, no *sir*.
Dubious sheets filthy tablecloths sleep in other people's
sweat in other people's filth eat with badly-washed knives
and forks you might catch lice or the pox and the smells
make me sick: quite apart from the fact that I get deadly
constipated because those loos where everybody goes turn
me off like a tap: the brotherhood of shit only a very little
for me please. Then what earthly point is there in travelling
alone? We had fun Dédé and I it's terrific two pretty girls
in a convertible their hair streaming in the wind: we made
a terrific impression in Rome at night on the Piazza del
Popolo. I've had fun with other friends too. But alone?
What sort of impression do you make on beaches in casinos
if you haven't got a man with you? Ruins museums I had
my bellyful of them with Tristan. I'm not an hysterical
enthusiast I don't swoon at the sight of broken columns or
tumble-down old shacks. The people of former times my
foot they're dead that's the only thing they have over the
living but in their own day they were just as sickening.
Picturesqueness: I don't fall for that not for one minute.
Stinking filthy dirty washing cabbage-stalks what a pretentious fool you have to be to go into ecstasies over that!
And it's the same thing everywhere all the time whether
they're stuffing themselves with chips paella or pizza it's
the same crew a filthy crew the rich who trample over you
the poor who hate you for your money the old who dodder
the young who sneer the men who show off the women who
open their legs. I'd rather stay at home reading a thriller
although they've become so dreary nowadays. The telly
too what a clapped-out set of fools! I was made for
another planet altogether I mistook the way.

Why do they have to make all that din right under my
windows? They're standing there by their cars they can't
make up their minds to put their stinking feet into them.
What can they be going on and on about? Snotty little
beastesses grotesque in their mini-skirts and their tights I
hope they catch their deaths haven't they any mothers
then? And the boys with their hair down their necks. From
a distance those ones seem more or less clean. But all those
louse-breeding beatniks if the chief of police had any sort
of drive he'd toss them all into the brig. The youth of
today! They drug they stuff one another they respect
nothing I'm going to pour a bucket of water on their heads.
They might break open the door and beat me up I'm
defenceless I'd better shut the window again. Rose's
daughter is one of that sort it seems and Rose plays the
elder sister they're always together in one another's pockets.
Yet she used to hold her in so she even boxed her ears she
didn't bother to bring her to reason she was impulsive
arbitrary: I loathe capriciousness. Oh, Rose will pay for it
all right as Dédé says she'll have Danielle on her hands
pregnant . . . I should have made a lovely person of Sylvie.
I'd have given her dresses jewels I'd have been proud of
her we should have gone out together. There's no justice in
the world. That's what makes me so mad—the injustice.
When I think of the sort of mother I was! Tristan acknowl-
edges it: I've forced him to acknowledge it. And then after
that he tells me he's ready for anything rather than let me
have Francis: they don't give a damn for logic they say
absolutely anything at all and then escape at the run. He
races down the stairs four at a time while I shout down
the well after him. I won't be had like that. I'll force him
to do me justice: cross my heart. He'll give me back my
place in the home my place on earth. I'll make a splendid
child of Francis they'll see what kind of a mother I am.

They are killing me the bastards. The idea of the party
tomorrow destroys me. I must win. I must I must I must
I must. I'll tell my fortune with the cards. No. If it went

wrong I'd throw myself out of the window no I mustn't it
would suit them too well. Think of something else. Cheerful things. The boy from Bordeaux. We expected nothing
from one another we asked one another no questions we
made one another no promises we bedded down and made
love. It lasted three weeks and he left for Africa I wept
wept. It's a memory that does me good. Things like that
only happen once in a lifetime. What a pity! When I think
back over it it seems to me that if anyone had loved me
properly I should have been affection itself. Turds they
bored me to death they trample everyone down right left
and centre everyone can die in his hole for all they care
husbands deceive their wives mothers toss off their sons not
a word about it sealed lips that carefulness disgusts me
and the way they don't have the courage of their convictions. 'But come really your brother is too close-fisted' it
was Albert who pointed it out to me I'm too noble-minded
to bother with trifles like that but it's true they had stuffed
down three times as much as us and the bill was divided
fifty-fifty thousands of little things like that. And afterwards he blamed me—'You shouldn't have repeated it to
him.' On the beach we went at it hammer and tongs.
Etiennette cried you would have said the tears on her
cheeks were melting suet. 'Now that he knows he'll turn
over a new leaf,' I told her. I was simple-minded—I
thought they were capable of turning over new leaves I
thought you could bring them up by making them see
reason. 'Come Sylvie let's think it over. You know how
much that frock costs? And how many times will you ever
put it on? We'll send it back.' It always had to be begun
again at the beginning I wore myself out. Nanard will go on
being close-fisted to the end of his days. Albert more de-
ceitful lying secretive than ever. Tristan always just as self-
satisfied just as pompous. I was knocking myself out for
nothing. When I tried to teach Etiennette how to dress
Nanard bawled me out—she was twenty-two and I was

dressing her up as an elderly school-teacher! She went on
cramming herself into little gaudy dresses. And Rose who
shouted out 'Oh you are cruel!' I had spoken to her out of
loyalty women have to stand by one another. Who has ever
shown me any gratitude? I've lent them money without
asking for interest not one has been grateful to me for it
indeed some have whined when I asked to be paid back.
Girl-friends I overwhelmed with presents accused me of
showing off. And you ought to see how briskly they slipped
away all those people I had done good turns to yet God
knows I asked for nothing much in return. I'm not one of
those people who thinks they have a right to everything.
Aunt Marguerite: 'Would you lend us your flat while
you're on your cruise this summer?' Lend it hell hotels
aren't built just for dogs and if they can't afford to put up
in Paris they can stay in their own rotten hole. A flat's holy
I should have felt raped . . . It's like Dédé. 'You mustn't
let yourself be eaten up,' she tells me. But she'd be delighted to swallow me whole. 'Have you an evening coat
you can lend me? You never go out.' No I never go out but
I did go out: they're my dresses my coats they remind me
of masses of things I don't want a trull to take my place in
them. And afterwards they'd smell. If I were to die Mama
and Nanard would share my leavings. No no I want to live
until the moths have eaten the lot or else if I have cancer
I'll destroy them all. I've had enough of people making a
good thing out of me—Dédé worst of all. She drank my
whisky she showed off in my convertible. Now she's playing
the great-hearted friend. But she never bothered to ring me
from Courchevel tonight of all nights. When her cuckold
of a husband is travelling and she's bored why yes then she
brings her fat backside here even when I don't want to see
her at all. But it's New Year's Eve I'm alone I'm eating
my heart out. She's dancing she's having fun she doesn't
think of me for a single minute. Nobody ever thinks of me.
As if I were wiped off the face of the earth. As if I had

never existed. Do I exist? Oh! I pinched myself so hard I shall have a bruise.

What a silence! Not a car left not a footstep in the street not a sound in the house the silence of death. The silence of a death-chamber and their eyes on me their eyes that condemn me unheard and without appeal. Oh, how strong they are! Everything they felt remorse for they clapped it on to my back the perfect scapegoat and at last they could invent an excuse for their hatred. My grief has not lessened it. Yet I should have thought the devil himself would have been sorry for me.

All my life it will be two o'clock in the afternoon one Tuesday in June. 'Mademoiselle is too fast asleep I can't get her to wake up.' My heart missed a beat I rushed in calling 'Sylvie are you ill?' She looked as though she were asleep she was still warm. It had been all over some hours before the doctor told me. I screamed I went up and down the room like a madwoman. Sylvie Sylvie why have you done this to me? I can see her now calm relaxed and me out of my mind and the note for her father that didn't mean a thing I tore it up it was all part of the act it was only an act I was sure I am sure—a mother knows her own daughter—she had not meant to die but she had overdone the dose she was dead how appalling! It's too easy with these drugs anyone can get just like that: these teen-age girls will play at suicide for a mere nothing: Sylvie went along with the fashion—she never woke up. And they all came they kissed Sylvie not one of them kissed me and my mother shouted at me 'You've killed her!' My mother my own mother. They made her be quiet but their faces their silence the weight of their silence. Yes, if I were one of those mothers who get up at seven in the morning she would have been saved I lived according to another rhythm there's nothing criminal about that how could I have guessed? I was always there when she came back from school many mothers can't say as much always ready to talk to question her it was she who shut herself up in her room pretending she wanted to work. I never failed her. And my mother she who neglected me left me by myself how she dared! I couldn't manage any reply my head was spinning I no longer knew where I was. 'If I'd gone to give her a kiss that night when I came in . . .' But I didn't want to wake her and during the afternoon she had seemed to me almost cheerful . . . Those days, what a torment! A score of times I thought I was going to crack up. School-friends teachers put flowers on the coffin without addressing a word to me: if a girl kills herself the mother is guilty: that's the way their minds worked out of hatred for their own mothers. All in at the kill. I almost let myself be got down. After the funeral I fell ill. Over and over again I said to myself, 'If I had got up at seven . . . If I had gone to give her a kiss when I came in . . .' It seemed to me that everybody had heard my mother's shout I didn't dare go out any more I crept along by the wall the sun clamped me in the pillory I thought people were looking at me whispering pointing enough of that enough I'd rather die this minute than live through that time again. I lost more than twenty pounds, a skeleton, my sense of balance went I staggered. 'Psycho-somatic,' said the doctor. Tristan gave me money for the nursing-home. You'd never believe the questions I asked myself it might have driven me crazy. A phoney suicide she had meant to hurt someone—who? I hadn't watched her closely enough I ought never to have left her for a moment I ought to have had her followed held an inquiry un-masked the guilty person a boy or a girl maybe that whore of a teacher. 'No Madame there was no one in her life.' They wouldn't yield an inch the two bitches and their eyes were murdering me: they all of them keep up the con-spiracy of lies even beyond death itself. But they didn't deceive me. I know. At her age and with things as they are today it's impossible that there was no one. Perhaps she was pregnant or she'd fallen into the clutches of a lezzy or she'd got in with an immoral lot someone was blackmailing her and having her threatening to tell me everything. Oh, I must stop picturing things. You could have told me everything my Sylvie I would have got you out of that filthy mess. It must certainly have been a filthy mess for her to have written to Albert, 'Papa please forgive me but I can't bear it any more.' She couldn't talk to him nor to the others: they tried to get round her, but they were strangers. I was the only one she could have confided in.

Without them. Without their hatreds. Bastards! You nearly got me down but you didn't quite succeed. I'm not your scapegoat; your remorse—I've thrown it off. I've told you what I think of you each one has had his dose and I'm not afraid of your hatred I walk clean through it. Bastards! They are the ones who killed her. They flung mud at me they put her against me they treated her as a martyr that flattered her all girls adore playing the martyr: she took her part seriously she distrusted me she told me nothing. Poor poppet. She needed my support my advice they deprived her of it they condemned her to silence she couldn't get herself out of her mess all by herself she set up this act and it killed her. Murderers! They killed Sylvie my little Sylvie my darling. I loved you. No mother on earth could have been more devoted: I never thought of anything but your own good. I open the photograph-album I look at all the Sylvies. The rather drawn child's face the closed face of the adolescent. Looking deep into the eyes of my seventeen-year-old girl they murdered I say 'I was the best of mothers. You would have thanked me later on.'

Crying has comforted me and I'm beginning to feel sleepy. I mustn't go to sleep in this armchair I should wake everything would be mucked up all over again. Take my suppositories go to bed. Set the alarm-clock for noon to have time to get myself ready. I must win. A man in the house my little boy I'll kiss at bed-time all this unused affection. And then it would mean rehabilitation. What? I'm going to sleep I'm relaxing. It'll be a swipe in the eye for them. Tristan is somebody they respect him. I want him to bear witness for me: they'll be forced to do me justice. I'll call him. Convince him this very night.

'Was it you who phoned me? Oh, I thought it was you. You were asleep forgive me but I'm glad to hear your voice it's so revolting tonight nobody's given the slightest sign of life yet they know that when you've had a great sorrow you can't bear celebrations all this noise these lights did you notice Paris has never been so lit up as this year they've money to waste it would be better if they were to reduce the rates I shut myself up at home so as not to see it. I can't get off to sleep I'm too sad too lonely I brood about things I must talk it over with you without any quarrelling a good friendly talk listen now what I have to say to you is really very important I shan't be able to get a wink until it's settled. You're listening to me, right? I've been thinking it over all night I had nothing else to do and I assure you this is an absurd position it can't go on like this after all we are still married what a waste these two flats you could sell yours for at least twenty million and I'd not get in your way never fear no question of taking up married life again we're no longer in love I'd shut myself up in the room at the back don't interrupt you could have all the Fanny Hills you like I don't give a hoot but since we're still friends there's no reason why we shouldn't live under the same roof. And it's essential for Francis. Just think of him for a moment I've been doing nothing else all night and I'm tearing myself to pieces. It's bad for a child to have parents who are separated they grow sly vicious untruthful they get complexes they don't develop properly. I want Francis to develop properly. You have no right to deprive him of a real home . . . Yes yes we do have to go over all this again you always get out of it but this time I insist on your listening to me. It's too selfish indeed it's even unnatural to deprive a son of his mother a mother of her son. For no reason. I've no vices I don't drink I don't drug and you've admitted I was the most devoted of mothers. Well then— Don't interrupt. If you're thinking about your fun I tell you again I shan't prevent you from having girls. Don't tell me I'm impossible to live with that I ate you up that I wore you out. Yes I was rather difficult it's natural for me to take the bit between my teeth: but if you'd had a little patience and if you'd tried to understand me and had known how to talk to me instead of growing pig-headed things would have gone along better between us you're not a saint either so don't you think it: anyhow that's all water under the bridge I've changed. As you know very well I've suffered I've matured I can stand things I used not to be able to stand let me speak you don't have to be afraid of scenes it'll be an easy-going coexistence and the child will be happy as he has a right to be I can't see what possible objection you can have . . . Why isn't this a time for talking it over? It's a time that suits me beautifully. You can give up five minutes of sleep for me after all for my part I shan't get a wink until the matter's settled don't always be so selfish it's too dreadful to prevent people sleeping it sends them out of their minds I can't bear it. Seven years now I've been rotting here all alone like an outcast and that filthy gang laughing at me you certainly owe me my revenge let me speak you owe me a great deal you know because you gave me the madly-in-love stuff I ditched Florent and broke with my friends and now you leave me flat all your friends turn their backs on me: why did you pretend to love me? Sometimes I wonder whether it wasn't a put-up job . . . Yes a put-up job—it's so unbelievable that terrific passion and now this dropping me . . . You hadn't realized? Hadn't realized what? Don't you tell me again that I married you out of interest I had Florent I could have had barrow-loads and get this straight the idea of being your wife didn't dazzle me at all you're not Napoleon whatever you may think don't tell me that again or I shall scream you didn't say anything but I can hear you turning the words over in your mouth don't say them it's untrue it's so untrue it makes one scream you gave me the madly-in-love jazz and I fell for it . . . No don't say listen Murielle to me I know your answers by heart you've gone over and over them a hundred times no more guff it doesn't wash with me and don't you put on that exasperated look yes I said that exasperated look I can see you in the receiver. You've been even more of a cad than Albert he was young when we married you were forty-five you ought to understand the nature of your responsibilities. But still all right the past's past. I promise you I shan't reproach you. We wipe everything out we set off again on a fresh footing I can be sweet and charming you know if people aren't too beastly to me. So come on now tell me it's agreed tomorrow we'll settle the details . . .

'Swine! You're taking your revenge you're torturing me because I haven't drooled in admiration before you but as for me money doesn't impress me nor fine airs nor fine words. "Never not for anything on earth" we'll see all right we'll see. I shall stand up for myself. I'll talk to Francis I'll tell him what you are. And if I killed myself in front of him do you think that would be a pretty thing for him to remember? . . . No it's not blackmail you silly bastard with the life I lead it wouldn't mean a thing to me to do myself in. You mustn't push people too far they reach a point when they're capable of anything indeed there are mothers who kill themselves with their children . . .'

Swine! Turd! He's hung up . . . He doesn't answer he won't answer. Swine. Oh! My heart's failing I'm going to die. It hurts it hurts too much they're torturing me to death I can't bear it any longer I'll kill myself in his drawing-room I'll slash my veins when they come back there'll be blood everywhere and I shall be dead . . . Oh! I hit it too hard I've cracked my skull it's them I ought to bash. Head against the wall no no I shan't go mad they shan't get me down I'll stand up for myself I'll find weapons. What weapons swine swine I can't breathe my heart's going to give I must calm down . . .

O God. Let it be true that You exist. Let there be a

heaven and a hell I'll stroll along the walks of paradise with my little boy and my beloved daughter and they will all be writhing in the flames of envy I'll watch them roasting and howling I'll laugh I'll laugh and the children will laugh with me. You owe me this revenge, God. I insist that you grant it me.

THE WOMAN
DESTROYED

Monday 13 September. Les Salines.

It is an astonishing setting, this rough draft of a town
lying deserted here, on the edge of a village and outside the
flow of the centuries. I went along one half of the hemi-
cycle and climbed the steps of the central building; for a
long while I gazed at the quiet splendour of these structures
that were put up for functional purposes and that have
never been used for anything at all. They are solid; they
are real: yet their abandoned state changes them into a
fantastic pretence—of what, one wonders. The warm grass
under the autumn sky and the smell of dead leaves told me
that I had certainly not left this world; but I had gone back
two hundred years into the past. I went to fetch things out
of the car: I spread a rug on the ground, cushions, the
transistor, and I smoked, listening to Mozart. Behind two
or three dusty windows I could make out people moving to
and fro—offices, no doubt. A lorry stopped in front of one
of the massive doors; men opened it; they loaded sacks into
the back. Nothing else disturbed the silence of that afternoon: I travelled away, a great way off, to the shores of an
unknown river; and then when I looked up there I was
among these stones, far from my own life.

For the most surprising thing about it is my being here,
and the cheerfulness of my being here. I had not looked
forward to the loneliness of this drive back to Paris at all.
Hitherto, if Maurice were not there, the girls were always
with me, in all my journeys. I had thought I was going to
miss Colette's raptures and Lucienne's demandingness. And
here I am with happiness of a forgotten kind given back to
me. My freedom makes me twenty years younger. So much
so that when I closed the book I began writing just for
myself, as I did when I was twenty.

I never part from Maurice with a light heart. The congress is only going to last a week, yet there was a lump in my throat as we drove from Mougins to the Nice airfield. He too, he was moved. When the loudspeaker summoned the travellers for Rome he squeezed me tight. 'Don't get killed on the road.'—'Don't get killed in the plane.' Before he vanished he turned round to look at me again: there was anxiety in his eyes, and I caught it at once. The take-off seemed to me dramatic. Four-engined planes rise gently into the air—it is a long-drawn-out au revoir. This jet left the ground with the violence of a last good-bye.

But presently I began to bubble with happiness. No, my daughters' absence did not sadden me at all—quite the reverse. I could drive as fast or as slowly as I liked, go where I liked, stop when the whim took me. I made up my mind to spend the week wandering about. I get up as soon as it is light. The car is waiting for me in the street or in the courtyard like a faithful animal; it is wet with dew; I wipe its eyes and full of delight I tear away through the growing sunlight. Beside me there is the white bag with the Michelin maps, the Guide Bleu, some books, a cardigan and my cigarettes—a reticent companion. No one grows impatient if I ask the owner of the little hotel for her receipt for chicken with crayfish.

Dusk is about to fall, but it is still warm. It is one of these heart-touching moments when the world is so well attuned to mankind that it seems impossible that they should not all be happy.

Tuesday 14 September

One of the things that really pleased Maurice was the intensity of what he called 'my awareness of life'. It has revived during this short colloquy with myself. Now that Colette is married and Lucienne is in America I shall have all the time in the world to cultivate it. 'You'll be bored.

You ought to look for a job,' Maurice said to me at Mougins. He went on and on about it. But I do not want one; not for the moment, anyhow. I want to live for myself a little, after all this time. And for us, Maurice and I, to make the most of this double solitude that we have been deprived of for so long. I have plans by the dozen in my mind.

Friday 17 September

On Tuesday I telephoned Colette: she had 'flu. She protested when I said I was coming straight back to Paris—Jean-Pierre was looking after her very well. But I was worried and I got back that same day. I found her in bed, much thinner: she has a temperature every evening. When I went into the mountains with her in August—even then I was anxious about her health. I can't wait for Maurice to examine her, and I should like him to call Talbot in for a consultation.

Here I am with still another protégée on my hands. When I left Colette after dinner on Wednesday it was so mild that I drove down to the Latin quarter: I sat on the terrace of a café, and I smoked a cigarette. At the next table there was a teen-age girl who gazed longingly at my packet of Chesterfields: she asked me for one. I talked to her; she evaded my questions and got up to go. She was about fifteen, neither a student nor a prostitute and she aroused my curiosity—I suggested giving her a lift home in my car. She refused, hesitated, and then in the end confessed that she did not know where she was going to sleep. She had escaped that morning from the Centre where the Public Assistance had put her. I kept her here for two days. Her mother, who is more or less mentally deficient, and her step-father, who loathes her, have given up their rights over her. The judge who is in charge of her case promised to send her to a Home where she will be taught a trade. Meanwhile for these six months past she has been living 'provisionally' at this Centre, where she *never* goes out—except on Sunday, to church, if she wishes—and where she is given nothing to do. There are some forty of them there, adolescent girls, physically well looked-after, but pining away from boredom, weariness and despair. At nights each is given a sleeping-pill. They manage to keep them by. And one fine day they swallow all they have saved. 'Running away or trying to commit suicide—that's what you have to do in our place for the judge to remember you,' Marguerite told me. It is easy to run away; it often happens; and if it does not last long the escapee is not punished.

I promised her I should move heaven and earth to get her transferred to a Home and she let herself be persuaded to go back to the Centre. I boiled with anger when I saw her go through the door, her feet dragging, her head bowed. She is a pretty girl, not stupid at all, very sweet-tempered, and all she asks is to work—her youth is being hacked to pieces: hers and the youth of thousands like her. Tomorrow I shall ring up Judge Barron.

How hard Paris is! Even on these balmy days this hardness weighs me down. I feel obscurely low-spirited this evening. I have made plans for changing the girls' room into a cosier place to sit in than Maurice's consulting-room or the waiting-room. And I am coming to see that Lucienne will never live here any more. The house will be quiet, but very empty. But above all I am racked with anxiety about Colette. What a good thing Maurice is coming home tomorrow.

Wednesday 22 September

Here is one of the reasons—indeed the main reason—why I have not the least wish to be tied down to a job: I should find it hard to bear if I were not entirely free to help the people who need me. I spent almost all my days at Colette's bedside. Her temperature will not go down. 'It's nothing serious,' says Maurice. But Talbot wants analyses. Terrifying notions run through my mind.

Judge Barron saw me this morning. Very friendly. He thinks Marguerite Drin's case heart-breaking; and there are thousands like it. The shocking thing is that there is no place designed for these children and no staff capable of looking after them properly. The government does nothing. So the efforts of the juvenile courts and the social workers come to nothing—run up against a wall. The Centre where Marguerite is staying is only a transit-point; after three or four days she ought to have been sent on elsewhere. But where? It is a complete vacuum. These girls stay on at the Centre, where nothing has been arranged in the way of occupation or amusement. But still he will try to find Marguerite some sort of a place somewhere. And he is going to advise the workers at the Centre to let me see her. The parents have not signed the paper that would finally do away with their rights, but there is no question of their taking the child back: they do not want her and from her point of view too it would be the worst possible solution.

I left the law courts vexed with the system's ineptitude. The number of juvenile delinquents is rising: and the only measure contemplated is greater severity.

I happened to find myself in front of the door of the Sainte Chapelle, so I went in and climbed the spiral staircase. There were foreign tourists and a couple gazing at the stained glass, hand in hand. For my part I could not concentrate upon it. I was thinking of Colette again, and I was worried.

And I am worried now. Reading is impossible. The only thing that could ease my mind would be talking to Maurice: he will not be here before midnight. Since he came back from Rome he spends his evenings at the laboratory with Talbot and Couturier. He says they are getting near to their goal. I can understand his giving up everything to his research. But this is the first time in my life that I have a serious worry that he does not share.

Saturday 25 September

The window was black. I had expected it. Before—before what?—when by some extraordinary chance I went out without Maurice there was always a streak of light between the red curtains when I came back. I would run up the two flights of stairs and ring, too impatient to look for my key. This time I went up the stairs without running; I pushed my key into the lock. How empty the flat was! How empty it is! Of course it is, since there is no one in it. No, that's not it: usually when I come home I find Maurice here, even when he is out. This evening the doors open on to wholly empty rooms. Eleven o'clock. Tomorrow the results of the analyses will be known and I am afraid. I'm afraid and Maurice is not here. I know. His research must be carried through. Still, I am angry with him. 'I need you, and you aren't here!' I feel like writing those words on a piece of paper and leaving it in an obvious place in the hall before I go to bed. Otherwise I shall be bottling it in, as I did yesterday, and as I did the day before that. He always used to be there when I needed him.

. . . I watered the pot-plants; I began to tidy the books and I stopped dead. I had been astonished by his lack of interest when I talked to him about arranging this sitting-room. I must tell myself the truth; I have always wanted the truth and the reason why I have had it is that I desired it. Well then. Maurice has changed. He has let himself be eaten up by his profession. He no longer reads. He no longer listens to music. I used so to love our silence and his attentive face as we listened to Monteverdi or Charlie Parker. We no longer go out together in or around Paris.

It might almost be said we no longer have any real conversation. He is beginning to be like his colleagues who are merely machines for getting on and for making money. I'm being unfair. He doesn't give a damn for money or social success. But ever since he decided, ten years ago, against my wishes, to specialize, gradually (and that was what I had been afraid of) he has grown hard. Even at Mougins this year I thought him remote—intensely eager to get back to the hospital and the laboratory, absent-minded and indeed moody. Come! I might as well tell myself the truth right through to the end. The reason why my heart was so heavy at Nice airfield was those dismal holidays behind us. And the reason why I had so vivid a happiness in the deserted salt-works was that Maurice, hundreds of miles away, was close to me again. (What an odd thing a diary is: the things you omit are more important than those you put in.) Anyone would say he was no longer interested in his private life. How easily he gave up our trip to Alsace last spring! Yet my disappointment grieved him deeply. I said cheerfully, 'A cure for leukaemia is certainly worth a few sacrifices!' But there was a time when for Maurice medicine meant the relief of men and women made of flesh and blood. I was so disappointed, so taken aback, when I did my course at the Cochin, by the professors' cold-hearted jollity and the students' uncaring attitude; and in that dresser's fine dark eyes I saw distress and fury of the same kind as mine. I believed I loved him from that moment on. I am afraid that now his patients are merely cases for him. Knowing concerns him more than healing. And even in his relations with people close to him he is growing remote, he who was so alive, so cheerful, as young at forty-five as when I first met him . . . Yes, something has changed, since here I am writing about him, about myself, behind his back. If he had done so, I should have felt betrayed. Each of us used to be able to see entirely into the other.

So we can still; it is my anger that is keeping us apart—he will soon make it die away. He will ask me to be patient a little longer; after spells of furious over-work come the calm, easy days. Last year too he often worked in the evenings. Yes, but then I had Lucienne. And above all there was nothing tormenting me. He knows very well that at present I can neither read nor listen to a record, because I am afraid. I shall not leave a note in the hall, but I shall talk to him. After twenty—twenty-two—years of marriage one relies too much upon silence—it is dangerous. I believe these last years I was too wrapped up in the girls—Colette was so lovable and Lucienne so difficult. Perhaps I was not as free, as available, as Maurice might have wished. He ought to have pointed it out instead of flinging himself into work that now cuts him off from me. We must have it out together.

Midnight. I am in such a hurry to be at one with him again and to stifle the anger that is still rumbling inside me that I keep my eyes fixed on the clock. Its hands do not move: I grow irritated, all on edge. My mental image of Maurice falls to pieces: what sense is there in fighting against illness and suffering if you behave so stupidly towards your own wife? It's indifference. It's hardness of heart. No point in losing one's temper. Stop it. If Colette's analyses are not good, I shall need all my self-control tomorrow. I must try to go to sleep, then.

Sunday 26 September

So it's happened. It's happened to me.

Monday 27 September

Yes, here I am! It's happened to me. It is *perfectly usual*. I must convince myself of that and strangle this fury that shattered me all yesterday. Maurice lied to me: yes, that too is perfectly usual. He might have gone on doing so instead of telling me. However late it is, I ought to feel grateful to him for his candour.

In the end I did go to sleep on Saturday. From time to time I stretched out to touch the other bed—its sheet was flat. (I like going to sleep before him when he is working in his consulting-room. Through my dreams I hear water running, smell a faint whiff of eau de Cologne; I reach out, his body moulds the sheet and I sink deep down into happiness.) The front door slammed. I called 'Maurice!' It was three in the morning. They had not been working until three; they had been drinking and gossiping. I sat up in bed. 'What kind of time is this to come home? Where have you been?'

He sat down in an armchair. He was holding a glass of whisky in his hand.

'It's three o'clock, I know.'

'Colette is ill, I'm racked with anxiety, and you come home at three. You haven't all been working until three?'

'Is Colette worse?'

'She's not better. You don't care! Clearly, when you take the health of all mankind under your wing an ill daughter doesn't amount to much.'

'Don't be inimical.' He looked at me with a rather saddened gravity. And I melted as I always do melt when he envelops me in that dark, warm light. Gently I asked, 'Tell me why you have come home so late.'

He made no reply.

'Were you drinking? Playing poker? Did you all go out? Did you forget the time?' He went on being silent, as it were emphatically silent, twirling his glass between his fingers. I flung out nonsensical words to make him lose his temper—to jerk an explanation out of him. 'What's the matter? Is there a woman in your life?'

Looking at me steadily he said, 'Yes, Monique, there is a woman in my life.'

(Everything was blue above our heads and beneath our feet, on the other side of the strait loomed the coast of

Africa. He squeezed me against him. 'If you were to deceive me I should kill myself.' 'If you were to deceive me I should have no need to kill myself. I should die of grief.' Fifteen years ago. Already? What do fifteen years count? Twice two is four. I love you, I love you alone. Truth cannot be destroyed: time has no effect upon it.)

'Who is it?'

'Noëllie Guérard.'

'Noëllie! Why?'

He shrugged. Of course I knew the answer—pretty, dashing, bitchy, available. The sort of adventure that has no importance and that flatters a man. Did he need flattery?

He smiled at me. 'I'm glad you questioned me. I hated lying to you.'

'Since when have you been lying to me?'

He scarcely hesitated at all. 'I lied to you at Mougins. And since I came back.'

That made five weeks. Was he thinking about her at Mougins? 'Did you go to bed with her when you stayed in Paris by yourself?'

'Yes.'

'Do you see her often?'

'Oh, no! You know very well I am working . . .'

I asked him to be more exact. Two evenings and one afternoon since he came back; that seems often enough to me.

'Why didn't you tell me right away?'

He looked at me shyly, and with sorrow in his voice he said, 'You used to say you would die of grief . . .'

'One says that.'

Suddenly I wanted to cry: I should not die of it—that was the saddest thing about it. We gazed at Africa, a great way off through the blue haze, and the words we uttered were merely words. I lay back. The blow had stunned me. My head was empty with shock. I had to have a pause, a break in time, to understand what had happened to me. 'Let's go to sleep,' I said.

Anger woke me early. How innocent he looked lying there, with his hair tangled over a forehead that sleep had made young again. (In August, when I was away, she woke up at his side: I can't bring myself to believe it! Why did I go to the mountains with Colette? It was not as though she very much wanted to—I was the one who insisted.) For five weeks he had been lying to me. 'This evening we made an important step forward.' And he had just come from Noëllie's. I felt like shaking him, insulting him, shrieking. I took myself in hand. I left a note on my pillow: 'See you this evening.' I was sure my absence would affect him more than any reproaches: there is no possible reply to absence. I walked through the streets, wherever chance led me, obsessed by the words 'He lied to me.' Mental images pierced me through—Maurice's eyes set on Noëllie, his smile. I dismissed them. He doesn't look at her as he looks at me. I did not want to suffer; I did not suffer; but I choked with bitterness. 'He lied to me!' I had said, 'I should die of grief'; yes, but he had made me say it. He had been more eager than I in drawing up our pact—no compromise, no deviating. We were driving along the little road to Saint-Bertrand-de-Comminges and he pressed me—'Shall I always be enough for you?' He blazed up because there was not enough ardour in my reply (but what a reconciliation in our room at the old inn, with the scent of honeysuckle coming in at the window! Twenty years ago—it was yesterday.) He has been enough for me: I have lived only for him. And for a mere whim he has betrayed our vows. I said to myself, I shall insist upon his breaking it off, right away . . . I went to Colette's flat; all day long I looked after her, but inside I was boiling. I came home, quite worn out. 'I'm going to insist upon his breaking it off.' But what does the word insist mean after a whole life of love and understanding? I

have never asked anything for myself that I did not also
wish for him.

He took me in his arms, looking quite distraught. He had
telephoned to Colette's several times and no one had
answered (I had jammed the bell, so that she would not be
disturbed). He was out of his mind with anxiety.

'But you didn't really imagine I was going to do myself
in?'

'There was nothing I didn't imagine.'

His anxiety went to my heart and I listened to him without hostility. Of course he had been wrong to lie, but I had
to understand: the first reluctance snowballs—you no
longer dare confess because then you would also have to
admit to having lied. It is an even more impossible hurdle
for people who rate sincerity so very high, as we do. (I
admit that: how furiously I should have lied to conceal a
falsehood.) I have never made proper allowance for
untruth. Lucienne's and Colette's first fibs utterly flabbergasted me. I found it very hard to accept that all children
lie to their mothers. Not to me! I am not the kind of
mother that is lied to; not a wife that is lied to. Idiotic
vanity. All women think they are different; they all think
there are some things that will never happen to them; and
they are all wrong.

I have spent a great deal of today thinking. (What luck
Lucienne is in America. I should have had to play a part
with her. She would never have left me in peace.) And I
went to have a talk with Isabelle. She helped me, as she
always does. I was afraid she might not really understand
me, since she and Charles put their money on freedom and
not on faithfulness, as Maurice and I did. But she tells me
that that has not prevented her from flying into rages
with her husband nor from sometimes feeling that she was
in danger—five years ago she thought he was going to leave
her. She advised me to be patient. She has a great regard
for Maurice. She thinks it natural that he should have
wanted an adventure and excusable that he should have

hidden it from me at first: but he will certainly soon grow tired of it. What gives this sort of affair its piquancy is its novelty; time works against Noëllie; the glamour she may have in Maurice's eyes will fade. But if I want our love to emerge from this trial unhurt I must play neither the victim nor the shrew. 'Be understanding, be cheerful. Above all be friendly,' she said to me. That was how she won Charles back in the end. Patience is not my outstanding virtue. But I certainly must do my best. And not only from a tactical point of view, but from a moral one too. I have had exactly the kind of life I wanted—now I must deserve that privilege. If I fail at the first little snag everything I have thought about myself will have been mere vapouring. I am uncompromising: I take after Papa, and Maurice respects me for it; but even so I must understand others and learn to adjust myself to them. Isabelle is quite right—it is perfectly natural for a man to have an affair after twenty-two years of marriage. It is I who would be un-natural—childish, really—if I were not to accept this.

When I left Isabelle I did not feel much like going to see Marguerite; but she had written me a touching little letter and I did not want to disappoint her. The sadness of that visiting-room and of the oppressed faces of those girls. She showed me some drawings—not bad at all. She would like to take up decoration; or at least be a window-dresser. Work at all events: I told her about the judge's promises. I told her about the steps I had taken to be allowed to have her on Sundays. She trusts me; she really likes me; she will be patient; but not indefinitely.

This evening I am going out with Maurice. The advice of Isabelle and of Miss Loneliheart's column—to get your husband back, be cheerful and elegant and go out with him, just the two of you. I don't have to get him back: I have never lost him. But I still have masses of questions to ask him and the talk will be easier if we dine out. Above all I don't want it to look like a formal summons to confess.

There is one idiotic detail that nags my mind—why did he have a glass of whisky in his hand? I called out 'Maurice!' Since I had been woken up at three in the morning he must have guessed I was going to question him. Usually he does not slam the front door so noisily.

Tuesday 28 September

I had too much to drink: but Maurice laughed and told me I was charming. It's funny: he had to deceive me for us to be able to revive the nights of our youth. There is nothing worse than the daily round: shocks wake one up again. Saint-Germain-des-Prés had changed since '46: a different sort of people go there. 'And it's another era,' said Maurice, rather sadly. But I had not set foot in a night-club for nearly fifteen years and I was delighted with everything. We danced. At one moment he squeezed me very tight and said, 'Nothing has changed between us.' And we talked of all sorts of things at random: but I was half-seas over and I have rather forgotten what he told me. Generally speaking it was just what I had imagined. Noëllie is an outstanding barrister and she is eaten up with ambition; she is a woman on her own—divorced, with one daughter—with very free and easy ways, fashionable, very much in the swim. Exactly my opposite. Maurice had wanted to know whether he could be attractive to a woman of that kind. 'If I wanted to . . .'—I had asked myself that question when I flirted with Quillan: the only time I ever flirted in my life, and I soon stopped it. Slumbering in Maurice, as in most men, there is a young man who is far from certain of himself. Noëllie reassured him. And obviously it is also a question of direct desire—she is appetizing.

Wednesday 29 September

It was the first time Maurice spent the evening with Noëllie, me knowing about it. I went to see an old Bergman film with Isabelle and we ate *fondue bourguignonne* at the Hochepot. I always liked being with her. She has preserved the eagerness of our teen-age days, when every film, every book, every picture was so immensely important: now that my daughters have left me I shall go to shows and concerts with her more often. She too left off her studies when she married, but she has kept up a more vigorous intellectual life than I have. Though it is true that she only had one son to bring up, not two daughters. Then again she is not hung about with lame ducks as I am; with an engineer for a husband she has few opportunities of coming across any. I told her that I had easily adopted the tactics of the smile because I was sure that in fact this affair had not much importance for Maurice. 'Nothing has changed between us,' he told me the day before yesterday.

To tell the truth I was much more affected ten years ago: the reason why he had fresh ambitions, the reason why his work at Simca (unexciting, run-of-the-mill, poorly paid, but with plenty of free time—a job that he carried out with immense conscientiousness) was not enough for him, was that he was bored at home and that his feelings for me had weakened. (Later years showed me that this was not the case. Only I am sorry that I no longer take any part in what he does. He used to talk to me about his patients; he told me of deserving cases; I tried to help them. Now I am shut out from his research and the people in his outpatients' department do not need me.) Isabelle helped me at that time, too. She convinced me that I ought to respect Maurice's freedom. That meant giving up the old ideal of which my father was the embodiment and which remains still alive in me. It was harder than turning a blind eye on a passing piece of nonsense.

I asked Isabelle whether she were happy. 'I never ask myself, so I suppose the answer is yes.'

At all events she likes the moment of waking up. That seems to me a pretty good definition of happiness! It is the same with me: every morning, when I open my eyes, I smile.

I did so this morning. Before going to bed I took a little Nembutal and I went off right away. Maurice tells me he came back about one o'clock. I asked him no questions.

One thing that helps me is that I am not physically jealous. My body is no longer thirty: nor is Maurice's. They come together with pleasure—not very often, to be sure—but without fire. Oh, I have no illusions. Noëllie has the attraction of novelty: Maurice grows younger in her bed. The idea leaves me unmoved. I should take offence at a woman who brought Maurice anything. But my meetings with Noëllie and what I have heard of her tell me all I need to know. She is the incarnation of everything we dislike—desire to succeed at any price, pretentiousness, love of money, a delight in display. She does not possess a single idea of her own; she is fundamentally devoid of sensitivity—she just goes along with the fashion. There is such barefacedness and exhibitionism in her capers with men that indeed I wonder whether she may not be frigid.

Thursday 30 September

Colette's temperature was right down this morning; she is getting up. Maurice says it is an illness that is running about Paris—temperature, loss of weight, and then recovery. I don't know why, but seeing her walking around that little flat made me understand something of Maurice's regret. She is no less intelligent than her sister: chemistry interested her and her studies were going well; it is a pity she stopped. What is she going to do with her days? I ought to be on her side—she has chosen the same path as I did. But then I had Maurice. She has Jean-Pierre, of course. It is difficult to imagine that a man one does not care for can possibly be enough to fill anyone's life.

A long letter from Lucienne, utterly delighted with her course and with America.

Look for a table for the sitting-room. Go and see the paralysed old woman from Bagnolet.

Why go on with this diary, since I have nothing to put in it? I started it because I was taken aback by being alone: I went on with it because I was worried, Maurice's attitude leaving me altogether at a loss. But now that I know just where I am the worry has vanished, and I think I shall give it up.

Friday 1 October

I behaved badly for the first time. During breakfast Maurice told me that from now on, when he goes out with Noëllie in the evening, he is going to spend the whole night at her place. It is more seemly for her, just as it is for me, he says. 'Since you acquiesce in my having this affair, let me live it decently.'

Taking into account the number of evenings he spends at the laboratory and the number of lunches he skips, he is giving Noëllie almost as much time as me. I flared up. He bewildered me with calculations. If the actual number of hours is counted, all right, he is more often with me. But during a great many of them he is working, reading periodicals—or else we are seeing friends. When he is with Noëllie he gives himself entirely up to her.

In the end I gave way. Since I have adopted an understanding, kindly attitude I must stick to it. No head-on collision with him. If I spoil his affair for him distance will make it seem charming—he will regret it. If I let him 'live it decently' he will soon get tired of it. That's what Isabelle assures me. I repeat to myself 'Patience.'

Still, I must realize that at Maurice's age an infatuation means a good deal. At Mougins he was thinking of Noëllie, obviously. Now I understand the anxiety in his eyes at the Nice airfield—he was wondering whether I suspected anything. Or was he ashamed of having lied to me? Was it shame rather than anxiety? I can see his face once more, but I cannot make it out properly.

Saturday 2 October. Morning

They are in their pyjamas; they are drinking coffee, smiling at one another . . . There is an image that hurts me. When you hit against a stone at first you only feel the impact—the pain comes after. Now, with a week's delay, I am beginning to suffer. Before, I was more bewildered—amazed. I rationalized, I thrust aside the pain that is pouring over me this morning—these images. I pace up and down the flat, up and down, and at each step another strikes me. I opened his cupboard. I looked at his pyjamas, shirts, drawers, vests; and I began to weep. Another woman was stroking his cheek, as soft as this silk, as warm and gentle as this pull-over—that I cannot bear.

I was not watchful enough. I thought Maurice was ageing, that he was over-working, that I ought to adapt myself to his lack of warmth. He took to thinking of me as a sister, more or less. Noëllie awoke his desires. Whether she has any sexual appetite or not she certainly knows how to conduct herself in bed. He has rediscovered the proud delight of fully satisfying a woman. Going to bed does not mean only going to bed. Between them there is that intimacy that used to belong only to me. When they wake up does he snuggle her against his shoulder calling her his doe, his honey-mouth? Or has he invented other names that he says in the same voice? Or has he found himself another voice? He is shaving, smiling at her, with his eyes darker and more brilliant, his mouth more naked under the mask of white foam. He appeared in the doorway holding a great bunch of red roses in his arms, wrapped in cellophane: does he take her flowers?

My heart is being sawn in two with a very fine-toothed saw.

Saturday evening

Mme Dormoy's arrival jerked me out of my obsessions. We gossiped, and I gave her the things Lucienne has not taken away, for her daughter. Having had one daily woman who was half blind, another a mythomaniac who overwhelmed me with the tale of her woes, and another mentally-deficient who stole, I value this straightforward, well-balanced woman—the only one I have not taken on to do her a kindness.

I went to do the shopping. Usually I take my time strolling along this street full of smells, noises and smiles. I try to work up longings as varied as the fruits, vegetables, cheeses, pâtés and fish on the stalls. I buy the autumn itself at the flower-seller's by the armful. Today my movements were automatic. Hastily I filled my shopping-basket. A feeling that I had never experienced before—other people's cheerfulness oppressing me.

At lunch-time I said to Maurice, 'Really, you know, we did not talk at all. I know nothing about Noëllie.'

'Oh yes you do; I told you everything of importance.'

It is true that he talked to me about her at the Club 46: I am sorry I listened so vaguely. 'But after all I do not understand what seems to you so special about her: there are quantities of women just as pretty.'

He reflected. 'She possesses one quality you ought to like —a way of giving herself up entirely to what she is doing.'

'She is ambitious, I know.'

'It's something other than ambition.' He stopped, no doubt feeling awkward at praising Noëllie to me. It must be admitted that I probably did not look very encouraging.

Tuesday 5 October

I am spending rather too much time at Colette's, now that she is no longer ill. In spite of her great sweetness I feel that my anxious concern is on the edge of being a nuisance. When one has lived so much for others it is quite hard to turn oneself back again—to live for oneself. I must not plunge into the pitfall of devotion—I know very well that the words *give* and *receive* are interchangeable, and I know very well how much I needed the need my daughters had of me. On that point I have never played false. 'You're wonderful,' Maurice used to say to me—he used to say it to me so often, on one pretext or another—'because giving others pleasure is in the first place a pleasure to you.' I would laugh. 'Yes, it's a form of selfishness.' That tenderness in his eyes—'The most enchanting form there is.'

Wednesday 6 October

Yesterday the table I found at the flea-market on Sunday was delivered, a genuine rough wood farm table, rather patched, heavy and enormous. The sitting-room is even pleasanter than our bedroom. In spite of my unhappiness (cinema, Nembutal—that's a routine I shall soon tire of), yesterday evening I was delighted with the pleasure he would have this morning. And to be sure he did congratulate me. But what of it? Ten years ago I rearranged this room when he was staying with his sick mother. I remember his face, his voice—'How splendid it will be to be happy here!' He lit a huge wood fire. He went out to buy

champagne; and he brought me back red roses then, too.
This morning he looked, he said it was fine with an air of
—how shall I put it?—meaning well.

Has he really changed, then? In one way his confession
had comforted me—he was having an affair: that explained everything. But would he have had an affair if he
had remained the same? I had had a fore-knowledge of the
change and that was one of the hidden reasons for my
resistance—you cannot transform your life without being
transformed yourself. Money; belonging to a brilliant set—
he has grown dulled, surfeited. When we were terribly
poor, quite broke, my shifts enchanted him—'You're wonderful!' A single flower, a fruit, a pull-over I had knitted
him—they were immense treasures. This sitting-room that
I arranged so carefully . . . well, it's nothing very marvel-
lous, compared with the Talbots' flat. And Noëllie's?
What is that like? More luxurious than ours, for sure.

Thursday 7 October

When all is said and done, what has it profited me, his
telling me the truth? He spends whole nights with her now
—it suits them splendidly. I wonder . . . Oh, really, it's too
obvious. He brought on my questions, provoked them.
And I, poor fool, I thought he was just telling me out of
fairness . . .

. . . God, how painful it is, being angry. I thought I
should never get over it before he came back. In fact I have
no reason for getting myself into such a state. He did not
know how to set about it: he used cunning to solve his
difficulties—that is not a crime.

Still, I should like to know whether he told me for my
sake or for his own ease and comfort.

Saturday 9 October

I was pleased with myself this evening because I had spent two untroubled, easy days. I wrote another letter to the social worker M Barron had mentioned and who had not answered. I lit a fine wood fire and I began knitting myself a dress. About half past ten the telephone went. It was Talbot asking for Maurice. I said, 'He is at the laboratory. I thought you were there too.'

'. . . What I mean is . . . I was supposed to go, but I have a cold. I thought Lacombe had gone home already— I'll call him at the laboratory. Forgive me for bothering you.'

The last sentences very quick—a very brisk voice. I heard only that silence—'. . . What I mean is.' And another silence after that one. I stayed there motionless, my eyes fixed on the telephone. Ten times over I repeated the two answers, like an old, worn-out record: 'That you were there too—. . . What I mean is . . .' And each time, merciless, that silence.

Sunday 10 October

He came back a little before midnight. I said to him, 'Talbot rang. I thought he was with you at the laboratory.'

He answered without looking at me, 'He wasn't there.'

I said, 'Nor were you.'

There was a short silence. 'Just so. I was at Noëllie's. She had begged me to drop in.'

'Drop in! You stayed three hours. Do you often go and see her when you tell me you are working?'

'What do you mean? It's the very first time,' he cried, as indignantly as if he had never told me a single falsehood.

'It's once too many. And what's the point of having told me the truth if you are going to go on lying?'

'You're right. But I didn't dare . . .'

I really did react at this—all that anger choked back, all those efforts to keep up the appearance of tranquillity. 'Didn't dare? Am I a shrew, then? Show me another woman who will stand being pushed around as much as this!'

His voice turned nasty. 'I did not dare because the other day you began to reckon everything up—"so many hours for Noëllie, so many hours for me . . ."'

'Oh, really! Really! You were the one who confused me with sums!'

He hesitated a moment and then said with a repentant air, 'All right. I plead guilty. I shall never lie any more.'

I asked him why Noëllie had wanted to see him all that much.

'It's not a very pleasant situation for her,' he replied.

Anger seized me again. 'That's the limit! She knew I existed when she went to bed with you.'

'She doesn't forget it: indeed it is that which she finds so painful.'

'I'm in her way? She wants you all to herself?'

'She likes me . . .'

Noëllie Guérard, that frigid little on-the-make climber, playing the love-lorn maiden—that was rather much to take!

'I can vanish, if that would make things easier for you two,' I said.

He laid his hand on my arm. 'I beg of you, Monique, don't take it like this.' He looked unhappy and tired, but I —I who go out of my mind if I hear him sigh—I was in no compassionate mood. I said coldly, 'And how would you like me to take it?'

'Without enmity. All right, so I was wrong to begin this affair. But now it's done I must try to manage things so as not to hurt anyone more than I can help.'

'I'm not asking you for pity.'

'It's not a question of pity! From a completely selfish

point of view, hurting you tears me to pieces. But do understand that I have to consider Noëllie too.'

I got up: I felt I was no longer in control of myself. 'Let's go to bed.'

And now, this evening, I tell myself that perhaps Maurice is in the act of repeating this conversation to Noëllie. How can it be that I had not thought of that before? They talk about themselves, and so necessarily about me. There are complicities between them, as there are between Maurice and me. It is not merely that Noëllie is a nuisance in our life: in their idyll, I am a problem and an obstacle. As she sees it, this is not just a passing thing: what she has in mind is a serious relationship with Maurice, and she is clever. My first reaction was the right one—I ought to have put a stop to it right away; to have said to Maurice 'Either her or me.' He would have been cross with me for a while but then no doubt he would have thanked me. I had not been able to bring myself to do it. My longings, wishes, interests have always been identical with his. On the few occasions when I have stood out against him it was for his own sake, for his own good. Now I ought to rise up in direct opposition I have not strength enough to enter into this battle. But I am not sure that my forbearance may not be a mistake. The bitterest thing about it is that Maurice scarcely seems to be grateful to me for it at all. I believe that with that splendid male illogicality he holds me responsible for the remorse he feels—holds it against me. Should I be still more understanding, more detached, more full of smiles? Oh, I can't tell any more. I have never hesitated so long about how I ought to behave. Yes I have, though: about Lucienne. But then I could ask Maurice's advice. The most staggering thing is my loneliness now that I am confronted with him.

Thursday 14 October

I am being manipulated. Who is directing the manipulation? Maurice? Noëllie? Both together? I do not know how to make the manoeuvre fail, whether by pretending to yield or by resisting. And where am I being led?

Yesterday as we came back from the cinema Maurice, speaking carefully, said he had a favour to ask me: he would like to go off for the week-end with Noëllie. By way of compensation he would arrange not to work these coming evenings so that we should have plenty of time to ourselves. I showed that my mind revolted against it. His face hardened. 'Let's not talk about it any more.' He grew amiable again, but having refused him something quite overwhelmed me. He was thinking me mean-minded, or at least unfriendly. He would not hesitate to lie to me the following week: the separation between us would be fully accomplished . . . 'Try to live this business *with* him,' Isabelle said to me.

Before going to bed I told him that on consideration I was sorry for my reaction—I should leave him free. He did not look happy about it: on the contrary, I thought I saw distress in his eyes. 'I know very well I am asking you a great deal. I ask you too much. Don't think I don't feel remorse.'

'Oh, remorse! What's the good of that?'

'No good, of course. I just said it, that's all. Maybe it's cleaner not to have any.'

I stayed awake a long while; so did he, it seemed to me. What was he thinking about? As for me, I was wondering whether I had been right to give way. Going from one concession to another, where should I end up?

And for the moment I am not getting anything out of it at all. It is too early, obviously. Before this affair can go bad it must be allowed to ripen. I tell myself that over and over again. And sometimes I think myself sensible, and sometimes I accuse myself of cowardice. In fact I am defenceless because I have never supposed I had any rights. I expect a lot of the people I love—too much, perhaps. I expect a lot and I even ask for it. But I do not know how to insist.

Friday 15 October

I had not seen Maurice so cheerful and affectionate for ages. He found two hours this afternoon to take me to the exhibition of Hittite art. No doubt he hopes to reconcile our life together with his affair. If it doesn't last too long, that's all right with me.

Sunday 17 October

Yesterday he slipped out of bed before eight. I caught a whiff of his eau de Cologne. He closed the door of the bedroom and the front door very gently. From the window I saw him scrupulously polishing the car, delighted. It seemed to me that he was probably humming.

Above the last autumn leaves there was a soft summer sky. (The golden rain of the acacia leaves on a pink and grey road, as we came back from Nancy.) He got into the car, he started the engine and I looked at my place next to him: my place, where Noëllie was going to sit. He shifted the gear lever, the car moved off, and I felt my heart lose its rhythm. He drove off very fast; he disappeared. For ever. He will never come back. It will not be he who comes back.

I killed the time as well as I could. Colette, Isabelle. I saw two films: the Bergman twice straight off, it struck me so. This evening I put on some jazz, lit a fire and knitted, watching the flames. Usually I am not afraid of being alone. Indeed, in small doses, I find it a relief—the presence of people I love overburdens my heart. I grow anxious about a wrinkle or a yawn. And so as not to be a nuisance—or absurd—I have to bottle up my anxieties, rein back my impulses. The times when I think of them from a distance are restful breaks. Last year, when Maurice was at a conference at Geneva, the days seemed short: this week-end is interminable. I threw my knitting aside, because it did not protect me: what are they doing, where are they, what are they saying to one another, what sort of looks do they exchange? I had thought I could preserve myself from jealousy: not at all. I searched through his pockets and his papers, without finding anything, of course. She must certainly have written to him when he was at Mougins: he went to fetch his letters at the post office, hiding it from me. And he has put them away somewhere at the hospital. If I asked to see them, would he show them to me?

Ask . . . whom? That man who is travelling with Noëllie, that man whose face, whose words I cannot even picture to myself—do not want to picture to myself? The man I love and who loves me? Are they the same one? I can no longer tell. And I do not know whether I am making a mountain out of a molehill or what I take to be a molehill is in fact a mountain.

. . . I sought shelter in our past. I spread out boxfuls of photographs in front of the fire. I found the one with Maurice wearing his arm-band: how much at one we were that day when we were looking after the wounded FFI near the Quai des Grands-Augustins. Here, on the Cap Corse road, is the gasping old motor-car his mother gave us. I remember that night when we broke down, near Corte. We sat there motionless, overawed by the solitude and the silence. I said, 'We must try to put it right.' 'Kiss me first,' said Maurice. We held one another tight, for a long while, and we felt that neither cold nor weariness nor anything on earth could touch us.

It's odd. Does it mean something? All these pictures that rise up in my heart are more than ten years old: Europa Point, the liberation of Paris, our return from Nancy, our house-warming, that breakdown on the Corte road. I can bring others to mind—our last summers at Mougins, Venice, my fortieth birthday. They don't move me in the same way. Perhaps the more remote memories always seem the loveliest.

I am tired of asking myself questions and not knowing the answers. I am out of my depth. I no longer recognize the flat. The things in it have the air of imitations of themselves. The massive table in the sitting-room—it is hollow. As though both I and the house had been projected into a fourth dimension. If I were to go out it would not astonish me to find myself in a prehistoric forest, or in a city of the year 3000.

Tuesday 19 October

Tension between us. My fault or his? I welcomed him with a fine air of naturalness: he told me about his weekend. They had been in the Sologne; it seems that Noëllie likes the Sologne. (So she possesses taste, does she?) I started when he told me that yesterday they had dinner and slept at the Hostellerie de Forneville.

'That pretentious, expensive place?'

'It's very pretty,' said Maurice.

'Isabelle tells me it's the kind of picturesqueness put on for Americans—stuffed with pot-plants, birds and phoney antiques.'

'There are pot plants, birds and antiques, real or false. But it's very pretty.'

I did not go on. I sense a hardness coming into his voice. What Maurice usually likes is finding a genuine little restaurant where you eat well, or an uncrowded hotel in a beautiful, remote situation. All right, I quite see that once

in a while he might do it for Noëllie; but he does not have
to pretend to like the vulgarities that delight her. Unless
she is acquiring an influence over him. He saw the latest
Bergman with her in August, at a private showing (Noëllie
only goes to private showings or galas) and he did not think
much of it. She must have told him that Bergman was out
of date—that's her only criterion. She dazzles him by
pretending to be completely with it—up to date in everything. I can see her now at that dinner of Diana's last year.
She gave a lecture upon these 'happenings'. And then she
held forth about the Rampal case, which she had just won.
A truly ludicrous act. Luce Couturier looked thoroughly
embarrassed and Diana gave me a knowing wink. But the
men listened, open-mouthed—Maurice among them. And
yet it's not like him, to allow himself to be taken in by that
kind of guff.

I ought not to go for Noëllie, but there are times when
I just can't help it. Over Bergman, I did not argue. But in
the evening, at dinner, I had a stupid quarrel with Maurice
because he would have it that it was quite possible to drink
red wine with fish. A typical Noëllie line—to know the
right way of behaving so perfectly that you don't have to
conform. So I stood up for the rule that says fish and white
wine. We grew heated. Such a pity. I don't like fish, anyhow.

Wednesday 20 October

The night Maurice spoke to me I thought I should have
an unpleasant but clear-cut situation to deal with. And now
I do not know where I stand in it nor what I have to fight
against nor whether I ought to fight or why. Are other
wives so bewildered in comparable cases? Isabelle tells me
again and again that time is on my side. I should like to
believe her. As for Diana, so long as her husband is kind
to her and her children and looks after them, she does not

care in the least whether he deceives her or not. She could
not possibly give me any advice. Still, I telephoned her
because I wanted information about Noëllie: she knows
her and dislikes her. (Noëllie made advances to Lemercier,
who would have none of it: he does not like women to
throw themselves at his head.) I asked her how long she
had known about Maurice. She pretended to be surprised
and said that Noëllie had not told her anything—they are
not at all intimate. She told me that when Noëllie was
twenty she married a very wealthy man. Her husband
divorced her—no doubt he was tired of being cuckolded—
but she got a handsome alimony; she forces him to give her
splendid presents; she gets along very well with his new
wife and often makes long stays at their villa at La
Napoule. She has gone to bed with quantities of men—
most of them useful in her career—and now she must be
wanting a steady relationship. But she will drop Maurice if
she hooks a richer or better-known man. (I should rather
he took the initiative.) Her daugher is fourteen and she is
being brought up on the most pretentious lines—riding,
yoga, Virginie dresses. She is at the Ecole Alsacienne with
Diana's second daugher and she shows off unbelievably.
And at the same time she complains that her mother
neglects her. Diana says that Noëllie asks her clients out-
rageous fees, that she takes immense care of her publicity,
and that she will do absolutely anything to succeed. We
talked about the way she boasted last year. Foolishly
enough this tearing of her to pieces eased my mind. It was
like a magic spell: where you stick in the pins your rival
will be maimed and disfigured, and the lover will see her
hideous wounds. It seemed to me impossible that our
portrait of Noëllie should not prevail with Maurice. (There
is one thing that I shall tell him though—it was not she
who argued the Rampal case at all.)

Thursday 21 October

Maurice was on the defensive right away. 'I can hear Diana from here! She loathes Noëllie!'

'That's true,' I said. 'But if Noëllie knows it, why does she go and see her?'

'And why does Diana go and see Noëllie? It's a fashionable acquaintance. And now what?' he asked me with a certain challenge. 'What has Diana been telling you?'

'You'll tell me it is mere spite.'

'That's for sure. Women who do nothing cannot bear those who work.'

(Women who do nothing: the expression stuck in my throat. It is not one of Maurice's expressions.)

'And married women don't like those who fling themselves at their husbands' heads,' I said.

'Oh, so that's the way Diana tells it?' asked Maurice, looking amused.

'Noëllie claims it was the other way around, obviously. Each has his own version of the truth . . .' I looked at Maurice. 'And in your case which of you started the flinging?'

'I told you how it happened.'

Yes, he did tell me at the Club 46: but it was not very clear. Noëllie brought him her daughter, who was anaemic; he suggested that she should spend an evening with him; she accepted; they ended up in bed. Oh, I don't care. I went on, 'If you want to know, Diana thinks Noëllie is self-seeking, on the make and pretentious.'

'And you take her word for it?'

'At all events she tells lies.' I told him about the Rampal case, which she pretended to have argued, whereas in fact she was only Brévant's junior.

'But she never said she was not. She looks upon it as her case in so far as she worked on it a great deal, that's all.'

Either he was lying or he had cheated with his own memory. I am almost certain that she spoke of her address to the court. 'In any case she arrogated the whole of the success to herself.'

'Listen,' he said cheerfully, 'if she has all the vices that you say she has how can you explain my spending five minutes with her?'

'I can't explain it.'

'I am not going to make a formal defence of her. But I do assure you she's a worth-while woman.'

Maurice will see anything I say against Noëllie as the effect of my jealousy. It would be better to say nothing. But I really do find her profoundly disagreeable. She reminds me of my sister—the same confidence, the same glibness, the same phonily off-hand elegance. It seems that men like this mixture of coquetry and hardness. When I was sixteen and she was eighteen Maryse swiped all my boy-friends; so much so that I was in a dreadful state of nerves when I introduced Maurice to her. I had a ghastly nightmare in which he fell in love with her. He was indignant. 'She is so superficial! So bogus! Paste diamonds, rhinestones! You—you're the real jewel.' Authentic: that was the word everyone was using in those days. He said I was authentic. At all events I was the one he loved and I was not envious of my sister any more; I was happy to be the person I was. But then how can he think a great deal of Noëllie, who is of the same kind as Maryse? He is altogether gone from me if he likes being with someone I dislike so very much—and whom he ought to dislike if he were faithful to our code. Certainly he has altered. He lets himself be taken in by false values that we used to despise. Or he is simply completely mistaken about Noëllie. I wish the scales would drop from his eyes soon. My patience is beginning to run out.

'Women who do nothing can't stand those who work.' The remark surprised and wounded me. Maurice thinks it right that a woman should have a calling: he was very sorry that Colette chose marriage and being a housewife, and he even rather resented my not having dissuaded her. But after all he does acknowledge that there are other ways in which a woman can fulfil herself. He never thought I was doing 'nothing': on the contrary, he was astonished at the thoroughness with which I looked after the cases he told me about while at the same time I looked after the house really well and took great care of our daughters—and that without ever appearing tense or overworked. Other women always seemed to him either too idle or too busy. As for me, I had a balanced life: he even used the word harmonious. 'With you, everything is harmonious.' I find it absolutely intolerable that he should adopt Noëllie's scorn for women 'who do nothing'.

Sunday 24 October

I am beginning to see through Noëllie's little game: she is trying to reduce me to the role of the affectionate, resigned, house-loving wife who is left at home. I do like sitting by the fireside with Maurice; but it vexes me that it should always be she that he takes to concerts and to the theatre. On Friday I cried out when he told me that he had been to a private view with her.

'But you loathe private views!' he replied.

'I love painting, though,' I said.

'If it had been good, I should have gone back with you.'

Easy enough to say. Noëllie lends him books—she plays at being the intellectual. All right, so I know less about modern writing and music than she does: but taken all in all I am not less cultured nor less intelligent. Maurice wrote to me once that he trusted in my judgment more than anyone else's because it was both 'enlightened and naïve'. I try to say exactly what I think, what I feel; so does he; and there is nothing that seems more precious to us than this sincerity. I must not let Noëllie dazzle Maurice with her showing-off. I asked Isabelle to help me to get back into the swim. Unknown to Maurice, of course: otherwise he would laugh at me.

She still urges me to go on being patient; she assures me that Maurice has not behaved very badly and that I ought still to retain my respect and liking for him. Her saying this about him did me good: I have so questioned myself about him, so distrusted him and blamed him, that in the end I was not really seeing what kind of a person he was at all. It is true that during our first years, between his consulting-room at Simca and the little flat with the children bawling in it, his life would have been grim if we had not loved one another so. After all it was for my sake, she said, that he gave up the idea of a staff appointment; he might have been tempted to hold it against me. There I just don't agree. The war had kept him back; he was beginning to find his studies exasperating—he wanted an adult life. We had both of us been responsible for my pregnancy, and under Pétain there was no question of risking an abortion. No: any resentment would have been quite unfair. Our marriage made him as happy as it made me. Still, it was very much to his credit to have been so cheerful and so affectionate in unpleasant and indeed even wretched circumstances. Until this business I never had the shadow of a complaint to make against him.

This talk with Isabelle gave me courage: I asked Maurice to let us spend next week-end together. I should like him to rediscover a happiness and closeness that he has rather tended to forget—rediscover it with me; and I should like him to remember our past, too. I suggested going back to Nancy. He had the worried, harassed look of a fellow who knows there will be scenes elsewhere. (I'd very much like her to prove to him that sharing is not possible.) He said neither yes nor no—it depended on his patients.

Wednesday 27 October

He positively cannot leave Paris this week-end. In other words Noëllie is against it. I broke out in rebellion; for the first time I cried in front of him. He looked horrified. 'Oh, don't cry! I'll try to find a locum.' In the end he promised he would manage somehow—he too wanted this week-end. That may be so or it may not. But what is quite certain is that my tears overwhelmed him.

I spent an hour in the visiting-room with Marguerite. She is growing impatient. How long the days must be! The social worker is kind, but she cannot let me take her out without an authorization that does not come. By mere carelessness, no doubt, for I provide all possible guarantees as to character.

Thursday 28 October

So we go for Saturday and Sunday. 'I managed!' he told me in a triumphant voice. He was obviously proud of having stood up to Noëllie—too proud. It means that there was a ferocious struggle and it therefore follows that she means a great deal to him. He seemed on edge all through the evening. He drank two glasses of whisky instead of one and smoked cigarette after cigarette. He was too jolly and high spirited by far discussing our route, and my reserve disappointed him. 'You're not pleased?'

'Of course I am.'

That was only half true. Has Noëllie taken up so much room in his life that he has to fight her so as to be able to take me away for a week-end? And have I myself reached the point of looking upon her as a rival? No, I won't have any recriminations, schemes, false-dealings, victories, defeats. I shall warn Maurice—'I shall not fight with Noëllie over you.'

Monday 11 *November*

It was so like the past: I almost believed the likeness was
going to bring the past to life again. We had driven
through fog and then beneath a beautiful cold sun. At Bar-
le-Duc and at Saint-Mihiel we looked at Ligier Richier's
sculptures again, and we were as deeply moved as we had
been in the old days: it was I who showed them to him
first. Since then we have travelled quite a lot; we have seen
a great deal; and yet the *Décharné* astonished us all over
again. In Nancy, as we stood in front of the wrought-iron
railings of the Place Stanislas, I felt something piercing
my heart—a happiness that hurt, so unaccustomed had it
become. In those old country-town streets I squeezed his
arm under mine; or sometimes he put his round my
shoulders.

We talked about everything, and about nothing, and
about our daughters a great deal. He cannot bring himself
to understand how Colette could have married Jean-
Pierre: with her chemistry and biology he had planned a
brilliant career for her; and we should have given her
complete romantic and sexual freedom, as she knew. Why
had she fallen for such a totally commonplace young fellow
—fallen for him to the point of giving up her whole future
to him?

'She is happy that way,' I said.

'I should have preferred her to be happy some other
way.'

The going of Lucienne, his favourite, saddens him still
more. Although he approves of her liking for independence
he would have preferred her to stay in Paris; he would
have preferred her to read medicine and work with him.

'Then she would not have been independent.'

'Oh yes she would. She would have had her own life at
the same time as she worked with me.'

Fathers never have exactly the daughters they want because they invent a notion of them that the daughters have to conform to. Mothers accept them as they are. Colette needed security above all and Lucienne needed freedom: I understand them both. And I think each perfectly successful in her own way—Colette so sensitive and kind, Lucienne so brilliant, so full of enegry.

We stopped at the same little hotel as we had stayed at twenty years ago, and we had—perhaps on another floor— the same room. I went to bed first and I watched him, walking to and fro in his blue pyjamas, bare-footed on the worn carpet. He looked neither cheerful nor sad. And I was blinded by the mental image—an image called up hundreds of times, set, but not worn-out, still shining with newness—of Maurice walking barefoot upon this carpet in his black pyjamas: he had pulled up the collar and its points framed his face; he talked nonsense, childishly worked up. I realized that I had come here in the hope of once more finding that man so hopelessly in love: I had not seen him for years and years, although this memory lies like a transparency over all the visions I have of him. That evening, for the very reason that the surroundings were the same, the old image, coming into contact with a flesh and blood man smoking a cigarette, fell to dust and ashes. I had a shattering revelation: *time goes by*. I began to weep. He sat on the edge of the bed and took me tenderly in his arms. 'Sweetheart, my sweetheart, don't cry. What are you crying for?' He stroked my hair, he gave me little fluttering kisses on the side of my head.

'It's nothing; it's over,' I said. 'I'm fine.'

I was fine; the room was bathed in a pleasant twilight, Maurice's hands and mouth were soft; I put my lips to his; and I slipped my hand under his pyjama jacket. And suddenly he was upright: he had thrust me away with a sudden jerk. I whispered, 'Do I disgust you as much as all that?'

'You're out of your mind, darling. But I'm dropping with tiredness. It's the open air—walking about. I just have to sleep.'

I buried myself under the blankets. He lay down. He turned out the light. I had the feeling of being at the bottom of a grave, with the blood frozen in my veins, unable either to stir or to weep. We had not made love since Mougins: and even then, that could hardly be called making love . . . About four o'clock I dropped off. When I woke up he was coming back into the bedroom, fully dressed: it was nine or thereabouts. I asked him where he had been.

'I went for a stroll.'

But it was raining outside and he did not have his mackintosh with him; he was not wet. He had been to telephone Noëllie. She had insisted upon his telephoning: she didn't even have the generosity to let me have him all to myself even for one wretched week-end. I said nothing. The day dragged along. Each realized that the other was making an effort to be pleasant and cheerful. We both agreed to go back to Paris for dinner and finish the evening at the cinema.

Why had he thrust me from him? Men still try to pick me up in the street; they squeeze my knee in the cinema. I have fattened a little—not much. My bosom went to pieces after Lucienne's birth; but ten years ago it stirred Maurice. And two years ago Quillan was wild to go to bed with me. No. The reason why Maurice jerked away was that he is infatuated with Noëllie; he could not bear sleeping with another woman. If he has her under his skin to that degree, and if at the same time he lets himself be dazzled by her things are far more serious than I had imagined.

Wednesday 3 November

I find Maurice's kindness almost painful—he is sorry for what happened at Nancy. But he never kisses me on the lips any more. I feel utterly wretched.

Friday 5 November

I behaved well, but what an effort it was! Fortunately Maurice had warned me. (Whatever he may say I still think he ought to have prevented her from coming.) I nearly stayed at home; he pressed me—we don't go out so very often; I ought not to cheat myself of this cocktail-party; my absence would not be understood. Or did he think it would be only too well understood? I watched the Couturiers, the Talbots, all those friends who have been at our house so often, and I wondered just how much they knew of what was going on, and whether Noëllie sometimes asked them with Maurice. As for Talbot, Maurice is not intimate with him: but obviously since that evening he made the gaffe on the telephone he has guessed that something is happening behind my back. As for Couturier, there is nothing Maurice hides from him. I can hear his collusive voice: 'I am supposed to be at the laboratory with you.' And what about the others—have they their suspicions? Ah, I was so proud of us as a pair—a model pair. We proved that love could last without growing weary. How often had I stood up for total faithfulness! Shattered, the ideal pair! All that is left is a husband who deceives his wife; and an abandoned wife who is lied to. And I owe this humiliation to Noëllie. It scarcely seems believable. Fair enough, she might be thought attractive; but really, quite objectively, what a phoney! That little sideways smile, her head rather leaning—that way of lapping up the other

person's words and then suddenly her head thrown back
and the pretty silvery laugh. An able woman, and yet *so*
feminine. With Maurice she was exactly as she had been
last year at Diana's—remote and intimate; and he wore the
same look of silly admiration. And like last year that fool
Luce Couturier looked at me with an air of embarrass-
ment. (Could it be that Maurice was already attracted by
Noëllie last year? Was it obvious? I had noticed his
wonder-struck appearance, certainly, but without thinking
it meant anything.) In an amused voice I said to her, 'I
think Noëllie Guérard delightful. Maurice has good taste.'

She opened her eyes very wide. 'Oh, you know about it?'
'Of course!'

I asked her to come and have a drink at the flat next
week. I should like to know who is aware and who isn't
and since when. Do they pity me? Laugh nastily? Maybe I
am mean-minded, but I should like them all to drop down
dead so that the awful picture they have of me just now
might be done away with for ever and ever.

Saturday 6 November

This talk with Maurice has left me quite at a loss, for he
was calm and friendly and he really seemed to believe what
he said. Talking over yesterday's cocktail-party I told him
—and I was speaking in all good faith, too—what I dis-
liked in Noëllie. In the first place I thought the barrister's
profession odious—for money you defend one fellow
against another, even if it is the second who is in the right.
This is immoral. Maurice replied that Noëllie ran her practice in a very agreeable way; that she did not accept just
any case; that she asked high fees from the rich, certainly,
but that there were masses of people she helped for nothing.
It is untrue that she is self-seeking. Her husband helped her
buy her practice: why not, since they have remained on

excellent terms? (But has she not remained on excellent terms just so that he should put up the money for her practice?) She wants to get to the top: there is nothing wrong about that, so long as one selects one's means. At this I found it hard to remain calm.

'You say that: but you have never tried to get to the top.'

'When I made up my mind to specialize I did so because I was sick of stagnating.'

'In the first place you weren't stagnating at all.'

'Intellectually I was. I was not getting nearly as much out of myself as I was capable of.'

'All right. But at all events you did not specialize out of vulgar ambition: you wanted to make intellectual progress and help towards the solving of certain problems. It was not a matter of money and career.'

'Success for a barrister is also something besides money and reputation: the cases they deal with grow more and more worthwhile.'

I said that in any case the social side counted immensely for Noëllie.

'She works very hard—she needs relaxation,' he replied.

'But why these galas, these first nights, these fashionable night-clubs? I think it ridiculous.'

'Ridiculous? By what standard? All amusements have something ridiculous about them.'

That really stung me. He who dislikes fashionable things as much as I do!

'But after all you only have to hear her talk for five minutes to realize that Noëllie is not an authentic person . . .'

'Authentic? What is that supposed to mean? It is a word that has been so misused.'

'By you to begin with.' He made no reply. I went on, 'Noëllie reminds me of Maryse.'

'Oh, no.'

'I promise you she is like her—she's the kind of person who never stops to look at a sunset.'

He laughed. 'It doesn't happen to me so often either, I can tell you.'

'Oh, come. You love nature as much as I do.'

'Well, I suppose I do. But I don't see that everybody else has to share our tastes.'

His lack of candour disgusted me. 'Listen,' I said to him, 'there is one thing I must warn you of: I shall not fight with Noëllie over you—if you prefer her to me, that's your affair. I shan't struggle.'

'Who's talking about struggling?'

I shan't struggle. But fear touched me all at once. Could it conceivably be that Maurice *does* prefer her to me? The idea had never occurred to me. I know that I possess—all right, let's leave that word authenticity out of it: maybe it is a trifle priggish—a certain *quality* that she does not. 'You have real quality, my dear,' my father used to say to me, proudly. And Maurice too, in other words. It is this *quality* that I value above anything else in people—in Maurice, and in Isabelle: and Maurice is like me. No. It is impossible that he should prefer someone as bogus as Noëllie to me. She is 'cheap', as they say in English. But it worries me that he should in her accept so many things that I consider unacceptable. For the first time I see that a gap has come into being between us.

Wednesday 10 *November*

I telephoned Quillan the day before yesterday. Oh, I'm not at all proud of it. I had to make sure that a man could still find me desirable. That has been proved. And where does it get me? It has not made me any more desirable to myself.

I had not made up my mind to go to bed with him at all: nor not to. I spent some time getting myself ready: bath-salts in my bath and lacquer on my toe-nails. It was enough

to make you weep! In these two years he had not aged but
grown more fine-drawn—his face is more interesting. I had
not remembered that he was so handsome. It was certainly
not from lack of being pleased with me that he asked me
out with such eagerness. It could have been because of his
remembering the past, and I was afraid—I was dreadfully
afraid—that he might be disappointed. Not at all.

'So all in all, you are happy?'

'I should be, if I were to see you more often.'

This was in a pleasant restaurant behind the Panthéon—
old New Orleans records, very funny funny-men, singers
with a good line of songs, anarchistic—that kind of thing.
Quillan knew almost everybody in the place—painters like
himself, sculptors, musicians: most of them young. He
sang himself, accompanied by a guitar. He remembered
what records I liked, what dishes; he bought me a rose; he
lavished little attentions on me, and I realized how very
few I got from Maurice, nowadays. He also paid me those
rather silly little compliments that I never hear any more—
compliments on my hands, my smile, my voice. Gradually
I let myself be smoothed by this tenderness. I forgot that at
that moment Maurice was smiling at Noëllie. After all I
was having my share of smiles too. He drew a pretty little
portrait of me on a paper napkin—I really did not look
like something on the scrap-heap. I drank a little, not much.
And when he asked if he might come in and have a drink
I said yes. (I had told him that Maurice was in the country.)
I poured us out two glasses of whisky. He never stirred,
but his eyes were on me all the time. It seemed to me
unnatural, seeing him there where Maurice usually sits:
my cheerfulness left me. I shivered.

'You're cold. I'm going to light you a huge fire.' He
darted towards the fire-place, but so eagerly and so clumsily
that he upset the little wooden statue I bought in Egypt
with Maurice and that I love so. I shrieked: it was broken!

'I'll mend it for you,' he said. 'It's perfectly simple.'

But he looked dreadfully upset. Because of my shriek, no doubt—I had shrieked very loud. A very little while later I said I was tired and that I had to go to bed.

'When shall we see one another again?'

'I'll ring you.'

'You won't ring me at all. Let's make a date at once.'

I said a day—just any day. I shall cry off. He left. I stayed there dazed, with a piece of my statue in each hand. And I began to sob.

It seemed to me that Maurice looked as though he didn't like it when I told him I had seen Quillan again.

Saturday 13 November

Each time I think I have got to the very bottom. And then I sink even farther down into doubt and unhappiness. Luce Couturier let herself be taken in like a child: so much so that I wonder whether she may not have done it on purpose . . . This business has been going on for more than a year. And Noëllie was in Rome with him in October! Now I understand Maurice's face at Nice airfield—remorse, shame, fear of being found out. One is inclined to invent hunches for oneself after the event. But in this case I am not inventing anything at all. I sensed something all right, because the going of the plane wrenched my heart out. One never mentions the disagreeable feelings and the uneasiness that one cannot give a name to, but that exist nevertheless.

When Luce and I parted I walked and walked, not knowing where I was going. I was stupefied. I realize it all now —I had not been altogether amazed when I heard that Maurice was going to bed with another woman. It had not been entirely by chance that I asked the question 'Is there a woman in your life?' Without ever being put into words the supposition had hovered there, fleeting and uncertain, half-seen through Maurice's absent-mindedness, his not being at home, and his coldness. It would be too much to say that I suspected it. But on the other hand I was not completely dumbfounded. While Luce talked to me I was falling, falling; and when I came to myself I was broken quite to pieces. I must look back over the whole of this year again in the light of this discovery—Maurice was going to bed with Noëllie. It is a question of a long-standing relationship. The journey to Alsace that we never carried out. I said, 'I will sacrifice myself to the cure of leukaemia.' Poor fool! It was Noëllie that kept him in Paris. At the time of the dinner at Diana's they were already lovers and Luce knew it. Diana too? I shall try to make her talk. Who knows but what this business may not go even farther back? Two years ago Noëllie was with Louis Bernard; but maybe she was a pluralist. When I think that I have to fall back on conjectures! And it is Maurice and I that are involved! Obviously all our friends knew what was going on! Oh, what does it matter? I'm beyond caring about what people think. I am too utterly destroyed. I don't give a damn for the picture they may draw of me. It's a matter of survival.

'Nothing has changed between us!' What illusions I built up for myself upon those words. Did he mean to say that nothing had changed because he had already been deceiving me for the past year? Or did he really mean nothing at all?

Why did he lie to me? Did he think me incapable of standing up to the truth? Was he ashamed? In that case why did he tell me? No doubt because Noëllie was tired of concealment. In any case what is happening to me is perfectly dreadful.

Sunday 14 November

Oh, perhaps it would have been better for me to have held my tongue! But I have never hidden anything from Maurice: at least nothing important. I could not bottle up the fact of his falsehood and my wretchedness. He banged the table. 'All this tittle-tattle!' His expression shattered me. I know that angry face of his and I love it: when Maurice is asked to make an unworthy compromise his mouth tightens and his eyes grow hard. But this time I was the object aimed at, or almost. No, Noëllie was not in Rome with him. No, he had not gone to bed with her before August. He saw her from time to time; possibly people may have seen them out together; there was nothing in it.

'Nobody met you together, but you told Couturier, who told Luce everything.'

'I said I was seeing Noëllie, not that I was going to bed with her. Luce has distorted it all. Telephone Couturier right away and ask him the truth.'

'You know perfectly well that's impossible.'

I wept. I had promised myself not to weep, but I wept. I said, 'You would do better to tell me everything. If I really knew the position I could try to face up to it. But suspecting everything, knowing nothing is unbearable. If you did no more than *see* Noëllie, what was the point of hiding it from me?'

'All right. I'll tell you the whole truth. But now you must believe me. I went to bed three times with Noëllie last year and it really did not amount to anything. I did not go to Rome with her. Do you believe me?'

'I don't know. You have lied to me so much!'

He flung his arms out in despair. 'What do you want me to do to convince you?'

'There's nothing you can do.'

Tuesday 16 November

When he comes in and he smiles at me and kisses me saying, 'Hallo, darling,' it is Maurice: these are his movements, his face, his warmth, his smell. And for a moment within me there is an immense sweetness: his presence.

Stay there: don't try to know—I can almost understand Diana. But I can't help it. I must know what is going on. In the first place does he really go to the laboratory in the evenings? When does he go to her place? I can't telephone: he would know it and he would be furious. Follow him? Hire a car and follow him? Or just find out where he is? It is base: it is degrading. But I have to get some kind of an idea.

Diana says she knows nothing. I asked her to make Noëllie talk.

'She's too clever by far: she would never give anything away.'

'You know about the affair through me. If you talk about it to her she will absolutely have to make some kind of an answer.'

At all events she promised me to get information about Noëllie—they have contacts in common. If only I were to discover things that would completely destroy her in Maurice's opinion!

No point in badgering Luce Couturier any more. Maurice will have had her told off by her husband. And he would tell Maurice that I had seen her again . . . No, that would be a blunder.

Thursday 18 November

The first time I went to check on Maurice at the laboratory the car was in the car-park. The second time it was not. I had myself driven as far as Noëllie's house. I did not have to search long. What a stab in my heart! I had loved our car: it was a faithful animal belonging to the house, a warm and comforting presence; and suddenly there it was, being used for betraying me; I hated it. I stayed there, standing under the big outer door, stupefied. I wanted to appear suddenly before him as he came from Noëllie's flat. It would only have sent him into a rage, but I was so bewildered that I had to do something—anything at all. I took myself in hand. I told myself, 'He is lying so as to ease things for me. If he eases things for me that means that he values me. In a way it would be worse if he were quite brazen.' I had almost succeeded in convincing myself when there was another stab at my heart—they came out together. I hid. They did not see me. They walked up the street to a big café. They went arm in arm, walking fast and laughing. I might have pictured them walking arm in arm and laughing a hundred times. In fact I had not really done so. No more than I really pictured them in bed: I haven't the courage. And anyway it's not the same as seeing. I began to tremble. I sat down on a bench in spite of the cold. I trembled and trembled. When I got home I went to bed and when he came in at midnight I pretended to be asleep.

But yesterday evening when he said to me, 'I'm going to the laboratory,' I asked, 'Really going?'

'Of course.'

'On Saturday you were at Noëllie's.'

He looked at me with a coldness that was even more terrifying than his anger. 'You are spying on me!'

There were tears in my eyes. 'It's a question of my life, my happiness. I want the truth. And you go on lying.'

'I try to avoid scenes,' he said in an intensely irritated tone.

'I don't make scenes.'

'Don't you?'

Every time we have things out he calls it a scene. And straight away, as I protested, my voice rose, and we had a scene. I talked about Rome again. He again denied it. Was she really not there? Or on the other hand was she in fact at Geneva? My ignorance is eating me away.

Saturday 20 November

Scenes, no. But I am clumsy. I am bad at controlling myself and I say things that vex him. I must admit that it is enough for him to have one opinion for me to have the other, imagining that he has it from her. In actual fact I have nothing against op-art. But Maurice's eager willingness to submit himself to this 'optical sadism' annoyed me: it was obviously Noëllie who had told him about the show. I stupidly maintained that it was not painting at all, and when he argued I went for him—did he suppose he was making himself younger by losing his head over everything that became fashionable?

'You're wrong to get cross.'

'I get cross because you're so desperately keen to be with it that you lose all sense of discrimination.'

He shrugged, without making any reply.

Saw Marguerite. Spent a good deal of time with Colette. But nothing worth recording.

Sunday 21 November

Talking about her relationship with Maurice, Noëllie— at least according to Diana, whom I don't altogether trust— only uttered dreary commonplaces. The situation was painful for everyone, but no doubt a balance would be reached. I was an admirable person, but men liked variety. What kind of a future did she envisage? She answered, 'Time will tell,' or words to that effect. She was on her guard.

Diana told me one story; but it is too vague for me to use. Noëllie was very nearly brought before the Bar Council because she had won the confidence of another barrister's client, an important man who took his business away and entrusted it to Noëllie. This sort of thing is thought very bad among lawyers, but it seems that Noëllie makes quite a practice of it. But Maurice would only reply, 'Tittle-tattle!' I did tell him Noëllie's daughter complained that her mother neglected her.

'At that age all girls complain of their mothers: remember your difficulties with Lucienne. In fact Noëllie does not neglect her daughter at all. She is teaching her to manage by herself and to stand on her own feet, and she is quite right to do so.'

That was a jab at me. He has often made fun of my hen-and-chicks attitude. We even had a certain number of disagreements over it.

'It doesn't worry the child that a man should spend the night in her mother's bed?'

'It is a big flat and Noëllie takes great care. Besides, she does not hide from her that since her divorce there are men in her life.'

'Quaint confidences from a mother to a daughter. Frankly, don't you find that a trifle shocking?'

'No.'

'I can't see myself ever having a relationship of that kind with Colette or Lucienne.'

He made no reply: his silence made it quite plain that he thought Noëllie's ideas on the bringing up of children were quite as good as mine. That wounded me. It is only too obvious that Noëllie behaves just as she chooses, without the least care for the interests of the child. Whereas I always did the very opposite.

'When all's said and done,' I said, 'everything Noëllie does is right.'

He waved his hand impatiently. 'Oh, don't always be talking to me about Noëllie!'

'How can I help it? She is part of your life and your life is my concern.'

'Oh, you can be interested in it and you can leave it alone.'

'How do you mean?'

'My professional life—that doesn't seem to matter to you. You never talk to me about it.'

It was an unfair counter-attack. He knows very well that when he took to specializing he moved on to ground where I could not follow him.

'What could I say to you about it? Your research is totally beyond me.'

'You don't even read my popular articles.'

'I was never really very interested in medicine as a science. It was the living relationship with the patients that fascinated me.'

'You might at least have had some curiosity about what I was doing.'

There was bitterness in his voice. I smiled at him affectionately. 'The thing is that I love you and prize you far beyond anything you can do. If you were to become a great scientist, famous and all that, I should not be in the least surprised—you're certainly capable of it. But in my eyes it would not add anything to you, that I do confess. Don't you understand me?'

He smiled too. 'Of course I do.'

This was not the first time he had complained of my indifference to his career; and up until now I have not been altogether sorry that it vexed him a little. All at once I told myself that it was a blunder. Noëllie reads his articles; she talks about them, with her head a little on one side and an admiring smile on her lips. But how can I change my attitude now? It would be terribly obvious. I found the whole of this conversation extremely disagreeable. I am sure Noëllie is not a good mother. So hard and cold a woman cannot possibly give her daughter what I gave mine.

Monday 22 November

No, I must not try to follow Noëllie on to her ground, but fight it out on my own. Maurice used to be touched by all the little things I did for him, and now I am neglecting him. I spent today tidying our wardrobes. I finally put away the summer things, brought the winter clothes out of their moth-balls and aired them, and drew up a list. Tomorrow I shall go and buy him the socks, pull-overs and pyjamas he needs. He also needs two good pairs of shoes; we'll choose them together the next time he has a free moment. Well-filled cupboards with everything in its place are a great comfort to one. Plenty: security . . . The heaps of delicate handkerchiefs and stockings and woollies gave me the feeling that the future could not possibly let me down.

Tuesday 23 November

It makes me sick with shame. I should have thought of it. When he came home to lunch Maurice had the face he wears on bad days. Almost at once he flung out, 'You're wrong to confide in your friend Diana. Noëllie has been told that she is conducting a positive inquiry about her among the lawyers and the contacts they have in common. And she tells everyone you have asked her to do it.'

I reddened and I felt ill. Maurice had never sat in judgment against me: he was my refuge. And here I was before him, pleading guilty. What utter misery!

'I only said I should like to know what kind of person Noëllie was.'

'You would have done better to have asked me rather than have stirred up all this gossip. Do you suppose I don't see Noëllie as she is? You're wrong. I know her faults as well as her virtues. I'm not a lovesick schoolboy.'

'Still, I don't imagine your opinion would be very objective.'

'And do you think Diana and her little friends are objective? They are malignance incarnate. And you can be sure they don't spare you, either.'

'All right,' I said. 'I'll tell Diana to hold her tongue.'

'You had better!'

He made an effort to change the conversation. We talked civilly. But I burn with shame. I am lowering myself in his eyes—doing it myself.

Friday 26 November

When I am with Maurice I cannot prevent myself from feeling I am in front of a judge. He thinks things about me that he does not tell me: it makes my head swim. I used to see myself so clearly through his eyes. Indeed I saw myself only through his eyes—too flattering a picture, perhaps, but one in which I recognized myself. Now I ask myself, 'Whom does he see?' Does he think me mean-minded, jealous, blabbing and even disloyal because I make inquiries behind his back? It's unfair. He forgives Noëllie so much—can't he understand my restless curiosity about her? I loathe gossip; and I have stirred it up, but I have plenty of excuse for doing so. He never mentions that business, by the way: he is as kind as can be. But I realize that he no longer talks to me quite without reserve. And sometimes I think I read in his eyes . . . not exactly pity. Shall I say a very faint mockery? (That odd look he gave me when I told him about going out with Quillan.) Yes: it's as though he saw right through me and found me touching and slightly ludicrous. For example, the time he came upon me listening to a Stockhausen record: in an indefinable tone of voice he asked, 'What? Are you taking to modern music?'

'Isabelle lends me records she likes.'

'She likes Stockhausen? That's new.'

'Yes, it is. Tastes do evolve, you know.'

'And what about you? Do you like it?'

'No. I don't understand it at all.'

He laughed: he kissed me, as though my frankness comforted him. In fact it was a calculated frankness. I know that he knew why I was listening to that music and he would not have believed me if I had pretended to like it.

Result: I can't bring myself to talk to him about what I have been reading recently, although in reality I have liked a certain number of these *nouveaux romans*. He would immediately think I was trying to go one better than Noëllie. How involved everything becomes as soon as one begins to have hidden motives!

Difficult, confused talk with Diana. She swears by everything she holds sacred that she never said she was getting the information for me. That was a supposition Noëllie must have thought up on her own account. She admitted having told a friend in confidence, 'Yes, just at present I am interested in Noëllie Guérard.' But that really did not compromise me at all. She has certainly been clumsy. I asked her to drop the whole thing. She looked hurt.

Saturday 27 November

I must learn to control myself. But it's so foreign to my nature! I always used to be spontaneous and completely open: serene, too. Whereas now my heart is filled with anxiety and bitterness. When he opened a magazine directly after leaving the table, I thought, 'He wouldn't do that at Noëllie's.' And I couldn't help it—I burst out, 'You wouldn't do that at Noëllie's!'

His eyes flashed. 'I just wanted to glance at an article,' he said evenly. 'Don't bristle like that over trifles.'

'It's not my fault. Everything makes me bristle.'

There was a silence. At table I had told him about how I had spent the day and now I could not find anything to say. He made an effort. 'Have you finished Wilde's *Letters*?'

'No. I didn't go on.'

'You said they were interesting . . .'

'If only you knew how unspeakably dreary I find Wilde, and how little I feel like talking to you about him!' I went to fetch a record out of the shelves. 'Would you like me to put on the cantata you brought?'

'All right.'

I did not listen for long; sobs rose in my throat; the music was now merely a refuge. We no longer had anything to say to one another, haunted as we were by this affair that he did not want to discuss.

'Why are you crying?' he asked, in a long-suffering voice.

'Because you're bored when you're with me. Because we can't talk to one another any more. Because you have built a wall between us.'

'It's you who built it: you never stop going over and over your grievances.'

I irritate him a little more every day. I don't mean to. And yet there is a part of me that does. When he seems too cheerful and unconcerned I say to myself, 'This is too easy.' And then any excuse is good enough for me to destroy his peace of mind.

Monday 29 November

I was very much surprised that Maurice had not yet spoken about winter sports. Coming back from the cinema yesterday evening I asked him where he would like to go this year. He answered evasively that he had not thought about it yet. I smelt a rat at once. I am growing very good at catching the scent—in any case it's not difficult: there are rats everywhere. I pressed him. Speaking very quickly, without looking at me, he said, 'We'll go wherever you like; but I must warn you that I also reckon on spending some days at Courchevel with Noëllie.'

I always expect the worst: and it's always worse than I had expected. 'How many days?'

'About ten.'

'And how long will you stay with me?'

'About ten days.'

'That's really too much! You are taking half our holidays away from me to give them to Noëllie!' Anger choked me. I managed to get out the words, 'Did you two decide that together, without consulting me?'

'No, I have not talked to her about it yet.'

I said, 'Fine! Keep it that way! Don't talk to her about it at all.'

Speaking quietly he said, 'I want those ten days with her.' The words held a scarcely-concealed threat—if you deprive me of them I will make our stay in the mountains hell. The idea that I was going to give in to this blackmail made me feel sick. No more concessions! It gets me nowhere and it disgusts me with myself. One has to look things in the face. This is not a mere affair. He is cutting his life into two, and I don't have the larger part. I've had enough. Presently I shall say to him, 'Her or me.'

Tuesday 30 *November*

So I was not wrong: he did manipulate me. Before reaching the point of the full confession he 'wore me down' as a bull is worn down. A suspicious confession that was in itself a manoeuvre. Is he to be believed? I did not keep my eyes shut for eight years on end. Then he told me that it was untrue. Or was it in saying *that* that he was lying? Where is the truth? Does it still exist?

What a rage I sent him into! Was I really so very insulting? It is hard to remember the things one says, above all in

3

the state I had reached. I wanted to hurt him, that's certain: I succeeded only too well.

Yet I started off very calmly. 'I don't want any sharing: you must make your choice.'

He had the overwhelmed look of a man who is saying to himself, 'Here we are! It had to happen. How can I get myself out of this one?' He adopted his most coaxing voice. 'Please, darling. Don't ask me to break with Noëllie. Not now.'

'Yes, now. This business is dragging on too much. I have borne it too long by far.' I looked at him challengingly. 'Come now, which do you like best? Her or me?'

'You, of course,' he said in a toneless voice. And he added, 'But I like Noëllie too.'

I saw red. 'Admit the truth, then! She's the one you like best! All right! Go to her! Get out of here. Get out at once. Take your things and go.'

I pulled his suitcase out of the wardrobe, I flung clothes into it higgledy-piggledy, I unhooked coat-hangers. He took my arm: 'Stop!' I went on. I wanted him to go; I really wanted it—it was sincere. Sincere because I did not believe in it. It was like a dreadful psychodrama where they play at truth. It is the truth, but it is being acted. I shouted, 'Go and join that bitch, that schemer, that dirty little shady lawyer.'

He took me by the wrists. 'Take back what you have said.'

'No. She's a filthy thing. She got you by flattery. You prefer her to me out of vanity. You're sacrificing our love to your vanity.'

Again he said, 'Shut up.' But I went on. I poured out everything I thought about Noëllie and him. Yes: I have a confused recollection of it. I said that he was letting himself be taken in like a pitiful fool, that he was turning into a vulgar, pretentious, on-the-make vulgarian, that he was no longer the man I had loved, that once upon a time he had possessed a heart and gave himself up to others—

now he was hard and selfish and concerned only with his career.

'Who's selfish?' he cried. And he shouted me down. I was the one who was selfish—I who had not hesitated to make him give up a resident post, who would have liked to confine him to a small-time career all his life long so as to keep him at home, I who was jealous of his work—a castrating woman . . .

I was shouting. As for the staff job he had dropped the idea of his own free will. He loved me. Yes, but he had not wanted to marry right away and I knew it; and as for the baby it would have been possible to manage somehow.

'Shut up! We were happy, passionately happy—you said yourself that you only lived for our love.'

'That was true—you hadn't left me anything else. You ought to have thought that one day I should suffer for it. But when I tried to escape you did everything you could to prevent me.'

I can't remember the exact words, but that was the meaning of this hideous scene. I was possessive, overbearing and encroaching with my daughters just as I was with him. 'You encouraged Colette to make an imbecile marriage; and it was to escape from you that Lucienne left.'

That put me beside myself; I shouted again, and I wept. At one moment I said, 'If you think all this evil of me, how can you still love me?'

And he flung this into my face—'But I don't love you any more. I stopped loving you after the scenes of ten years ago.'

'You're lying! You're lying so as to hurt me!'

'It's you who are lying to yourself. You claim to love the truth: so just you let me tell it you. After that we can make up our minds.'

So for eight years now he has not loved me and he has been going to bed with other women—with the little Pellerin for two years, with a South American patient that I know nothing about at all; with a nurse at the hospital;

and lastly *for eighteen months past* with Noëllie. I screamed. I was on the edge of hysteria. Then he gave me a tranquillizer and his voice altered. 'Listen, I don't really mean all I have just said. Only you are so unfair you make me unfair too.'

He deceived me, yes, that was true. But he had never stopped being fond of me. I asked him to go away. I stayed there, shattered, trying to grasp this scene, trying to disentangle the true from the false.

A recollection came back to me. Three years ago I came home without his hearing me. He was laughing on the telephone—that affectionate, collusive laugh I knew so well. I did not hear the words; only that tender complicity in his voice. The ground shifted under me—I was in another life, one in which Maurice could have deceived me and in which I could have been hurt to screaming-point. I walked in noisily. 'Who were you telephoning?'

'My nurse.'

'You're very matey with her.'

'Oh, she's a delightful girl—I adore her,' he said in an absolutely natural voice.

There I was back in my own life, beside the man who loved me. What is more, I should not have believed my eyes if I had seen him in bed with a woman. (And yet the memory is there, entire, painful.)

He went to bed with those women; but did he no longer love me? And how much truth was there in what he said against me? He knows very well that we both decided everything together as far as the resident post and our marriage were concerned—before this morning he has never for a moment claimed that this was not so. He has manufactured grievances for himself to excuse him for deceiving me—he is less guilty if I am at fault. But still, why did he pick on those? Why that dreadful remark about the children? I am so proud of having made a success of them, each in a different way, each according to her own character. Like me, Colette had a vocation for home life—by what right was I to thwart it? Lucienne wanted to stand on her own feet—I did not prevent her. Why all this unjust rancour on Maurice's part? My head aches and I can no longer think clearly at all.

I phoned Colette. She has just left me—midnight. She was good for me: she was bad for me. I can no longer tell which is good and which is bad as far as I am concerned. No, I was not bossy, possessive, encroaching; over and over again she assured me that I was an ideal mother and that her father and I got on perfectly well together. Family life *was* wearisome to Lucienne as it is to many young people, but that was not my fault. (Lucienne's relationship with me was complex, because she worshipped her father—a classical Oedipus. That proves nothing against me.) She grew cross. 'I think it's disgusting of Papa to say what he did to you.'

But she was jealous of Maurice, because of Lucienne: she is aggressive towards him—too eager to find him in the wrong. Too eager to comfort me too. Lucienne, with her hard sharpness, would have been a better informant. I talked to Colette for hours and hours and I'm no farther forward for it.

I am in a dilemma. If Maurice is a swine, then I have wrecked my life, loving him. But perhaps he had reasons for not being able to bear me any more. In that case I must look upon myself as hateful and contemptible, without even knowing why. Both suppositions are appalling.

Wednesday 1 December

Isabelle thinks—or at least that's what she says—that Maurice did not mean a quarter of what he said. He has had affairs without telling me—that is perfectly usual. She had always told me a faithfulness lasting twenty years is an impossibility for a man. Clearly Maurice would have done better to tell me, but he felt completely bound by his

promises. As for his grievances against me, he has no doubt
just made them up: if he had married me unwillingly I
should have sensed it—we should not have been so happy.
She advises me to wipe the slate clean. She still thinks I
have the winning position. Men choose the easiest solution
—it is easier to stay with one's wife than to plunge into a
new life. She made me telephone an old friend of hers for
an appointment. This friend is a gynaecologist; she has
great experience of marital problems and Isabelle thinks she
may be able to help me to understand my difficulties. Very
well.

Since Monday Maurice has been very attentive, as he
always is when he has gone too far.

'Why did you let me live eight years in falsehood?'

'I didn't want to hurt you.'

'You ought to have told me you didn't love me any
more.'

'But that's not true—I said it out of anger. I have always
been very fond of you indeed. I insist upon that.'

'You can't be fond of me if you think half of what you
said. Do you really think I have been a possessive mother?'
Of all the unkindnesses that he hurled at me, that was most
certainly the one that stung me most.

'Possessive; that is too strong.'

'What then?'

'I always said you coddled the children over much.
Colette's reaction was to model herself too tamely upon
you; Lucienne's was to be antagonistic—an attitude that
has often distressed you.'

'But which helped her find herself in the end. She is
happy with her lot and Colette with hers: what more do
you want?'

'If they really are happy . . .'

I did not go on. His mind is full of reservations. But
there are answers I would not have the strength to hear: I
do not ask the questions.

Friday 3 December

Pitiless memories. How did I manage to push them aside
and take away their sting? A certain look in his eye two
years ago at Mykonos, when he said to me, 'Do buy yourself a one-piece bathing-dress.' I know—I knew then. A
certain amount of fat on my thighs; my stomach no longer
completely flat. But I thought he didn't mind. When
Lucienne made fun of fat grannies in bikinis he cried out,
'What are you talking about? What harm does it do? Just
because you're growing old that's no reason to deprive your
body of sun and air.' I wanted sun and air; and it did no
harm. And yet—maybe because of those very pretty girls
who came on to the beach—he said that to me. 'Buy
yourself a one-piece bathing-dress.' And I didn't buy it, so
there.

And then there was that quarrel last year, the evening
when the Talbots came to dinner, together with the Couturiers. Talbot was playing the great big boss; he congratu-
lated Maurice on a paper about the origin of certain viruses,
and Maurice looked delighted, like a schoolboy who has
been awarded the form prize. That irritated me because I
don't like Talbot: when he says of someone 'He's an asset!'
I could slap him. After they had gone, I said to Maurice,
laughing, 'Soon Talbot will be saying of you "He's an
asset!" Lucky you!'

He grew cross. He reproached me more sharply than
usual for not caring about his work and for underestimating
his successes. He told me that it didn't interest him to be
prized in general, if I never gave a damn for what he did in
particular. There was so much bitterness in his voice that
all at once my blood froze.

'How inimical you are!'

He looked quite taken aback. 'Don't talk nonsense!'

Afterwards he persuaded me that it was just a quarrel

like so many others. But the chill of death had breathed upon me.

Jealous of his work: I must admit that that is not untrue. For ten years on end, through Maurice, I carried out an experiment that fascinated me—following the relationship of the doctor with the patient. I took part in it: I advised him. He saw fit to break this bond between us—such an important one for me. After that I confess that I was hardly very zealous about watching his progress passively and from afar. His progress left me cold: that was true. It is the human being I admire in him, not the scientist. But castrating woman—that is unfair, I only refused to feign enthusiasm I did not feel: he used to love my sincerity. I can't bring myself to believe that it wounded his vanity. There is no small-mindedness in Maurice. Or is there, and has Noëllie found out the best way of exploiting it? Revolting idea. My head is filled with confusion. I thought I knew what kind of person I was: what kind of person he was. And all at once I no longer recognize us, neither him nor me.

Sunday 5 December

When this happens to other people it seems to be a limited, bounded event, easy to ring around and to overcome. And then you find yourself absolutely alone, in a hallucinating experience that your imagination had not even begun to approach.

I am afraid of not sleeping and I am afraid of sleeping, on the nights that Maurice spends with Noëllie. That empty bed next to mine, these flat, cold sheets . . . I take sleeping-pills, but in vain; for I dream. Often in my dream I faint with distress. I lie there under Maurice's gaze, paralysed, with the whole world's anguish on my face. I expect him to rush towards me. He glances indifferently in my direction and walks off. I woke up and it was still night—I could feel the weight of the darkness; I was in a corridor, I hurried down it and it grew narrower and narrower; I could scarcely breathe. Presently I should have to crawl and I should stay wedged there until I died. I screamed. And I began calling him more quietly, weeping as I did so. Every night I call him: not him—the other one, the one who loved me. And I wonder whether I should not prefer it if he were dead. I used to tell myself that death was the only irremediable misfortune and that if he were to leave me I should get over it. Death was dreadful because it was possible; a break was bearable because I could not imagine it. But now in fact I tell myself that if he were dead I should at least know whom I had lost and who I was myself. I no longer know anything. The whole of my past life has collapsed behind me, as the land does in those earthquakes where the ground consumes and destroys itself —is swallowed up behind you as you flee. There is no going back. The house has vanished, and the village and the whole of the valley. Even if you survive there is nothing left, not even what had been your living-space on earth.

I am so destroyed by the morning that if the daily woman did not come at ten o'clock I should stay in bed every day until past noon, as I do on Sundays: or even all day long, when Maurice does not come back to lunch. Mme Dormoy senses that something is wrong. Taking away the breakfast-tray she says reproachfully, 'You haven't eaten anything!'

She presses me, and sometimes for the sake of peace I swallow a square of toast. But the mouthfuls won't go down.

Why doesn't he love me any more? The question is, why did he love me in the first place? One never asks oneself. Even if one is neither vain nor self-obsessed, it is so extraordinary to be oneself—exactly oneself and no one else— and so unique, that it seems natural that one should also be unique for someone else. He loved me, that's all. And for

ever, since I should always be me. (And I have been astonished at this blindness, in other women. Strange that one
can only understand one's own case by the help of other
people's experience—experience that is not the same as
mine, and that doesn't help.)

Stupid things fleeting through one's head. A film I saw
when I was a child. A wife going to see her husband's
mistress. 'For you it's only fun. But I love him!' And the
mistress is moved and she sends the wife to take her place
at the nocturnal rendezvous. In the darkness the husband
takes her for the other one and in the morning he comes
back to her, looking shamefaced. It was an old silent film
that the Studio put on for the laughs but that stirred me a
great deal. I can still see the wife's long dress, and her
bandeaux.

Talk to Noëllie? But it's not just fun for her: it's a major
undertaking. She would tell me that she loved him too; and
certainly she's very fond of all that he can give a woman
nowadays. For my part I loved him when he was twenty-
three—an uncertain future—difficulties. I loved him with
no security; and I gave up the idea of a career for myself.
Anyhow I regret nothing.

Monday 6 December

Colette, Diana, Isabelle: and I who did not like confid-
ing! And Marie Lambert this afternoon. She has had a
great deal of experience. I should so like it if she could
make things clear to me.

What appears from our long talk is how little I myself
understand my own case. I know the whole of my past by
heart and all at once I no longer know anything about it.
She asked me for a short written summary. Let's have a
try.

As Papa practised it at Bagnolet, medicine seemed to me
the finest calling in the world. But during my first year I

was shattered, sickened, and overwhelmed by its daily horror. Several times I could not take it. Maurice was a senior medical student and the very first time I saw him I was moved by what I saw in his face. We had neither of us had anything more than passing affairs. We fell in love. It was wild, passionate love and it was steady, sober love: love. He was bitterly unfair the other day when he said I had made him give up the idea of a resident post: up until then he had always taken complete responsibility for his decision. He was fed up with being a student. He wanted an adult life, a home. As for our solemn promise of faithfulness, it was he who was keener on it than I because his mother's second marriage had given him a morbid horror of breaks and separations. We married in the summer of '44, and the beginning of our happiness coincided with the intoxicating joy of the Liberation. Maurice liked the idea of social medicine. He found a job at Simca. It tied him down less than local practice and he liked the workingmen, his patients.

The period after the war was a disappointment to Maurice. His work at Simca began to bore him. Couturier—who had made a success of his staff job—persuaded him to join him in Talbot's hospital, to work as a member of his team and to specialize. No doubt (and Marie Lambert made this clear to me) I did struggle too violently against his decision, ten years ago now; no doubt I did show too plainly that in my heart of hearts I never really came to agree with it. But that is not an adequate reason for having stopped loving me. Precisely what relationship is there between the alteration in his life and the alteration in his feelings?

She asked me whether he often blamed me or criticized me. Oh, we quarrel—we're both of us quick-tempered. But it's never serious. At least not with me.

Our sexual life? I don't know exactly when it lost its warmth. Which of us wearied of it first? At one time I was vexed by his indifference—that was what caused my little affair with Quillan. But might he not have been disappointed by my coldness? That is of secondary importance, it seems to me. It would explain his going to bed with other women, but not his breaking away from me. Nor his losing his head over Noëllie.

Why her? If she were at least genuinely beautiful, really young and outstandingly intelligent I should understand it. I should suffer, but I should understand. She is thirty-eight; she is fairly pleasant to look at—no more; and she is very superficial. So why? I said to Marie Lambert, 'I'm certain that I am worth more than she is.'

She smiled. 'That is not where the question lies.'

Where did it lie? Apart from novelty and a pleasant body, what could Noëllie give Maurice that I do not give him? She said, 'Other people's loves are never comprehensible.'

But I am convinced of something that I cannot find adequate words for. With me Maurice has a relationship in depth, one to which his essential being is committed and which is therefore indestructible. He is only attached to Noëllie by his most superficial feelings—each of them might just as well be in love with someone else. Maurice and I are wholly conjoined. The flaw is that my relationship with Maurice is *not* indestructible, since he is destroying it. Or is it? Is not his feeling for Noëllie an infatuation that takes on the look of something greater but that will fade away? Oh, these splinters of hope that pierce my heart every now and then, more wounding than despair itself! There is another question I turn over and over in my mind, one that he did not really answer. Why did he tell me now? Why not before? There is no conceivable doubt that he ought to have warned me. I should have had affairs, too. And I should have worked: eight years ago I should have found the strength of mind to do something—there would not be this vacuum around me. That was what shocked Marie Lambert most—the fact that by his silence Maurice had refused me the possibility of confronting a break, armed with weapons of my own. As soon as he doubted his

own feelings he ought to have urged me to build myself up
a life that would be independent of him. She imagines, and
so do I, that Maurice remained silent in order to ensure a
happy home for his daughters. I got it wrong when I was
pleased about Lucienne's absence, at the time of his first
confession—it was not just a matter of chance. But in that
case it's appalling. He chose the very time when I no longer
had my daughters as the moment for leaving me.

Impossible to accept that I can have committed the
whole of my life to love so selfish a man as that. I must
certainly be being unfair! In any case Marie Lambert told
me so. 'His point of view ought to be known. There is
never anything to be understood in these cases of separation
when they are recounted by the wife.' It was the 'masculine
mystery', far more impenetrable than the 'feminine mystery'. I suggested that she should speak to Maurice, she
refused—I should have less confidence in her if she knew
him. She was very friendly; but with a certain amount of
holding back and hesitation, nevertheless.

Certainly Lucienne is the person who would be most
useful to me—Lucienne, with her penetrating critical sense.
She has lived all these years in a state of half-enmity towards me and this would allow her to enlighten me. But
by letter she would only say little commonplace things.

Thursday 9 December

Couturier lives not far from Noëllie, and as I was going
there I thought I recognized the car. No. But every time I
see a big dark-green Citroën with a grey roof and red and
green upholstery I think it is the one I used to call our car
and which is now his car because our lives are no longer
one. And it torments me. Before, I used to know exactly
where he was, what he was doing. Now he might be
absolutely anywhere—in the very place where I saw that
car for example.

It was almost indecent to go and see Couturier and he seemed very embarrassed when I telephoned to say I was coming. But I want to know.

'I know you are primarily Maurice's friend,' I said when I arrived. 'I have not come to ask you for information—only to give me a man's point of view about the situation.' He relaxed. But he told me nothing at all. Men need change more than women. Fourteen years of faithfulness is in itself uncommon. It is a usual thing to lie—one does not want to cause pain. And when a man is angry he says things he does not mean. Maurice certainly loves me still: it is possible to love two people, in different ways . . .

They all explain the usual to you—that is to say, what happens to others. And I am trying to use this master-key! Just as though it was not Maurice, me, and the unique aspect of our love that was in question.

How very low I must have fallen! I had a spurt of hope when I looked at a magazine and saw that as far as romance was concerned Sagittarius would win a considerable victory this week. On the other hand it depressed me when I looked into a little astrology book at Diana's—it would seem that Sagittarius and Aries were not really made for one another. I asked Diana whether she knew Noëllie's sign. No. She is not pleased with me since our disagreeable talk and she took a delight in telling me that Noëllie had spoken to her about Maurice at greater length. She will never give him up, nor he her. As for me, I am an admirable woman (she is fond of that formula, it seems) but I do not value Maurice at his true worth. I found it hard to control myself when Diana repeated that piece. Has Maurice complained of me to Noëllie? 'You at least, *you* take an interest in my career.' No, he could not have said that to her: I won't believe it. His true worth . . . Maurice's worth does not come down to his worldly success: as he knows very well himself, what he appreciates in people in something quite different. Or am I mistaken about him? Has he a trifling, social side that comes into flower when he is with Noëllie? I forced myself to laugh. And then I said that after all I should still like to understand what men see in Nollie. Diana gave me an idea—have our three handwritings analysed. She told me an address and gave me one of Noëllie's letters—nothing in it. I went to find one of Maurice's recent letters, wrote the graphologist a note in which I asked for a quick reply, and went and left the lot with the concierge.

Saturday 11

I am taken aback by the graphologist's analyses. The most interesting hand, according to him, is Maurice's—great intelligence, wide culture, capacity for work, tenacity, deep sensitivity, a mixture of pride and lack of self-confidence, on the surface very open but fundamentally reticent (I summarize). As for me, he finds I have many qualities—poise, cheerfulness, frankness and a lively care for others; he also mentions a kind of emotional demandingness that might make me rather wearisome to those around me. That agrees with what Maurice reproaches me for—that I am encroaching and possessive. I know perfectly well that there is that tendency in me: but I have fought against it so strongly! I tried so hard to leave Colette and Lucienne free, not to overwhelm them with questions, to respect their privacy. And with Maurice how often have I not choked back my anxiety, bottled up my impulses, avoided going into his study in spite of my longing, and prevented myself from gazing lovingly at him while he read at my side! For them I wanted to be both present and unobtrusive: have I failed? Graphology shows tendencies rather than actual behaviour. And Maurice went for me when he was in a rage. Their verdict leaves me still wondering. In any case even if I am rather over-zealous, over-demonstrative, over-attentive—in short, rather a nuisance—that is not an adequate reason for liking Noëllie more than me.

As for her, although her portrait is more sharply distinguished than mine and contains more faults, it seems to me, all things considered, more flattering. She is ambitious; she likes display, but she has a delicate sensitivity and a great deal of energy; she is generous and she has a very lively intelligence. I don't claim to be anything extraordinary, but Noëllie is so superficial that she cannot possibly be my superior, not even in intelligence. I shall have to get another expert opinion. In any case graphology is not an exact science.

I am torturing myself. What is the general opinion of me? Quite objectively, who am I? Am I less intelligent than I suppose? As for that, it is the kind of question it is no use asking anybody: no one would like to reply that I was a fool. And how can one tell? Everybody thinks he is intelligent, even the people I find stupid. That is why a woman is always more affected by compliments about her looks than by those about her mind—for she has inner certainties about her mind, those which everybody has and which therefore prove nothing. To know your limits you have to be able to go beyond them: in other words, you have to be able to jump right over your own shadow. I always understand what I hear and what I read; but perhaps I grasp it all too quickly, for want of being able to understand the full wealth and complexity of an idea. Is it my shortcomings that prevent me from seeing Noëllie's superiority?

Saturday evening

Is this the good fortune Sagittarius was promised this week? On the telephone Diana told me a piece of news that may be of decisive importance: it seems that Noëllie goes to bed with Jacques Vallin, the publisher. It was Mme Vallin herself who told a friend of Diana's—she happened to find some letters and she hates Noëllie. How to let Maurice know? He is so certain of Noëllie's love that he would be knocked all of a heap. Only he would not believe me. I should have to have proof. But I can't very well go and see Mme Vallin, whom I don't know, and ask her for the letters. Vallin is very wealthy. Of the two, Maurice and Vallin, he is the one Noëllie would choose if he were to agree to divorce. What a schemer! If only I could have any respect for her I should suffer less. (I know. Another woman, talking to herself about her rival, is saying, 'If only I could despise her I should suffer less.' Besides, I myself have thought 'I have too low an opinion of her to suffer.')

Sunday 12

I showed Isabelle the graphologist's replies: she did not look convinced—she does not believe in graphology. Yet as I pointed out to her the emotional demandingness shown in the analysis chimes in with the unkind things Maurice said the other day. And I know that in fact I do expect a lot from people: maybe I ask them too much.

'Obviously. Since you live very much for others, you also live a great deal through them,' she said. 'But that's what love and friendship is—a kind of symbiosis.'

'But for someone who doesn't want the symbiosis, am I a bore?'

'When you like them and they don't like you you bore people. It depends on situation, not on character.'

I begged her to make an effort and to tell me what kind of a person she saw me as—what she thought of me. She smiled. 'In fact I don't *see* you at all; you are my friend: and that's that.'

She maintained that when there is nothing at stake one either likes being with people or one does not like being with them; but one does not see them as being this or that. She likes being with me, that's all.

'Candidly, quite candidly now, do you think me intelligent?'

'Of course. Except when you ask me that. If we are both of us half-wits each will think the other very bright—what does that prove?'

She told me again that in this business my virtues and faults are not in question—it is novelty that is attracting Maurice. Eighteen months: that's still novelty.

Monday 13

The hideous fall into the abyss of sadness. From the very fact of being sad one no longer has the least wish to do anything cheerful. Now I never put on a record when I wake up. I never listen to music any more, never go to the cinema, never buy myself anything pleasant. I got up when I heard Mme Dormoy come in. I drank my tea and ate a piece of toast to please her. And I look forward over this day, still another day that I must get through. And I say to myself . . .

A ring at the bell. A delivery-boy put a great bunch of lilac and roses into my arms with a note saying 'Happy birthday. Maurice.' As soon as the door was shut I burst into tears. I defend myself with restless activity, horrid plans and hatred; and these flowers, this reminder of lost, hopelessly lost happiness, knocked all my defences to the ground.

Towards one o'clock the key turned in the lock and there was that horrible taste in my mouth—the taste of dread. (The same, exactly, as when I used to go to see my father dying in the nursing-home.) That presence, as familiar to me as my own reflection, my reason for living, my delight, is now this stranger, this judge, this enemy; my heart beats high with fear when he opens the door. He came quickly over to me, smiling as he took me in his arms. 'Happy birthday, darling.'

Gently I wept on his shoulder. He stroked my hair. 'Don't cry. I can't bear it when you're unhappy. I'm so very fond of you.'

'You told me that for the past eight years you had no longer loved me.'

'Oh, stuff. I told you afterwards it wasn't true. I *am* fond of you.'

'But you're not in love with me any more?'

'There are so many kinds of love.'

We sat down; we talked. I talked to him as I might have talked to Isabelle or Marie Lambert, full of trust and friendliness, quite detachedly—as if it were not a question of ourselves at all. It was a problem that we were discussing, objectively, impersonally, just as we have discussed so many others. Once again I said how surprising his eight years' silence was. Again he said, 'You used to say you would die of grief.'

'You made me say it. The notion of unfaithfulness seemed to torment you so . . .'

'It did torment me. That was why I remained silent—so that everything should be as though I were not deceiving you . . . There was magic in it . . . And of course I was ashamed, too . . .'

I said that above all I should like to know why he had told me this year. He admitted that it was partially because his relationship with Noëllie called for it; but also, he said, he thought I had a right to the truth.

'But you didn't tell me the truth.'

'Out of shame at having lied.'

He wrapped me in that dark, warm gaze that seems to open him to me to the very bottom of his heart—delivered up wholly and entirely, as it were, innocent and loving, as he used to be.

'The worst thing you did,' I said, 'was to let me lull myself in a sense of false security. Here I am at forty-four, empty-handed, with no occupation, no other interest in life apart from you. If you had warned me eight years ago I should have made an independent existence for myself and now it would be easier for me to accept the situation.'

'But Monique!' he cried, looking astonished. 'I urged you as strongly as I possibly could to take that job as secretary of the *Revue médicale* seven years ago. It was right up your street and you could have reached a worthwhile position. You wouldn't!'

The suggestion had seemed to me so untimely that I had almost entirely forgotten it. 'I couldn't see any point in spending the day away from the house and the children just for a hundred thousand francs a month,' I said.

'That was your answer then. I pressed you very hard.'

'If you had told me your real reasons—if you had told me I no longer meant everything to you and that I too should stand off a little myself, I should have accepted it.'

'I suggested your getting a job again when we were at Mougins. And again you refused.'

'At that time your love was enough for me.'

'It is not too late,' he said. 'I can easily find you something to do.'

'Do you suppose that that would console me? Eight years ago I might have thought it less ludicrous—I should have had more chance of getting somewhere. But now . . .'

We marked time for a great while over this. I feel no doubt that it would soothe his conscience if he got me something to do. I have not the least wish to soothe it.

I went back to our conversation of November 1—a date to remember. Did he really consider me selfish, domineering, encroaching? 'Even though you were in a rage, you didn't make that up entirely, did you?'

He hesitated, smiled, explained. I have the defects of my qualities. I am quick-witted and attentive, which is extremely valuable; but sometimes, when one is ill-tempered, it is wearing. I am so faithful to the past that the least forgetfulness seems a crime and one has a feeling of guilt if one changes a taste or an opinion. All right. But had he any grudges against me? He resented my conduct ten years ago, as I knew very well, for we had quarrelled about it often enough; but all that is over and done with because he did what he wanted to do and in the long run I have admitted that he was right. As for our marriage, did he think I had forced his hand? Not at all: we had made the decision together . . .

'What about your reproach the other day that I did not take an interest in your work?'

'I do rather regret it, that's true, but I should think it even more regrettable if you were to force yourself to take an interest in it just to please me.'

His voice was so encouraging that I asked the question that harasses me most. 'You are against me because of Colette and Lucienne? They are a disappointment to you and you hold me responsible?'

'What right have I to be disappointed? And what right would I have to hold it against you?'

'Then why did you speak to me with such hatred?'

'Oh, the position is not very easy for me either! I grow angry with myself and that very unfairly turns against you.'

'Still, you don't love me as you did before; you're fond of me, yes; but it's no longer love as we knew it in our twenties.'

'It's no longer the love of our twenties for you, either. When I was twenty I was in love with love at the same time that I was in love with you. I have lost the whole of that glowing, enthusiastic side of myself: that is what has changed.'

It was delightful talking with him, like two friends, as we used to do. Difficulties grew smaller; questions wafted away like smoke; events faded; true and false merged in an iridescence of converging shades. Fundamentally, nothing had happened. I ended up by believing that Noëllie did not exist . . . Illusions: sleight of hand. In fact this comfortable talk has not changed anything in the very least. Things have been given other names: they have not altered in any way. I have learnt nothing. The past remains as obscure as ever; the future as uncertain.

Tuesday 14

Yesterday evening I wanted to return to that afternoon's disappointing conversation. But Maurice had work to do after dinner, and when he finished he wanted to go to bed.

'We talked quite enough this afternoon. There is nothing to add. I must get up early tomorrow.'

'We didn't really say anything, when you come to look into it.'

He put on a look of resignation. 'What more do you want me to say?'

'Well, there is after all something that I should like to know. How do you envisage our future?'

He was silent. I had driven him into a corner. 'I don't want to lose you. I don't want to give up Noëllie, either. As for everything else, I just don't know where I am . . .'

'She puts up with this double life?'

'She is obliged to.'

'Yes: like me. And when I think that at the Club 46 you dared tell me that there was nothing changed between us!'

'I never said that.'

'We were dancing, and you said to me, "Nothing is changed." And I believed you!'

'Monique, it was you who said to me, "All that matters is that there is nothing changed between us." I did not contradict you: I remained silent. At that particular moment it was impossible to go into things thoroughly.'

'It was you who said it. I remember it perfectly.'

'You had drunk a lot, you know: you have built up . . .'

I dropped the subject. What did it matter? What does matter is that he does not want to give Noëllie up. I know it and yet I cannot bring myself to believe it. Curtly I told him that I had decided not to go ski-ing. I have thought it over thoroughly and I am glad I took that decision. I used so to love the mountains with him in the old days. To see them again in these conditions would be a torment. I couldn't bear going there with him first and then leaving, defeated, thrust out by the other woman and yielding the place to her. I should find it no less revolting to come after Noëllie, knowing that Maurice was regretting her absence, comparing her figure with mine, my sadness with her laughter. I should pile up blunder upon blunder and he would only feel more eager to get rid of me.

'Spend the ten days with her that you have promised, and come back,' I said.

It was the first time in this whole business that I had taken the initiative, and he seemed quite flabbergasted. 'But Monique, I *want* to take you with me. We have had such splendid days in the snow!'

'Exactly.'

'You won't go ski-ing this winter?'

'Just at present, you know, the joys of ski-ing don't mean very much to me.'

He argued with me, he pressed me, he looked wretched. He is used to my sadness of every day, but to deprive me of ski-ing—that crams him with remorse. (I am unfair : he is not used to it—he drips with guilty conscience, he takes pills to go to sleep, he looks like death warmed up. I am not touched by that; indeed I even rather resent it. If he tortures me knowing what he is at and torturing himself at the same time, then he must be disgustingly fond of Noëllie.) We argued for a long while. I did not give way. In the end he looked so exhausted—drawn face, rings under his eyes—that I sent him to bed. He sank down into sleep as though into a refuge of peace.

Wednesday 15

I watch the drops of water running down the window-pane—a moment ago the rain was beating upon it. They don't go straight down: they are like little creatures that for mysterious reasons of their own slant off to the right or the left, slipping between other motionless drops, stopping and then starting again as though they were in quest of something. It seems to me that I no longer have anything whatever to do. I always used to be busy. Now everything, knitting, cooking, reading, putting on a record—everything seems pointless. Maurice's love gave every moment of my life a meaning. Now it is hollow. Everything is hollow—things are empty: time is empty. And so am I.

I asked Marie Lambert the other day whether she thought me intelligent. She looked me straight in the eye. 'You are very intelligent . . .'

'There is a *but*,' I said.

'Intelligence withers if it is not fed. You ought to let your husband find you a job.'

'The kind of work I could do would bring me nothing.'

'That is very far from certain.'

Evening

I had an inspiration this morning: the whole thing is my fault. My worst mistake has been not grasping that *time goes by*. It was going by and there I was, set in the attitude of the ideal wife of an ideal husband. Instead of bringing our sexual relationship to life again I brooded happily over memories of our former nights together. I imagined I had kept my thirty-year-old face and body instead of taking care of myself, doing gymnastics and going to a beauty parlour. I let my intelligence wither away; I no longer cultivated my mind—later, I said, when the children have gone. (Perhaps my father's death was not without bearing on this way of letting things slide. Something snapped. I stopped time from that moment on.) Yes: the young student Maurice married felt passionately about what was happening in the world, about books and ideas; she was very unlike the woman of today, whose world lies between the four walls of this flat. It is true enough that I tended to shut Maurice in. I thought his home was enough for him: I thought I owned him entirely. Generally speaking I took everything for granted; and that must have irritated him intensely—Maurice who changes and who calls things in question. Being irritating—no one can ever get away with that. I should never have been obstinate about our promise of faithfulness, either. If I had given Maurice back his freedom—and made use of mine, too, perhaps—Noëllie would not have profited by the glamour of clandestinity. I should have coped with the situation at once. Is there still time? I told Marie Lambert that I was going to have it all out with Maurice and take steps to deal with the position. I have already taken to reading again a little and to listening to records: I must make a greater effort. Lose several pounds, dress better. Talk with Maurice more openly, refuse to have silences. She listened to me without enthusiasm. She wanted to know which of us was responsible for my first pregnancy, Maurice or I. Both of us. Or I was, if you like, in that I trusted in the calendar too much; but it was not my fault if it let me down. Had I insisted upon keeping the child? No. Upon not keeping it? No. The thing decided itself. She seemed sceptical. Her idea is that Maurice harbours a serious grudge against me. I countered that with Isabelle's argument—the beginning of our marriage would not have been so happy if he had not wanted it. Her reply seems to me very far-fetched: so as not to admit his disappointment Maurice staked everything on love—he went all out for happiness, and once this enthusiasm faded he rediscovered the resentment that he had repressed. She herself feels that her argument is weak. His old grievances would not have sprung up again with such strength as to separate him from me if there had been no new ones. I asserted that he had none whatever.

To tell the truth Marie Lambert rather annoys me. They all annoy me because they look as though they know things that I don't. It may be that Maurice or Noëllie pass around their version of the affair. It may be that the people I know have experience of matters of this kind and they apply their patterns to me. It may be that they see me from the outside, as I cannot manage to see myself, and that for that reason everything is plain to them. They are tactful with me and I feel them holding things back when I talk to them. Marie Lambert approves of my having given up the ski-ing, but only in so far as it prevents me from suffering; she does not think it will make any difference to Maurice's attitude.

I told Maurice that I understood all my faults. He stopped me—with one of those irritated gestures that I am getting so used to. 'You have nothing to blame yourself for. Don't let's always be going over and over the past.'

'What else do I possess?'

That heavy silence.

I possess nothing other than my past. But it is no longer pride nor happiness—a riddle, a source of bitter distress. I should like to force it to tell the truth. But can one trust one's memory? I have forgotten a great deal, and it would appear that sometimes I have gone so far as to distort the facts. (Who was it who said 'There is nothing changed'? Maurice or I? In this diary I wrote that it was he. Perhaps because I wanted to believe it . . .) To some extent it was out of hostility that I contradicted Marie Lambert. In fact I have more than once felt resentment in Maurice. He denied it, on my birthday. But there are remarks and tones of voice that still ring in my mind: I had not wanted to attribute any importance to them and yet I do in fact remember them. When Colette made up her mind to make that 'imbecile marriage' it is obvious that although he was vexed with her he was also indirectly attacking me—he held me responsible for her sentimentality, her need for security, her shyness and her passive attitude of mind. But above all it was Lucienne's leaving home that hit him hardest. 'It was to escape from you that Lucienne left.' I know that's what he really thinks. To what degree is it true? With a different kind of a mother, less anxious, less perpetually there, would Lucienne have put up with family life? Yet I had thought things were better between us during the last year, that she was less tense—perhaps because she was about to leave? I can no longer tell. If I have failed with the bringing up of my daughters, my whole life has been a mere failure. I cannot believe it. But as soon as doubt so much as touches me, how my mind reels!

Does Maurice stay with me out of pity? If so I ought to tell him to go. I could not bring myself to. If he stays, perhaps Noëllie will lose heart and turn to Vallin or some-one else. Or perhaps he will come to understand once more what we have been for one another.

What exhausts me is the way he is kind one day and surly and unaffectionate the next. I never know which is going to open the door. It is as though he were appalled at having hurt me and yet afraid of giving me too much hope. Should I settle down definitively into despair? But then he would quite forget what I was once and why he had loved me.

Thursday 16

Marguerite has run away again and they can't find her. She went off with a girl who is a real tramp. She will go on the streets, steal things. It's heartbreaking. Yet my heart is not broken. Nothing touches me any more.

Friday 17

I saw them again yesterday evening. I was prowling about L'An 2000, where they often go. They got out of Noëllie's convertible; he took her arm; they were laughing. At home, even when he is being pleasant, he has a grim expression: his smiles are forced. 'It's not an easy position . . .' When he is with me he never forgets it for a moment. With her, he does. He laughed, unconstrained, careless, easy. I felt like doing her an injury. I know that is female and unfair; she has no duty towards me—but there it is.

What cowards people are. I asked Diana to introduce me to the friend Mme Vallin had talked to about Noëllie. She looked embarrassed. The friend is no longer so sure of her facts. Vallin goes to bed with a young woman barrister, very much in the swim. Mme Vallin did not mention her name. It is reasonable to suppose that it is Noëllie, who has often appeared in court for the publishing house. But it may be someone else . . . The other day Diana was perfectly definite. Either it is the friend who is frightened of stirring up trouble or it is Diana who is afraid that I will. She swore it was not so—she only wants to help me! No doubt. But they all have their own ideas of the best way of setting about it.

Sunday 19

Every time I see Colette I overwhelm her with questions. Yesterday it almost made her cry. 'I never thought you coddled us too much; I liked being coddled . . . What did Lucienne think of you during the last year? We weren't very intimate—she sat in judgment on me, too. She thought us too soft-centred; she acted the tough girl. Anyhow, what does it matter what she thought? She's not an oracle.'

Of course. Colette never felt herself ill-treated because of her own free will she complied with what I expected of her. And obviously she cannot think that it is a pity that she is what she is. I asked her whether she did not get bored? (Jean-Pierre is a worthy soul, but not much fun.) No: it was rather that she can hardly cope with all she has to do. Keeping house is not as easy as she had thought. She no longer has time to read or to listen to music. 'Try to find it,' I told her, 'otherwise one ends up by growing completely stupid.' I said that I really knew what I was talking about. She laughed—if I was stupid, then she was quite happy to be stupid too. She loves me dearly: that at least will not be taken away from me. But have I crushed her? Certainly I foresaw a completely different kind of life for her—a more active, richer life. At her age mine, with Maurice, was far more so. Has she lost her vitality, living in my shadow?

How I should like to see myself as others see me! I showed the three letters to a friend of Colette's who goes in for graphology a little. It was chiefly Maurice's hand that interested her. She said pleasant things about me: much less about Noëllie. But the results were falsified because she had certainly grasped the meaning of the consultation.

Sunday evening

I had a sudden spurt of happy surprise just now, when Maurice said to me, 'We'll spend Christmas Eve and New Year's Eve together, of course.' I think he is offering me a compensation for the ski-ing I have given up. What does the reason matter? I have determined not to hold aloof from my pleasure.

26 *December—Sunday*

It was rather pleasure that held aloof from me. I hope
Maurice did not notice it. He had booked a table at the
Club 46. Magnificent supper, excellent cabaret. He was
lavish with his money and his kindness. I had on a pretty
new dress and I smiled, but I was in an unbearable state of
distress. All those couples . . . These women, all well-
dressed, well-jewelled, well made-up, their hair well-done
—they laughed, showing their well-tended teeth, looked
after by excellent dentists. The men lit their cigarettes for
them, poured them out champagne: they exchanged affectionate looks and little loving remarks. Other years it had
seemed to me that the bond that joined each him to each
personal her, each her to each personal him was positively
tangible. I believed in unions, because I believed in ours.
Now what I saw was individuals set down by chance
opposite one another. From time to time the old illusion
came to life again: Maurice seemed welded to me—he was
my husband just as Colette was my daughter, in a way
that could not be undone: a relationship that could be
forgotten, that could be twisted, but that could never be
done away with. And then there was no current between
him and me any more—nothing passing whatever; two
strangers. I felt like shouting 'It's all untrue, it's all play-
acting, it's all a farce—drinking champagne together does
not mean taking Communion.' As we came home Maurice
kissed me. 'That was a good evening, wasn't it?'

He looked pleased and relaxed. I said yes, of course. On
December 31 we go to the New Year's Eve party at
Isabelle's.

1 *January*

I ought not to be delighted at Maurice's good temper: the
real reason for it is that he is going away for ten days with
Noëllie. But if at the cost of a sacrifice I rediscover his
affection and cheerfulness, whereas so often he is unyield-
ing and surly, why then I gain by it. We were a pair once
again when we arrived at Isabelle's. Other pairs, more or
less limping, more or less patched up, but united for all
that, surrounded us. Isabelle and Charles, the Couturiers,
Colette and Jean-Pierre, and others. There were excellent
jazz records; I let myself drink a little, and for the first
time since—how long?—I felt cheerful. Cheerfulness—a
transparent quality in the air, a smooth flowing in the
passage of time, an ease in breathing: I asked no more of
it. I don't know how I came to be talking about the Salines
de Ledoux and describing them in detail. They listened to
me and asked me questions, but suddenly I wondered
whether it did not look as though I were imitating Noëllie,
trying to shine as she does, and whether Maurice would not
think me ridiculous once again. He seemed rather tense. I
took Isabelle aside. 'Did I talk too much? Did I put on a
ludicrous act?'

'No, no!' she protested. 'What you told us was very
interesting.'

She was dreadfully concerned at seeing me so upset.
Because I was wrong to be uneasy? Or because I was
right? Later on I asked Maurice why he had looked vexed.

'But I wasn't!'

'You say that as though you were.'

'No. Not at all.'

Perhaps it was my question that vexed him. I cannot tell
any more. From now on, always, everywhere, there is a
reverse side to my words and my actions that escapes me.

2 January

Yesterday we had dinner with Colette. The poor child had taken a very great deal of trouble and nothing went right. I looked at her through Maurice's eyes. Her flat certainly lacks charm. She scarcely possesses any ideas of her own, even for her clothes or her furniture. Jean-Pierre is very kind; he adores her—a heart of gold. But it is impossible to know what to talk to him about. They never go out; they have few friends. A very dismal, very narrow existence. Once again, and with terror, I ask myself, 'Is it my fault that the brilliant fifteen-year-old schoolgirl has grown into this lifeless young woman?' It is a metamorphosis that happens often enough, and I have seen plenty like it: but perhaps each time it was the parents' fault. Maurice was very cheerful, very friendly all through the evening, and when we left he said nothing about them. I imagine that did not stop him thinking, however.

I thought it strange that Maurice should spend all yesterday at home and the evening at Colette's with me. A suspicion came into my mind and I have just telephoned Noëllie's flat: if she had answered I should have hung up. I got her secretary. 'Mme Guérard will not be back in Paris until tomorrow.'

What an utter simpleton I must be! Noëllie was away, and there I was, acting as the stop-gap. I choke with rage. I feel like flinging Maurice out—finishing with him for good and all.

I went for him furiously. He replied that Noëllie had gone because he had decided to spend Christmas and New Year's Eve with me.

'Oh no! I remember now: she always spends the holidays with her daughter, at her husband's place.'

'She had only meant to stay four days.' He gazed at me with that sincere look that comes so easily to him.

'In any case you worked this out together!'

'Obviously I spoke to her about it.' He shrugged. 'A woman is never happy unless what she is given has been violently wrenched from another. It is not the thing in itself that counts: it is the victory won.'

They had settled it together. And it is true that that spoils all the pleasure these days have brought me. If she had reacted strongly he would certainly have yielded. So I am dependent on her, upon her whims, her magnanimity or her mean-mindedness—upon her interests, in fact.

They leave tomorrow evening for Courchevel. I wonder whether my decision was not utterly mistaken. He is only taking a fortnight's holiday instead of three weeks (which is a sacrifice, he pointed out to me, seeing how passionately he loves ski-ing). So he is spending five days longer than he had planned with Noëllie. And I lose ten days alone with him. She will have ample time to get round him entirely. When he comes back he will tell me that everything is over between us. I have put the finishing touches to my own destruction! I tell myself this with a kind of heavy inertness. I feel that in any case I am done for. He is kind and tactful with me; perhaps he is afraid that I will kill myself —which is out of the question: I do not want to die. But his attachment to Noëllie does not lessen.

15 *January*

I ought to open a tin, or run myself a bath. But in that case I should go on pursuing my thoughts round and round. If I write it fills up my time, it lets me escape. How many hours without eating? How many days without washing? I sent the daily woman away; I shut myself up; people have rung at the door twice, telephoned several times, but I never answer except at eight o'clock in the evening, when it is Maurice. He rings me up punctually every day, speaking anxiously.

'What have you done today?'

I reply that I have seen Isabelle, Diana or Colette; that I have been to a concert—to the cinema.

'And this evening, what are you doing?'

I say I am going to see Diana or Isabelle, that I shall go to the theatre. He presses me. 'You're all right? You sleep well?'

I reassure him, and I ask what the snow is like. Not terribly good; and the weather is nothing much either. There is gloom in his voice, as though he were carrying out some tolerably dreary task there at Courchevel. And I know that as soon as he has hung up he goes laughing into the bar where Noëllie is waiting for him and they drink martinis, talking twenty to the dozen about what has happened during the day.

That's what I chose, isn't it?

I chose going to ground: I no longer know when it is day and when it is night: when things are too bad, when it becomes unbearable, I gulp down spirits, tranquillizers or sleeping-pills. When things are a little better I take stimulants and plunge into a detective-story—I have laid in a stock. When the silence stifles me I turn on the radio and from a remote planet there come voices that I can hardly understand: that world has a time, set hours, laws, speech, anxieties and amusements that are essentially foreign to me. How far one can let oneself go, when one is entirely alone and shut in! The bedroom stinks of stale tobacco and spirits; there is ash everywhere; I am filthy, the sheets are filthy; the sky is filthy behind the filthy windows: this filth is a shell that protects me; I shall never leave it again. It would be easy to slide just a little farther into the void, as far as the point of no return. I have all that is needed in my drawer. But I won't, I won't! I'm forty-four; it's too early to die—it's unfair; I can't live any longer. I don't want to die.

For a fortnight I have written nothing in this notebook because I read over what I had written before. And I saw

that words say nothing. Rages, nightmares, horror—words
cannot encompass them. I set things down on paper when
I recovered strength, either in despair or in hope. But the
feeling of total bewilderment, of stunned stupidity, of
falling to pieces—these pages do not contain them. And
then these pages lie so—they get things so wrong. How I
have been manipulated! Gently, gently Maurice brought
me to the point of saying 'Make your choice!' so that he
could reply 'I shall not give up Noëllie . . .' Oh, I am not
going over the whole business again, with comments.
There is not a single line in this diary that does not call for
a correction or a denial. For example, the reason why I
began to keep it, at Les Salines, was not that I had suddenly recovered my youth nor that I wanted to fill my loneliness with people, but because I had to exorcize a certain
anxiety that would not admit its own existence. It was
hidden deep under the silence and the warmth of that disturbing afternoon, bound up with Maurice's gloom and
with his departure. Yes: throughout these pages I meant
what I was writing and I meant the opposite; reading them
again I feel completely lost. There are some remarks that
make me blush for shame . . . 'I have always wanted the
truth; and the reason why I have had it is that I desired it.'
Is it possible to be so mistaken about one's life as all that?
Is everybody as blind as this or am I an outstanding prize
half-wit? And not only a half-wit. I was lying to myself.
How I lied to myself! I said that Noëllie did not amount
to anything and that Maurice preferred me; and I knew
perfectly well that was untrue. I have taken to my pen
again not to go back over the same ground but because the
emptiness within me, around me, is so vast that this movement of my hand is necessary to tell myself that I am still
alive.

Sometimes I stand at that window from which I saw him
leave, one Saturday morning an eternity ago. I said to
myself then, 'He will not come back.' But I was not certain
of it. It was the lightning-flash of intuition—the intuition

of what would happen later, or what has happened. He has not come back. Not him: and one day there will no longer be even this semblance of him at my side. The car is there, parked against the pavement: he left it. It used to mean his presence, and the sight of it warmed me. Now it only emphasizes his absence. He is gone. For ever he will be gone. I shall not live without him. But I do not wish to kill myself. What then?

Why? I batter my head against the walls of this blind alley. I have not loved a scoundrel all through these twenty years! I am not, unknown to myself, a fool or a shrew! This love between us was real: it was solid—as indestructible as truth. Only there was time going by and I—I did not know it. The river of time, the erosion caused by the river's current: there you have it—there has been an erosion of his love by the flow of time. But why not of mine too, in that case?

I brought out the boxes from the cupboard where we keep our old letters. All those sayings of Maurice's that I know by heart date back at least ten years. It is the same as the memories. So it must be supposed that the passionate love between us—or at least his for me—lasted only ten years, and its memory echoed on through the next ten, giving things a tone that they did not really possess. Yet he smiled in the same way, looked at me in the same way during those last years. (Oh, if only I were to recover those looks and those smiles!) The more recent letters are amusing and affectionate, but meant for his daughters as much as for me. From time to time a really warm-hearted phrase stands out against the usual tone: but there is something forced about them. My letters—tears blinded me when I tried to re-read them.

I did re-read them, and the feeling of uneasiness is still with me. The early letters are in tune with Maurice's, eager, loving and happy. Later they give an odd sort of a ring, vaguely whining, almost querulous. I assert with altogether too much rapture that we love one another as we did the

first day; I insist upon his assuring me of this; I ask questions that call for given replies—how can I have been
satisfied by them, knowing I had wrenched them out of
him? But I did not realize. I forgot. I have forgotten a
great deal. What was that letter he sent me and I tell him
I burnt after our talk on the telephone? I only remember it
vaguely: I was at Mougins with the children; he was
finishing his preparation for an examination; I reproached
him for not writing often enough; he answered roughly.
Very roughly. Distraught, I sprang to the telephone; he
said he was sorry, he begged me to burn his letter. Are
there other occurrences that I have buried? I always
imagined myself to be honest. It is dreadful to think that
behind me my own past is no longer anything but shifting
darkness.

Two days later

Poor Colette! I had taken care to telephone her twice,
speaking cheerfully, so that she should not worry. But still
it astonished her that I no longer went to see her nor asked
her to come to me. She rang and beat on the door with such
force that I let her in. She looked so shocked and amazed
that I saw myself through her eyes. I saw the flat, and I
too was stupefied. She made me wash and do my hair and
pack a bag and go and stay with her. The daily woman will
put everything straight. As soon as Jean-Pierre had left I
seized upon Colette and overwhelmed her with questions.
Did we quarrel a great deal, her father and I? At one time,
yes: it had frightened her because up until then we had got
on so well together. But after that period there had never
been any more scenes, at least not when she was there.

'Still, it wasn't the same as before?'

She said she was too young to realize fully. She does not
help me. She could give me the key to this if she would

make an effort. I think I can tell from her voice that she is holding something back—it is as though she too had notions of her own that she meant to conceal. What notions? Had I become too revolting? Really too revolting? At present I am, of course—haggard, my hair dead, my complexion muddy. But eight years ago? That I daren't ask her. Or am I stupid? Or at least not bright enough for Maurice? Terrible questions when one is not used to asking about oneself.

19 January

Can it be true? Am I going to be rewarded for my effort at leaving Maurice free, not clinging to him? For the first time in weeks I slept with no terrible dreams last night, and something loosened in my throat. Hope. Still frail, but it is there. I had been to the hairdresser, to the beauty-parlour: I was very trim, the house was shining with cleanliness and I had even bought some flowers when Maurice came back. Yet his first words were, 'How ill you look!'

It is true that I had lost nine pounds. I had made Colette swear not to tell him about the state she found me in, but I am almost sure she did. Well, perhaps it was not so wrong of her! He took me in his arms. 'My poor dear!'

'But I'm fine,' I said. (I had taken some Librium: I wanted to be relaxed.) And to my utter astonishment it was in his eyes that I saw tears.

'I have been behaving like a swine!'

I said, 'It's not being a swine to love another woman. You can't help it.'

Shrugging his shoulders he said, 'Do I really love her?'

I have been feeding on that remark for the last two days. They spent a fortnight together, in the freedom and the beauty of the mountains, and he comes back saying, 'Do I really love her?' It is a line I should never have dared play deliberately; but my desperation has worked on my side. This long tête-à-tête has begun to wear out his passion. Again he said, 'I didn't want this! I didn't want to make you unhappy.' As for that, it is a stock phrase which hardly moves me at all. If he had felt only an upsurge of pity I should not have taken hope again. But there in front of me, speaking aloud, he said 'Do I really love her?' And I tell myself that perhaps this is the beginning of the decrystal-lization that will detach him from Noëllie and give him back to me.

23 *January*

He has spent all the evenings at home. He bought some new records and we listened to them. He promised that we should go on a little tour in the south at the end of February.

People are more willing to sympathize with misery than happiness. I told Marie Lambert that Noëllie has shown herself in her true colours at Courchevel and that Maurice was without any doubt returning to me for good. She said unwillingly, 'If it is for good, so much the better.'

In the end she gave me no sound advice. I am sure they are talking about me behind my back. They have their own little notions about my trouble. They don't confide them to me. I said to Isabelle, 'You were right to prevent me from doing the irreparable. Fundamentally Maurice never did stop loving me.'

'I dare say,' she answered in a somewhat dubious tone.

I reacted violently. 'You dare say? You think he doesn't love me any more? You always used to assure me that he did . . .'

'I don't think anything exact. I have a feeling that he doesn't know what he wants himself.'

'What? Have you heard something new?'

'Absolutely nothing!'

I can't see what she could have heard. She merely has the spirit of contradiction: she comforted me when I was in doubt—she produces doubts now I begin to have some confidence again.

24 *January*

I ought to have hung up: I ought to have said 'He's not in' or even not have answered at all. What a nerve! And Maurice's thunderstruck look! Must speak firmly to him presently when he comes home. He was reading the papers by my side when the telephone rang: Noëllie. It was the first time: and once too often. Very polite. 'I should like to speak to Maurice.'

Stupidly I passed him the receiver. He scarcely spoke at all; he looked terribly embarrassed. Several times he repeated, 'No, it's impossible.' And in the end he said, 'All right. I'll come.' As soon as he put the receiver down I cried, 'You shan't go! Daring to pester you here!'

'Listen. We had a violent quarrel. She's desperate because I haven't given any sign of life.'

'I've been desperate too often enough and I've never rung you up at Noëllie's.'

'I beg you—please don't make things to hard for me. Noëllie is capable of killing herself.'

'Oh come.'

'You don't know her.'

He walked up and down; he kicked one of the armchairs, and I understood that whatever happened he was going to go. We had got along so well together for days that once again I was cowardly. 'Go on, then,' I said. But as soon as he is back I shall speak. No scenes. But I won't be treated like a doormat.

25 January

I am shattered. He telephoned to tell me that he was
spending the night at Noëllie's—that he *could not* leave her
in her present state. I protested; he rang off; I telephoned
in my turn; I let the bell ring on and on, and then they
unhooked it. I very nearly jumped into a cab to go and peal
away at Noëllie's door. But I dared not face Maurice's
look. I went out, I walked in the cold of the night, seeing
nothing, not stopping, until I was exhausted. A cab brought
me back and I dropped, fully dressed, on to the divan in
the sitting-room. Maurice woke me up. 'Why didn't you go
to bed?' There was reproach in his voice. A dreadful scene.
I said he had spent his time with me because he had
quarrelled with Noëllie; that at the first snap of her fingers
he came running; that as far as I was concerned I might
perfectly well die of grief.

'You are unjust,' he said indignantly. 'If you want to
know, it was because of you that we quarrelled.'

'Me?'

'She wanted us to stay on in the mountains.'

'You might just as well say that she wanted you to finish
with me!' I wept, wept . . . 'I know very well that in the
end you will leave me.'

'No.'

30 January

What's happening? What do they know? They are not the
same with me any more. Isabelle, the day before yesterday
. . . I was aggressive with her. I blamed her for having
given me bad advice. I granted everything, accepted everything, from the very first day: result—Maurice and Noëllie
treat me like a doormat. She stood up for herself a little; at

first she had not known that it was a question of a long-standing relationship.

'But you didn't want to admit that Maurice was a swine, either,' I said.

She protested. 'No. Maurice is not a swine! He's a man caught between two women: no one is a very shining light in cases of that kind.'

'He never ought to have got himself into that position.'

'It happens to very decent creatures.'

She is indulgent with Maurice because she has put up with a great deal from Charles. But their relationship was a completely different story.

'I don't believe Maurice is a decent creature any more,' I said. 'I am discovering small-minded aspects in him. I wounded his vanity by not going into ecstasies over his successes.'

'There you are unjust,' she said, with a kind of sternness. 'If a man likes to talk about his work, that is not vanity. It has always surprised me that you care so little for what Maurice does.'

'I've nothing of any interest to say to him about it.'

'No. But he would certainly have liked to tell you about his difficulties, and the things he had discovered.'

A suspicion crossed my mind. 'Have you been seeing him? Has he been talking to you? Has he got round you?'

'You're out of your mind!'

'I am astonished that you should take his side. If he is a decent fellow, then I am the one who is altogether in the wrong.'

'Not at all. It's possible for people not to get along together without either of them being in the wrong.'

She sang a different tune before. What are the words they have on the tip of their tongue, and that they do not bring out?

I went home, very low. What a relapse! He spends virtually all his time with Noëllie. During the few moments he grants me, he avoids our being alone together—he takes me to a restaurant or a theatre. He is right: it is less painful than being together in what was our home.

Colette and Jean-Pierre are really very kind. They take great care of me. They took me to have dinner in a pleasant little eating-place in Saint-Germain-des-Prés where excellent records were put on: one was a blues that I had often heard with Maurice and I realized that it was my past and my whole life that were going to be taken away from me—that I had already lost. Suddenly I fainted, having uttered a little cry, it seems. I came to almost directly. But it had shocked Colette. She grew very angry. 'I can't bear seeing you tearing yourself to pieces in this way. With Papa treating you like this, you ought to send him packing. Let him go and live with that woman: you will be much quieter in your mind.'

She would not have given me that advice only a month ago.

The fact is that if I were a good loser I should tell Maurice to go. But my last chance is that Noëllie, for her part, should grow exasperated, make scenes and show herself in an unpleasant light. And also that the way I stick it out should touch Maurice. And then even if he is not often here, this is, after all, still his home. I am not living in a desert. Weakness; cowardice; but there is no reason why I should torture myself—I am trying to survive.

I look at my little Egyptian statue: it has taken the glue very well. We bought it together. It was filled through and through with loving kindness, and with the blue of the sky. It stands there, naked, desolate. I take it in my hands and I weep. I can no longer put on the necklace that Maurice gave me for my fortieth birthday. All the things, all the pieces of furniture around me have had their surfaces taken off by some acid. There is nothing left of them but a kind of heart-breaking skeleton.

31 *January*

I am losing all grasp on things. I am falling lower, lower
all the time. Maurice is kind, full of consideration. But he
can hardly conceal his delight at having recovered Noëllie.
Now he would no longer say to me, 'Do I really love her?'
Yesterday I was having dinner with Isabelle and I collapsed
on to her shoulder, sobbing. Fortunately it was in a fairly
dark bar. She says I am overdoing the stimulants and the
tranquillizers and that I am racking myself to pieces. (It is
true that I am terribly out of order. I began bleeding again
this morning, a fortnight earlier than I ought to have.)
Marie Lambert advises me to see a psychiatrist—not for an
analysis but an immediate palliative treatment. But what
could he do for me?

2 *February*

Once upon a time I had some strength of mind, and I
should have turned Diana out of the house: but I am nothing but a limp rag nowadays. How can I ever have been
friends with her? She amused me, and in those days
nothing mattered.

'Oh, how thin you've grown! How ill you look!'

She had come out of curiosity, out of ill nature—I felt
that at once. I ought not to have let her in. She started
prattling away: I did not listen. Suddenly she attacked me.
'It's too painful to see you in this state. You must cope, pull
yourself together—go off and travel, for example. Otherwise you'll have a nervous breakdown.'

'I am very well.'

'Oh come, come! You're eating your heart out. Believe
me, there comes a moment when one has to know how to
give in.' She pretended to hesitate. 'No one dares tell you

the truth: for my part I think that trying to be too tactful with people often only does them harm in the end. You must get it firmly into your head that Maurice loves Noëllie—it's very serious.'

'Was it Noëllie who told you that?'

'Not only Noëllie. Friends who saw a great deal of them at Courchevel. They seemed absolutely determined to make their life together.'

I did my best to look unconcerned. 'Maurice lies as much to Noëllie as he does to me.'

Diana looked at me pityingly. 'At all events I have warned you. Noëllie is not the sort of girl to let herself be trifled with. If Maurice doesn't give her what she wants, she'll drop him. And of course he knows it. I should be astonished if he doesn't act accordingly.'

She left almost immediately after that. I can hear her from here. 'That poor Monique! How ghastly she looks! She still refuses to open her eyes.' The cow. Of course he loves Noëllie; he would not torture me for nothing.

3 February

I ought not to ask questions. They are holds that I reach out to him and that he grasps at once. I asked Maurice, 'Is it true what Noëllie says, that you have made up your mind to live with her?'

'She certainly can't be saying that, since it is not true.' He hesitated. 'What I should like—I have not spoken of it to her: you are the one it concerns—is to live by myself for a certain time. There is a tension between us that would vanish if—just for the time being, of course—we were to give up living together.'

'You want to leave me?'

'No, of course not. We should see just as much of one another.'

'I can't bear it!'

I screamed. He took me by the shoulders. 'Stop! Stop!' he said gently. 'It was just a thought in the air. If you find it so very disagreeable I will abandon it.'

Noëllie wants him to leave me; she is pressing him; she is making scenes: I'm sure of it. It is her pushing him on. I shall not give way.

6 *February*: *then with no date*

What useless energy you need for even the simplest things, when all liking for life is gone! In the evening I get the teapot, the cup and the saucepan ready; I put each thing in its place so that life may start in the morning with the least possible effort. And even so it is almost more than I can bring myself to do, creeping out of my bed, starting the day. I get the daily woman to come in the afternoon so that I can stay in bed as long as I like in the morning. Sometimes I get up just as Maurice is coming home to lunch at one o'clock. Or if he does not come back, then at the very moment Mme Dormoy turns the key in the lock. Maurice frowns when he sees me at one o'clock in a dressing-gown and with my hair undone. He thinks I am putting on a desperation act for his benefit. Or at least that I am not making the necessary effort 'to live the situation decently'. He too tells me over and over again, 'You ought to see a psychiatrist.'

I go on bleeding. If only my life could run out of me without my having to make the slightest effort!

There must exist a truth in all this. I ought to take the plane for New York and ask Lucienne the truth. She does not love me: she will tell me. Then I should wipe out all that is bad, all that does me harm: I should put everything between Maurice and me back in its place.

Yesterday evening when Maurice came home I was sitting in the living-room, in the darkness, wearing my dressing-gown. It was Sunday; I had got up in the middle of the afternoon: I had eaten a slice of ham and drunk some cognac. And then I had stayed sitting there, following the thoughts that went round and round in my head. Before he came in I took some tranquillizers and went back to sit in the armchair, without even thinking of turning on the light.

'What are you doing? Why don't you turn on the light?'

'Why should I?'

He scolded me, affectionately, but with irritation behind his kindness. Why don't I see my friends? Why haven't I been to the cinema? He told me the names of five films worth seeing. It's impossible. There was a time when I could go to the cinema and even to the theatre all by myself. For I was not alone. His presence was there in me and all around me. Now when I am by myself I say to myself, 'I am alone.' And I am afraid.

'You can't go on like this,' he said.

'Like what?'

'Not eating, not dressing, shutting yourself up in this flat.'

'Why not?'

'You'll get ill. Or go off your head. As for me, I can't help you because I'm part of it. But I beg you, do see a psychiatrist.'

I said no. He pressed me and pressed me. In the end he grew impatient. 'How do you expect to get out of it? You do nothing to help.'

'Get out of what?'

'Out of this depression. Anyone would say you were sinking deeper and deeper into it on purpose.'

He shut himself up in his study. He thinks I am trying to blackmail him with misery, so as to frighten him and prevent him from leaving me. Maybe he's right. Do I know what I am? Perhaps a kind of leech that feeds on the life of others—on Maurice's, on our daughters', on the life of all those lame ducks I claimed to be helping. An egoist who will not let go: I drink, I let myself slide, I make myself ill with the unadmitted intention of softening his heart. Completely phoney through and through, rotten to the bone, play-acting, exploiting his pity. I ought to tell him to go and live with Noëllie, to be happy without me. I can't bring myself to do so.

In a dream the other night I had on a sky-blue dress and the sky was blue.

Those smiles, looks, words—they cannot have vanished. They float here in the air of this flat. As for the words, I often hear them. In my ear a voice says, very distinctly, 'Darling; sweetheart, my sweetheart . . .' As for the looks and the smiles, I ought to catch them as they pass and clap them suddenly on to Maurice's face, and then everything would be the same as before.

I still go on bleeding, I am afraid.

'When one is so low any movement must be upwards,' says Marie Lambert. What foolishness! You can always go lower, and lower still, and still lower. There is no bottom. She says that to get rid of me. She is sick of me. They are all sick of me. Tragedies are all right for a while: you are concerned, you are curious, you feel good. And then it gets repetitive, it doesn't advance, it grows dreadfully boring: it is so very boring, even for me. Isabelle, Diana, Colette, Marie Lambert—they are all fed to the teeth; and Maurice

. . .

There was once a man who lost his shadow. I forget what happened to him, but it was dreadful. As for me, I've lost my own image. I did not look at it often; but it was there, in the background, just as Maurice had drawn it for me. A straightforward, genuine, 'authentic' woman, without mean-mindedness, uncompromising, but at the same time understanding, indulgent, sensitive, deeply feeling, intensely aware of things and of people, passionately devoted to those she loved and creating happiness for them. A fine life, serene, full, 'harmonious.' It is dark: I cannot see myself any more. And what do the others see? Maybe something hideous.

There are plottings that go on behind my back. Between Colette and her father, Isabelle and Marie Lambert, Isabelle and Maurice.

20 *February*

I have ended up by yielding to them. I was afraid of my blood, and the way it flowed away from me. Afraid of the silence. I had taken to telephoning Isabelle three times a day and to Colette in the middle of the night. And now I am paying someone to listen to me: it's killingly funny.

He urged me to take up this diary again. I see the gimmick perfectly well—he is trying to give me back an interest in myself, to reconstruct my identity for me. But the only thing that counts is Maurice. My self, what does that amount to? I have never paid much attention to it. I was safe, because he loved me. If he does not love me any more . . . It is only the transition that haunts my mind— how have I deserved it that he should no longer love me? Or have I deserved it that he should no longer love me? Or have I not deserved it, and is he a swine—a swine that should be punished, and his accomplice with him? Dr Marquet sets about it at the other end—my father, my mother, my father's death: he wants to make me talk about myself and I only want to talk to him about Maurice and Noëllie. Still, I did ask him whether he thought me intelligent. Yes, undoubtedly; but intelligence is not a quality with an independent existence: when I go on and on pursuing my obsessions my intelligence is no longer available to me.

Maurice treats me with that mixture of tactfulness and muffled irritation that one puts on for invalids. He is patient, so patient that I feel like shrieking; and indeed I do sometimes. Go mad. That would be a good way out. But Marquet assures me there is no danger of it—my structure is too sound. Even with drink and drugs I have never pushed myself very far off the middle line. It is a way out that is closed to me.

23 February

The haemorrhage has stopped. And I manage to eat a little. Mme Dormoy was delighted yesterday, because I got down the whole of her cheese soufflé. I find her touching. No one, throughout this long nightmare from which I am just beginning to emerge, has been more kind and helpful than she. Every evening I found a perfectly clean nightgown under my pillow. So sometimes, instead of going to bed fully dressed, I would put it on, and by its whiteness it would force me to wash and do my teeth. In the afternoon she used to say to me, 'I have run you a bath,' and I would take it. She thought up appetizing dishes. Without the slightest remark or the least question. And I was ashamed; I was ashamed of the way I let myself go, I being rich and she having nothing at all.

'Collaborate,' says Dr Marquet. All right. I am quite willing to try to find myself again. I stand in front of the looking-glass: how ugly I am! How unlovely my body is! Since when? I seem quite agreeable in my photographs of two years ago. I don't look so bad in those of last year; but they were amateur snapshots. Is it the misery of these five months that has changed me? Or had I begun to go downhill fast well before that?

I wrote to Lucienne a week ago. She answered with a very affectionate letter. She is really distressed about what has happened to me and she asks nothing better than to talk it over, although she has nothing particular to tell me. She suggests that I should come to New York to see her;

she could arrange to spend a fortnight there; we would talk and then again it would take my mind off things. But I don't want to leave now. I want to fight here, on the spot.

When I think that I used to say 'I shan't struggle!'

26 February

I have obeyed the psychiatrist; I have accepted a job. I go to the periodicals room in the Bibliothèque Nationale and I comb through the back numbers of medical magazines for a fellow who is writing on the history of medicine. I can't see how this can do anything towards solving my problems. When I have written up two or three index-cards I don't get the least satisfaction out of it.

3 March

Here we are! I was sent to the psychiatrist, I was made to recover a little strength before the final blow was struck. It's like those Nazi doctors who brought the victims back to life so that they could be tortured again. I shouted at him, 'Nazi! Torturer!' He looked shattered. Really it was he who was the victim. He even went so far as to say to me, 'Monique! Have some pity for me!'

Once again, with innumerable precautions, he had explained to me that living together did neither of us any good; that he was not going to move into Noëllie's flat, no; but he was going to find a little place for himself. That would not prevent us from seeing one another nor even prevent us from spending parts of the holidays together. I said no, I screamed, I insulted him. This time he did not say he would give up his idea.

What stuff, their ergotherapy! I have dropped this idiotic job.

I think of Poe's tale—the iron walls that come together and the knife-edged pendulum that swings above my heart. At certain moments it stops but it never withdraws. Now it is only a few inches from my skin.

5 March

I told the psychiatrist about this last scene. He said to me, 'If you have spiritual strength enough for it, it would certainly be better for you to be at a distance from your husband, at least for a while.' Did Maurice pay him to tell me this?

I looked him straight in the eye. 'It is strange that you should not have said that before.'

'I wanted the idea to come from you.'

'It doesn't come from me, but from my husband.'

'Yes. But still it is you that have spoken to me about it.' And then he began to muddle me with tales of lost and recovered personalities, distances to be taken, returns to oneself. Claptrap.

8 March

The psychiatrist has put the last touches to my demoralization. I no longer have any strength; I no longer attempt to struggle. Maurice is looking for a furnished flat—he has several in view. This time I did not even protest. Yet our conversation was appalling. Without any anger, totally reduced, empty, I said to him, 'It would have been better if you had told me at the end of the holidays, or even at Mougins, that you had made up your mind to leave me.'

'To begin with I am not leaving you.'

'That's quibbling.'

'And then again I had not made up my mind about anything.'

A mist floated in front of my eyes. 'Do you mean you have been putting me on trial these six months and that I have wrecked my chances? That is atrocious.'

'Not at all. It is me I was thinking about. I hoped I should manage somehow with Noëllie and you. And I'm going off my head. I can't even work any more,'

'It's Noëllie who insists on your leaving.'

'She can't bear the situation any more than you can.'

'If I had stood it better, would you have stayed?'

'But you couldn't. Even your kindness and your silence tore my heart out.'

'You're leaving me because the pity you feel for me makes you suffer too much?'

'Oh, I beg you to understand me!' he said in an imploring voice.

'I understand,' I said.

Maybe he was not lying. Perhaps he had not made up his mind this summer: indeed, in cold blood the idea of breaking my heart for me must have seemed to him appalling. But Noëllie has badgered him. Has she perhaps threatened to break? So that at last he is throwing me overboard.

I repeated, 'I understand. Noëllie says you must say yes or no. You leave me or she drops you flat. Well then, quite candidly she is an odious beast! She might perfectly well have agreed that you should keep a little place for me in your life.'

'But I do keep one for you—a very big one.'

He hesitated: was he going to deny that he was giving in to Noëllie or admit it? I spurred him on. 'I should never have believed that you would yield to blackmail.'

'There was no question of an ultimatum, nor of blackmail. I need a little solitude and quiet; I need a place of my own—you'll see, everything will be better between us.'

He had chosen the version that he thought would hurt me least. Was it true? I shall never know. But on the other hand what I do know is that in a year or two, when I have

got used to it, he will live with Noëllie. Where shall I be?
In my grave? In an asylum? I don't care. I don't care
about anything at all.

He presses me to go and spend a fortnight in New York:
so do Colette and Isabelle; they have more or less plotted
this together, and perhaps they even suggested her invitation to Lucienne—her invitation to spend a fortnight in
New York. They explain to me that it would be less painful
if he were to move while I was away. And in fact if I were
to see him emptying his cupboards I should not escape a
nervous breakdown. All right. I give way once more. Perhaps Lucienne will help me understand myself, although
now that has not the slightest importance.

15 March, New York

I can't prevent myself looking out for the telegram, the
telephone-call from Maurice that will tell me, 'I have
broken with Noëllie' or just, 'I have changed my mind. I
am staying at home.' And of course it does not come.

To think that once I should have been so happy to see
this city. And here I am, blind.

Maurice and Colette took me to the airport; I was
stuffed with tranquillizers: Lucienne would take delivery
of me at the other end—a parcel that is trundled about, an
invalid, or a half-wit. I slept, I thought about nothing, and
I landed in a fog. How elegant Lucienne has grown! Not
a girl any more at all: a woman, very sure of herself. (She
who loathed adults. When I used to say to her, 'Admit I
was right' she would fly into a rage—'You're wrong!
You're wrong to have been right!') She drove me to a
pleasant flat on 50th Street that a friend had lent her for a
fortnight. And as I unpacked my bags I thought, 'I shall
force her to explain everything to me. I shall know why I
have been condemned. That will be less unbearable than
ignorance.'

She said, 'It really suits you, being thinner.'

'Was I too fat?'

'A little. You look better now.'

Her steady, collected voice overawed me. Still, that evening I did try to talk to her. (We were drinking martinis in a terribly hot, noisy bar.)

'You saw our life together,' I said. 'And indeed you were very critical as far as I was concerned. Don't be afraid of hurting me. Try to explain why your father has stopped loving me.'

She smiled rather pityingly. 'But Mama, after fifteen years of marriage it is perfectly natural to stop loving one's wife. It's the other thing that would be astonishing!'

'There are people who love one another all their lives.'

'They pretend to.'

'Listen, don't answer me with generalities, like everybody else. *It's normal, it's natural*: that doesn't satisfy me. I'm sure I must have had faults. What were they?'

'Your fault was believing that love could last. I've grasped the situation: as soon as I begin to grow fond of a man, I find another.'

'Then you'll never love anyone.'

'No, of course not. *You* know where that gets you.'

'What's the point of living if you don't love anyone?'

I am incapable of wishing that I had not loved Maurice or even of wishing that I did not love him now: I just want him to love me.

I persisted during the days that followed. 'Still, look at Isabelle, look at Diana: and the Couturiers. There are marriages that stick.'

'It's a matter of statistics. When you put your money on married love you take the risk of being left flat at forty, empty-handed. You drew a losing ticket: you're not the only one.'

'I haven't crossed the Atlantic to hear you utter commonplaces.'

'It is so far from being a commonplace that you had

never thought of it and that you don't even want to believe it now.'

'Statistics don't explain why it should happen to me personally!'

She shrugs; she changes the conversation; she takes me to the theatre, to the cinema; she shows me the town. But I go relentlessly on. 'Did you have the feeling that I did not understand your father? That I was just not up to it?'

'When I was fifteen of course I did, like all girls who are in love with their fathers.'

'What exactly did you think?'

'That you didn't admire him enough: for me he was a kind of superman.'

'I was certainly wrong in not taking a greater interest in his work. Do you think he turned against me?'

'Because of that?'

'That or anything else.'

'Not that I know of.'

'Did we quarrel a lot?'

'No. Not when I was there.'

'Still, in '55, Colette remembers . . .'

'Because she was always clinging to your apron-strings. And she was older than me.'

'Then why do you imagine your father is leaving me?'

'At about that age men often feel like starting a new life. They suppose it will go on being new for the rest of their lives.'

Really I can get nothing out of Lucienne. Does she think so badly of me that she finds it impossible to tell me?

16 *March*

'You just won't talk to me about myself: do you think so very badly of me, then?'

'What a notion!'

'I know I am being a bore. But I do want to see clearly into my past.'

'It's the future that counts. Find yourself some man. Or take a job.'

'No. I need your father.'

'Maybe he'll come back to you.'

'You know perfectly well he won't.'

We have had this conversation ten times over. I bore her too; I exasperate her. Perhaps if I were to push her far enough she would end up by breaking out and telling me. But she has such patience that I lose heart. Who knows but they may have written to her to tell her about my case and beg her to bear with me?

Dear God! How smooth life is, now clear—it runs so naturally, when everything is going well. And all that's needed is just one hitch. Then you discover that it's thick and dark, that you know nothing whatever about anybody, either yourself or anyone else—what they are, what they think, what they do, how they look upon you.

I asked her what she thought of her father.

'Oh, for my part, I don't sit in judgment on anyone.'

'You don't think he has behaved like a swine?'

'Frankly, no. He is certainly kidding himself about this woman. He's a simple-minded soul. But not a swine.'

'You think he has the right to sacrifice me?'

'Obviously it's tough on you. But why should *he* sacrifice himself? I know very well *I* should not sacrifice myself for anyone on earth.'

She said that with a kind of boasting air. Is she really as hard as she likes to make out? I wonder. She seems much less sure of herself than I had thought at first. Yesterday I questioned her about herself. 'Listen, I want you to be straight with me: I need it—your father has lied to me so much. Was it because of me that you went off to America?'

'What a notion!'

'Your father is sure of it. And he holds it against me

terribly. I know very well that I was burdensome to you. I always was, from the very beginning.'

'Let's put it that I had no talent for family life.'

'It was my presence you couldn't bear. You left to get away from me.'

'Don't let's exaggerate anything. You didn't crush me. No. I only wanted to know whether I could stand on my own feet.'

'Now you know.'

'Yes; I know that I can.'

'Are you happy?'

'There you are, that's one of your words. It really has no meaning as far as I am concerned.'

'Then that is to say you're not happy.'

Aggressively she replied, 'My life suits me splendidly.'

Work, going out, brief encounters: it seems an arid sort of an existence to me. She has rough ways, spurts of impatience—not only with me—that seem to betray a conflict. This is certainly my fault too, this refusal of love: my sentimentality sickened her and she has warped herself in trying not to be like me. There is something stiff, almost unpleasing, about her ways. She has introduced some of the men she knows and I have been struck by her attitude with them—always on the watch, remote, hard; there is no mirth in her laughter.

20 March

Something is out of beat in Lucienne. There is evil in her—the word horrifies me and I hesitate to write it; but it is the only one that fits. I have always seen her critical, scornful and fleering; but now it is with genuine ill nature that she tears those she calls her friends to pieces. She delights in telling them unpleasant truths. In fact they are no more than common acquaintances. She has made an effort to display people for my benefit; but usually she lives very much alone. Ill nature. It is a defence: against what? At all events she is not the capable, brilliant, well-balanced girl I had imagined in Paris. Have I failed with both of them? No, oh no!

I asked her, 'Do you agree with your father that Colette has made a dreadfully silly marriage?'

'She made just the marriage anyone would have expected her to make. Love was the only thing she ever thought about, so it was inevitable that she should lose her head over the first fellow she came into contact with.'

'Was it my fault, if she was like that?'

She laughed her mirthless laugh. 'You've always had a very exaggerated notion of your own responsibilities.'

I persisted. According to her it is the psychoanalytical situation that really matters in a childhood—the situation that exists outside the parents' range of knowledge and almost in spite of them. The bringing up, in its deliberate, conscious aspect, comes very far behind. My responsibility is nil. Cold comfort. I had never imagined I should ever have to deny guilt—my daughters were my pride.

I also asked her, 'What do you see me as?' She stared at me, amazed. 'I mean, how would you describe me?'

'You're very French, very *soft*, as they say here. Very idealistic, too. You have no defences, that's your only fault.'

'The only one?'

'Yes, of course. Apart from that you are full of life, gay and charming.'

It was pretty concise, her description. I repeated, 'Full of life, gay and charming . . .'

She seemed embarrassed. 'And what about you—how do you see yourself?'

'As a marshland. Everything is buried in the mud.'

'You'll find yourself again.'

No: and perhaps that is the worst side of it all. It is only now that I realize how much value I had for myself, fundamentally. But Maurice has murdered all the words by which I might try to justify it: he has repudiated the standards by which I measured others and myself. I had never dreamt of challenging them—that is to say of challenging myself. And now what I wonder is this: what right had I to say that the inner life was preferable to a merely social life, contemplation to trifling amusements, and self-sacrifice to ambition? My only one had been to create happiness around me. I have not made Maurice happy. And my daughters are not happy either. So what then? I no longer know anything. Not only do I not know what kind of a person I am but also I do not know what kind of a person I ought to be. Black and white merge into one another, the world is an amorphous mass, and I no longer have any clear outlines. How is it possible to live without believing in anything or in myself?

It shocks Lucienne that New York should interest me so little. Before, I used to come out of my burrow very often, but when I did I was interested in everything—the country-side, people, museums, the streets. Now I am a dead woman. A dead woman who still has years to drag out—how many? Even a single day, when I open my eyes in the morning, seems to me something whose end I can never possibly reach. In my bath yesterday the mere act of lifting my arm faced me with a problem—why lift an arm: why put one foot in front of another? When I am by myself I stand there motionless for minutes on end at the edge of the pavement, utterly paralysed.

23 March

I leave tomorrow. The night all round me is as dark as ever. I cabled to ask that Maurice should not come to Orly. I haven't the moral strength to face him. He will be gone. I am going back and he will be gone.

24 *March*

There. Colette and Jean-Pierre were waiting for me. I had dinner at their flat. They brought me here. The window was dark: it always will be dark. We climbed the stairs; they put my bags down in the sitting-room. I would not let Colette stay and sleep here: I just have to get used to it. I sat down at the table. I am sitting there now. And I look at those two doors—Maurice's study, our bedroom. Closed. A closed door: something that is watching behind it. It will not open if I do not stir. Do not stir: ever. Stop the flow of time and of life.

But I know that I shall move. The door will open slowly and I shall see what there is behind the door. It is the future. The door to the future will open. Slowly. Unrelentingly. I am on the threshold. There is only this door and what is watching behind it. I am afraid. And I cannot call to anyone for help.

I am afraid.

Simone de Beauvoir

She Came to Stay
The passionately eloquent and ironic novel she wrote as an act of revenge against the woman who so nearly destroyed her life with the philosopher Sartre. 'A writer whose tears for her characters freeze as they drop.' *Sunday Times*

Les Belles Images
Her totally absorbing story of upper-class Parisian life. 'A brilliant sortie into Jet Set France.' *Daily Mirror*. 'As compulsively readable as it is profound, serious and disturbing. *Queen*

The Mandarins
'A magnificent satire by the author of *The Second Sex. The Mandarins* gives us a brilliant survey of the post-war French intellectual . . . a dazzling panorama.' *New Statesman*. 'A superb document . . . a remarkable novel.' *Sunday Times*

The Woman Destroyed
'Immensely intelligent, basically passionless stories about the decay of passion. Simone de Beauvoir shares, with other women novelists, the ability to write about emotion in terms of direct experience . . . The middle-aged women at the centre of the three stories in *The Woman Destroyed* all suffer agonisingly the pains of growing older and of being betrayed by husbands and children.' *Sunday Times*

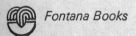 *Fontana Books*

Anthony Powell

'Powell is very like a drug, the more compelling the more you read him.' *Sunday Times*

A Dance to the Music of Time

'The most remarkable feat of sustained fictional creation in our day.' *Guardian*

A Question of Upbringing
A Buyer's Market
The Acceptance World
At Lady Molly's
Casanova's Chinese Restaurant
The Kindly Ones
The Valley of Bones
The Soldier's Art
The Military Philosophers
Books Do Furnish a Room
Temporary Kings
Hearing Secret Harmonies

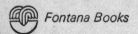 *Fontana Books*

Morris West

'A great writer.' *Daily Mirror*. 'An able novelist . . . skilled in characterization and in generating an atmosphere of emotional tension.' *New York Times*. 'A first-class, professional writer.' *BBC*. 'A craftsman.' *Time*

The Navigator

The Big Story

Children of the Sun

Daughter of Silence

The Devil's Advocate

Harlequin

The Second Victory

The Shoes of the Fisherman

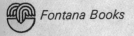 *Fontana Books*

Fontana Paperbacks

Fontana is a leading paperback publisher of fiction and non-fiction, with authors ranging from Alistair MacLean, Agatha Christie and Desmond Bagley to Solzhenitsyn and Pasternak, from Gerald Durrell and Joy Adamson to the famous Modern Masters series.

In addition to a wide-ranging collection of internationally popular writers of fiction, Fontana also has an outstanding reputation for history, natural history, military history, psychology, psychiatry, politics, economics, religion and the social sciences.

All Fontana books are available at your bookshop or newsagent; or can be ordered direct. Just fill in the form and list the titles you want.

FONTANA BOOKS, Cash Sales Department, G.P.O. Box 29, Douglas, Isle of Man, British Isles. Please send purchase price, plus 8p per book. Customers outside the U.K. send purchase price, plus 10p per book. Cheque, postal or money order. No currency.

NAME (Block letters)

ADDRESS